M000308211

DARK DESIRE

Surrender Series - Book 5

LAUREN SMITH

This book is a work of fiction. Names, characters, places, and incidents are the product of the author's imagination or are used fictitiously. Any resemblance to actual events, locales, or persons, living or dead, is coincidental.

Copyright © 2021 by Lauren Smith

Cover design by Cover Couture

All rights reserved. In accordance with the U.S. Copyright Act of 1976, the scanning, uploading, and electronic sharing of any part of this book without the permission of the publisher constitutes unlawful piracy and theft of the author's intellectual property. If you would like to use material from the book (other than for review purposes), prior written permission must be obtained by contacting the publisher at lauren@laurensmithbooks.com. Thank you for your support of the author's rights.

The publisher is not responsible for websites (or their content) that are not owned by the publisher.

ISBN: 978-1-952063-64-0 (e-book edition)

ISBN: 978-1-952063-13-8 (trade paperback edition)

IMPORTANT AUTHOR'S NOTE

Dear Readers,

Within these pages, there are topics that can be hard to read about. Elena, the heroine, is a survivor of two months of sexual assault and captivity. Those events are not part of this story. (They are only referenced in inner thought or dialogue.) Elena suffers from nightmares and trauma stemming from that past. If you do not want to read about a heroine who overcomes these traumas, then do not read on. If you wish to see how she conquers her fears and finds love again, then keep reading.

Why did I choose to write this? Because I am a survivor, like Elena. My situation was nothing compared to hers, but it is a part of my history, and I know many women out there have experienced similar situations of harassment or worse. I believe women can overcome these traumas, but I am by no means saying it is easy. However, I believe the power of fiction gives writers and readers the chance to explore topics that can be uncomfortable but important. I assure you, this book has a happily ever after for Elena and her hero, Dimitri.

What you should know about this book: Elena, the heroine, had a previous interest in BDSM before she was sexually assaulted. Dimitri is a dominant alpha male, but he fully respects her decisions and her choices. In no way is this book intended to suggest that sexual assault victims will be drawn to BDSM, nor does it suggest that the only way to overcome the trauma of sexual assault is by having a romantic relationship.

Please remember, this is a *fictional* romance novel, and everyone's ways of overcoming trauma are different. Elena's choices work for her character. She is in charge of her timeline of recovery, and Dimitri fully respects that she is the one who decides if and when she is ready to have intimacy with a man again. I do not intend to make light of sexual assault trauma or to romanticize it. Dimitri does not use violence against Elena, nor does he try to push her boundaries for his own desires.

Writing a book like this has been on my mind for many years. I met Elizabeth Smart a few years ago when she visited my hometown to give a speech. I had the greatest honor and humbling experience of meeting with her privately after her speech, and I had a chance to speak with her and also hug her. She exuded warmth and love, and I began to cry upon embracing her. She was strength and life, beauty and courage all at once.

The lesson I learned from her that day has stuck with me: assault survivors don't have to remain victims the rest of their lives, and they don't have to be defined by their trauma. This doesn't mean that the trauma wasn't horrific or that it ceases to matter after you overcome it. But it does mean that you aren't inevitably trapped within it, and you can regain your courage to live the life you deserve to live.

As a writer, my gift is being able to reach people through the power of my stories. I hope Elena's story touches you. I also hope you enjoy Elena and Dimitri's romance, the story of two souls who feel lost and find each other. They say time heals all wounds, but I believe that love is the greater healing force, especially love for oneself. So as you read each chapter, take a moment and remind yourself how wonderful you are, how amazing you are, and that each day you are alive on this earth, you are a gift to someone, including yourself.

With all my love to you, dear reader,

Lauren Smith

April 2021

PROLOGUE

Clutching her pregnant belly, soaked in blood, a young woman stumbled into the emergency room as night fell outside the rural hospital. She could barely breathe as rolling waves of labor pains threw her body into spasms. It felt as though two giant hands were trying to rip her body apart. Everything felt heavy, and she couldn't move, couldn't even walk another step.

"Help! Please—help me . . ." She collapsed, her hands braced against the wall as two men in scrubs rushed toward her. Nurses? They had that efficient, pragmatic air about them. Sweat poured off her skin, dampening her bloodstained maternity dress. The instinctive need to push was so overpowering that she whimpered and dug her nails into the arm of the nearest man as he helped her stand.

"Save my baby," the woman pleaded. "Please . . . don't

let anyone find me . . ." She relaxed in the hold of the strong nurse who was holding her upright. This place was safe—these people would help her.

If she could just hold on, stay alive a little longer, then it wouldn't matter that she'd hurt two men who'd tried to kill her. For a brief moment, she was safe, safe enough to do what she needed to.

She doubled over, the strength leaving her legs, and she again sagged against the nurse who was supporting her. The man shifted his arm to lift her onto the approaching gurney. Her fingers tangled in the soft blue of his scrubs as he deposited her onto the gurney, and she noticed the blue was now streaked with red from her clothing. He wheeled her out of the lobby and back toward the examination area.

"Ma'am, is this your blood?" one nurse asked as he cut the soaked dress off her body and began to examine her.

She squirmed on the gurney as another contraction hit her. "No. Not mine."

"What's your name?"

"Tatiana . . . Anderson." She collapsed back, momentarily unable to breathe. Only then did she realize her mistake. She never should have said her name, but everything was happening so fast, so painfully, that she couldn't think straight.

One of the nurses began to push the gurney back out of the exam room, telling her they were taking her to a delivery room.

"What happened, Tatiana?" someone asked her as she closed her eyes.

"They tried to kill me . . . I got away." How those men had found her, she would never know. She was supposed to be safe, supposed to be protected. This wasn't Russia—this was the United States. The Red Army shouldn't be able to touch her here, but somehow they had.

"Who tried to kill you?"

"Can't say . . . Not safe . . ." She'd already said too much. Her brain wasn't functioning right. She was tired, frightened, and desperate.

"All right, we're going to help you deliver the baby," a woman explained as a doctor came into the room and scrubbed up at a sink.

"Mrs. Anderson?" the doctor asked.

Tatiana nodded. She was so tired. She'd been on the run for weeks, and now the baby was coming. She couldn't keep running, not from this, and not from the men who wanted her and her child dead. She grabbed the doctor's sleeve.

"If they come for her, don't let them take her."

His brows rose in concern at her white-knuckled grip on his arm. "Who?"

But she couldn't answer him. She could only scream as another wave of pain hit her. Her child was *here*.

What felt like an eternity later, Tatiana fell back on the bed and listened with exhausted joy to the cries of her new baby.

"Mrs. Anderson, congratulations. You have a healthy baby girl." The doctor placed a tiny bundle in her arms.

Tatiana curled her fingers into the blanket under the baby's chin, pulling the cloth down to better see her child's face. She was the most beautiful creature she had ever seen. Looking upon her, so new and innocent to this world, it shattered Tatiana's heart.

"Doctor," she breathed, "you must take her away. She must be given up for adoption immediately."

"What? Why?" The doctor and the nurses simply stared at her.

"Please, it isn't safe. She must be as far away from me as she can be. Take her now. Do not put my name on her wrist. Do you understand?"

"Look, Mrs. Anderson, you really should speak to a counselor first before you make that kind of decision . . ."

"If you do not do it, she will be dead within a week. Do it!" Tatiana declared so forcefully that one of the nurses rushed to take the baby from her.

The child was carried away, and Tatiana let out a bone-weary sigh. That was when her body gave out and the bleeding started. She drifted away, her last thoughts on the future of her child, a child who held one of the world's greatest secrets within her DNA.

Two miles south of Lake Kardyvach, Russia

Sergei Razin watched his son with pride. The boy held a fencing sword at the ready. At only eight years old, he was already proficient in a dozen weapons, three years ahead in his schooling, and only two years away from entering the ranks of the White Army. With his dark hair and pale, clear blue eyes, the boy looked so much like his beloved mother that it made Sergei's heart swell with even more love than before.

"Attack!" the fencing master bellowed.

Sergei's son lunged forward and in a few moves disarmed the fencing master. The adult man's fencing foil clattered to the ground.

Sergei clapped his hands together and beamed at his son. The fencing instructor turned Sergei's way.

"He bests me every time, Sergei. I cannot teach him anything new. He passes his fencing course." The teacher collected his foil, and with an elegant flick of his blade, he saluted Sergei's son. The boy smiled, but his cheeks were stained with a blush at the praise. He was a good boy, a humble child, but smart and talented, the best son a man could ask for.

"Dimitri, come with me." Sergei motioned for his boy to follow him. Dimitri set his foil on a stand by the wall of the training room and rushed after his father.

The palace was quiet that afternoon. Most of the servants were busy at their tasks, and the few other people who lived in the palace permanently were currently away on missions. The remote location of the palace meant that they could largely live their lives away from the prying eyes of the Kremlin. That was key. If they were to ever defeat the corrupt men who sat in power in Red Square, the White Army would need to have the best men and women ready.

The Kremlin's forces focused on breaking down people, especially women, turning them into creatures so damaged that they were empty-shelled puppets that danced to the tune of political leaders in their spy games.

The men and women of the White Army were the opposite. Individual skills were praised and cultivated. Everyone was valued, and everyone had a place. They fought for a Russia that had been murdered long ago in a basement, but they also believed in change for the better and not remaining stagnant in the past. The day the last of the Romanovs had been slain was the day the White Army had gone underground, to wait, to hope, to plan for a truly free Russia.

"Am I doing well, Father?" Dimitri asked.

"Very well. It's time you meet the other boys. They will be like brothers to you."

"How many will there be?"

"Three others. Four, including you."

Dimitri kept pace with Sergei as they entered a long portrait gallery. "Why so few?"

"All of us in the White Army must keep one another safe. These other boys will be your world. The four of you will trust in each other. Do you understand?"

"I think so," Dimitri replied.

Someday Dimitri would know how dangerous this life could be, but not today. He was still young and innocent. Today it was still a game to him.

Sergei pulled the frame on one of the paintings to reveal a secret passageway. He'd spoken to the parents of the other three boys and sent for them this morning so that they could all meet each other. Sergei and his son walked through the darkness together until they reached another door.

Sergei opened the door, and he and Dimitri stepped into a sunny atrium. It was a sacred room in the palace, and the skylights far above let golden sunlight streak down through the room, illuminating the white marble floor and making the blue-and-red painted walls shimmer. It was a room full of books and cozy armchairs and a table. There were drinks and a few light foods prepared by the palace cook.

Three other boys were there, each around eight years of age, standing by the table, waiting respectfully for Sergei to address them.

"Dimitri, these are the sons of my closest and most trusted friends. Now they will be your friends, your confidants, your brothers in all but blood. This is Leo." He pointed at a blond-haired boy with light-brown eyes who watched Dimitri with open curiosity. "And this is Maxim." An intense black-haired, brown-eyed boy nodded in silent greeting. "And this is Nicholas." The last boy, with dove-gray eyes and light-brown hair, grinned and waved at Dimitri. Nicholas was much like his mother, a charmer who befriended and enchanted all who knew her.

"This is my son, Dimitri," Sergei said and then stepped back.

It was time to let his son forge his own fate with these boys. They were the future of the White Army. They would rise from the ashes and save Russia one day. They would protect the past and fight for a better world, and Sergei would make sure each boy had the training to survive and thrive.

Dimitri left his father's side and moved into the room, a little shy at first, but then within moments he and the others were talking excitedly. The bond between the four boys was almost instantaneous, as it was supposed to be.

Sergei held back a smile. He wanted to laugh with joy at the sight, but this was a serious moment, and he did not want Dimitri to mistake his joy for something else. So he kept quiet and watched as the future unfolded.

Can't breathe . . . can't . . . need air . . .

Elena Allen bolted upright in the uncomfortable seat in the gate area of the Moscow airport. One hand clutched her chest. Her heart was pounding so hard it felt like someone was beating her ribs from the inside. The fragments of the nightmare were still scattered in her thoughts as she fought to remember where she was. She was in an airport. She wasn't chained up. She wasn't in the dark. She caught her breath and glanced around her, instinctively searching for any threat before she finally calmed.

Several passengers nearby watched her with open concern. She managed a shaky smile before she glanced down at her lap where her cell phone rested. She had ten minutes before boarding her flight back to the United

States. Then she could start to feel a bone-deep sense of relief at the thought of getting out of Moscow.

Flashes of the dream that had woken her still lurked in her mind. The nightmare of what she had recently endured for two months had burned her so deeply that the scars ran straight through her soul. If she had never gone to that club that night, then she never would have been kidnapped, raped, tortured, and starved by that sadistic rich Russian mobster, Vadym. She never would have endured the dark, evil things that had nearly killed her.

A cold numbness settled over her each time she was swamped by memories of what Vadym had done.

A gate attendant began to speak in Russian, and Elena collected her bag when she realized it was the call for boarding.

As she queued up with the other passengers, she felt a prickling on her scalp. Someone was watching her. She turned her head just enough to glance to her right and then her left, her movements economical, so slight that the people around her wouldn't notice the fear she felt. She'd had this funny feeling on and off since she'd arrived at the airport, but whenever she looked, she could see no one showing any particular interest in the twenty-year-old American college student at the gate for the Los Angeles flight.

But that didn't mean someone wasn't watching her, and the thought of a hidden voyeur edged her toward panic. Maybe Vadym was holding to that promise he'd made, that he would kill her, and he was finally coming after her. She wasn't the first woman he had captured, and she wouldn't be the last, but according to him she had survived the longest. He hadn't lost interest in her because of the fire in her eyes.

"Like emeralds burning me up. You won't break so easily. I like that about you," Vadym had growled. She had been chained to the wall in a secret hidden room in his office, suffocating slowly in the dark until he opened the door. That was the horror she'd faced every day. Wishing to die quietly, alone in peace in that dark little chamber, breathing in stale air, and not having to face the violence of the man who had stolen her life. There were so many days that she had longed for death, but it never came.

Now she was free, thanks to a paleontology professor named Royce Devereaux and his graduate student, Kenzie Martin. They had been kidnapped by Vadym and forced to help him smuggle fossils out of Mongolia, but Vadym's plan had backfired. Royce and Kenzie had saved her life, and the three of them had made it safely to the US embassy in Ulaanbaatar, Mongolia, about a week and a half ago. From there, they'd traveled to the US embassy in Moscow, where the staff had helped to sort out the logistics for her return home to the United States. So much of the days since her escape were blurry.

Once she'd been able to move around without constant pain, the US embassy in Moscow had moved her to one of their apartments while they worked on helping her get the documents necessary to return to the United States. Slowly, she'd begun to feel safe behind the gates of the secured building. And now, she'd started her journey back home by leaving those who had helped her.

Elena stepped onto the plane behind the other passengers and examined her seat number on her boarding pass. She paused in confusion because her seat number led her to business class. The US embassy had said they could only offer her economy, and her parents didn't have enough money to pay for business class either.

"Miss, can I help you?" one of the flight attendants asked as he came toward her.

"Yes, um . . . My boarding pass says this is my seat." She gestured to the expensive leather chair that could convert into a small bed.

The flight attendant examined her boarding pass and nodded. "Yes, that is correct. Please go ahead and take your seat." He started to reach for her backpack to put it above her, but Elena clutched it to her chest. This was a mistake. It had to be. She sank into the seat by the window and waited for someone to come and tell her to leave. This couldn't be her seat. She stared at the other men and women coming down the aisle. One of these people would have her seat. She just needed to wait for confirmation.

One by one the passengers walked by, but no one claimed her seat. She peered around the back of her headrest, noticing the plane was now completely full except for the seat next to hers. Why was she still in this seat? It made no sense. Airlines didn't grant surprise upgrades, not for free, and she definitely hadn't paid for this seat. Even though she was on the plane and should relax now, she couldn't. Something was wrong—it had to be.

"We have one last passenger coming," one of the cabin crew said to another as they started closing the overhead bins.

This had to be it, the last passenger on the plane. She blew out a relieved breath. Soon she'd find out where her real seat was, and she'd be all right.

She stared at the door expectantly, waiting for someone to come down the aisle and claim her seat. She mentally rehearsed her apology for taking the person's seat. It was silly, but in the two months with Vadym she'd gotten used to apologizing for everything and begging for mercy. Now she felt she had to plan every encounter and rehearse every scenario so nothing bad could happen to her again.

Her breath suddenly caught in her throat as a tall, dark-haired man stepped through the hatch and into the cabin. He had a casual elegance to his clothes and movements that screamed *old money*. He smiled at one of the flight attendants, his lazy grin so charming that the poor woman nearly swooned as she offered to help him find his seat.

So this was the person who owned her seat. His gaze

zeroed in on her. He came down the aisle to stop at her row. It was impossible not to notice the casual tightness of his charcoal trousers pulled against his thighs, and his white button-up shirt was what a rich man would wear to travel to a resort. His sleeves were rolled up, exposing the lightly tanned skin of his forearms. This man was an exercise in sexy elegance. Her throat ran dry, and she swallowed. Her heart kicked up a beat as something began to hum in her blood—attraction. She'd never imagined she'd feel attraction to any man ever again after what she'd been through.

Elena stood as the man checked his boarding pass and murmured a polite "Excuse me" before he sat down in the empty seat next to her, blocking her from exiting the row of their pair of seats.

"Excuse me, are you sure this isn't your seat?" She pointed to her own.

The man faced her, his pure blue eyes so soft but also so intense that they made all the thoughts in her head flutter away.

"*This* is my seat." He placed his hand on the armrest. His accent was Russian, but his voice was smooth, rich, like whiskey, not like Vadym's guttural tones. This man was a true specimen of masculinity, with a jawline sharp enough to cut stone. He had the kind of face that she could see on a *GQ* magazine spread for Armani suits, Burberry coats, or Breitling watches.

"Oh . . . okay." Elena collapsed back in the chair beside

him, stunned. The hatch to the boarding ramp closed. So this was it. Somehow she had gotten insanely lucky, and for the next twelve and a half hours she was flying back to Los Angeles in business class next to this man. Maybe karma realized she owed her.

"You had better latch your belt," the man beside her said as he put on his seatbelt.

"What? Oh, right." She fumbled, shoving her backpack under the seat in front of her. She rushed to buckle herself, but her hands started to tremble and she had trouble getting the buckle to fit.

"Allow me." The man suddenly leaned over, his muscled forearms right in her face as his hands gently brushed hers out of the way, then he clicked her belt into place. She flinched away at first, then relaxed. His fingers, even only briefly in contact with hers, made her skin tingle in a wonderful way rather than a bad way. She had the sudden urge to stroke her hands down his corded forearms and trace the veins that just barely showed on his tanned skin.

This was insane. Why wasn't she panicking? A strange man being so close, touching her, should have sent her into a dizzying spiral of PTSD, causing her to pass out. But it hadn't. Ever since she'd escaped Vadym, she hadn't been able to let any man touch her. And now . . . ?

Was it because his eyes were kind? It sounded silly, but maybe it was the truth. Lips could lie, but cold, calculating malice couldn't be hidden in a person's eyes.

"Thank you." She turned her face to the window to watch the ground crew load the final suitcases on the plane.

"Of course. My pleasure, *kiska*," the man beside her replied.

Kiska? That was a word she didn't recognize. She had studied two years of Russian, but there was still so much she didn't know. She opened her backpack and pulled out her small pocket dictionary and searched for the word. When she found it, she shot another glance at the man.

He'd called her *kitten?* She shivered, yet not out of fear. A couple of years ago, when Elena had turned eighteen, she'd learned that she had a submissive tendency, but only in the bedroom. She hadn't experimented, at least not officially, in the BDSM lifestyle. She'd had sex a few times with a college boyfriend that first year, and he'd tied her up once or twice, but while she'd enjoyed it, he hadn't been that interested in the experience. She'd started researching about BDSM and learned that many Doms saw themselves as wolves and their subs as kittens or sweet things they would fiercely protect.

She had gone with a couple of friends to that bar in Moscow that night hoping to watch some BDSM play, to see if it excited her in real life the way it had in her fantasies. That had been her mistake. Even going with a group of friends, she hadn't been safe. She had been ambushed when leaving the restroom, and for the next two months she had lived at the mercy of a sadist.

Elena closed her eyes as the cabin crew was told to prepare for takeoff. She gripped her armrests tight, her hand brushing against the man's fingers. She stared at the point where their fingers connected before she flinched and moved her hand away.

"Afraid of flying?" the man asked.

"What?" It took Elena a second to process what he had asked her. "Oh, it's not that."

He watched her with those vivid blue eyes. She'd never seen a blue so pure and clear. "Then what?"

"I . . ." Elena bit her bottom lip. She shouldn't be talking to the stranger, yet something about him made her want to trust him.

"I really need to leave Moscow, and I'm just terrified that something will keep me here," she said as the plane rumbled down the runway.

A breath released from her lungs as she felt the plane accelerate, and she sagged back in boneless relief. It wasn't until she felt the plane leave the ground that she realized how tense she had been. Now every muscle in her body ached, and she tried to hold in a flood of emotions. Yet she couldn't stop the outpouring of fear and relief that overwhelmed her.

"Excuse me!" she gasped and unbuckled herself.

His eyes widened in surprise as she scrambled across his body and into the aisle, but she couldn't just sit. A flight attendant who had strapped himself in for takeoff waved his arm and told her to stay seated, but she turned away from him and headed toward the business-class bath-room. She couldn't stay seated any longer. The gnawing anxiety of the past months made her feel sick to her stom-ach, and she needed a private place to cry.

She yanked open the door, the interior lights snapping on and disorienting her.

"*Kiska.*"

The sound just behind her had her whirling toward the man from her row, and a scream welled up in her throat as he crowded her. Terrified thoughts raced through her mind, and the pain of her experiences with Vadym battered against her nerves. She brought up her arms to stop him—*Did he mean to strangle her? Rape her? Murder her?*—but her strength was depleted after being so long abused. She was tired, defeated, and when he gently pushed her into the bathroom and locked the door behind them, she let him do so without a fight. She pitched forward as a sob racked her body.

"*Kiska,*" he murmured again, and then his arms were around her stiff body, gentle and firm.

The sob turned into real cries as she fell into his embrace, knowing now he wouldn't hurt her and uncaring as to where his kindness originated. She leaned into his strength where hers was failing. The two months of having to be strong, of not allowing herself to cry or feel anything but terror or numbness and the threat of her imminent death, all washed over her. She was overwhelmed.

The plane hiccupped in its rise, the ding of the seatbelt warning lights sounding out, and she was reminded again that they were in the air, on the way home, far from the sadistic animal who had harmed her. She was safe. Her life was hers again. Even if she knew she'd never feel as alive as she used to.

"*Kiska*, please, dry your eyes," the beautiful Russian man begged. "You're too beautiful to cry." He pressed his lips to the crown of her hair as if standing in an airplane bathroom with a stranger while she sobbed her eyes out was the most normal thing in the world.

She felt the plane level out and knew they were high up in the sky. Moscow was behind her, and she was never going back. When her body stopped shaking, she became all too aware that she was still in the man's arms. A very strong and gorgeous man.

I should be afraid. I should be screaming.

Yet she wasn't. She looked up at his face. Those eyes were still unbearably tender, and his lips were fuller than most men's. Soft and kissable. But she didn't want to think about kissing anyone ever again. Even if she wanted a love life, she was certain she would never be able to have sex again. She had scars, both inside and out, and the thought of being with a man again sexually filled her mouth with a metallic taste.

"Please let go of me," Elena said.

The man instantly obeyed. "Do you feel better?" he asked in a low voice.

She nodded. He studied her a long moment before he

seemed to agree she was ready to go back to her seat. "Good, because the cabin crew will be very unhappy. Let me speak with them first."

Again she nodded, happy to let him deal with the mess she had created. She was too tired to face it herself. He opened the door, and she peeped around his shoulder to see one of the cabin crew glaring at them. The man who had come to her rescue spoke quickly in Russian to the flight attendant, and his glare faded.

"Are you feeling better, miss? Can I get you anything?" the flight attendant asked in English.

"Thank you. Can I just have some water?" she asked, her voice barely above a whisper.

"Of course." He went to the drink cart, and she and the mystery man returned to their seats. Everyone was staring at her, but she was too tired to care. She was unable to deal with the exhaustion and simply collapsed in her chair and closed her eyes.

"Thank you," she told the man beside her, who had remained silent. She was glad. He wasn't a talker, and for that she was relieved. She couldn't have handled trying to answer any questions he'd asked her just then.

"You're welcome," he replied. She drifted off to sleep a few seconds later.

DIMITRI RAZIN HELD HIS BREATH AS HE WATCHED Elena fall asleep. It was taking every ounce of control he possessed not to let his dominant side out. He knew about Elena's trauma, about her kidnapping, rape, and torture. He had been one of the people working behind the scenes to free her. And just today, as he watched her from a distance at the airport, he'd received confirmation that the man who'd done this to her, Vadym Andreikiv, was dead, by Dimitri's own command.

Elena was safe from all but herself now, and that would be the hardest battle. It took a warrior's heart to conquer pain and trauma such as what she had survived, but it was a battle he would not let her face alone. She didn't know him, didn't know he was friends with the professor who had freed her from Vadym, but that was a good thing for now.

She needed to look forward, not back. Learning who he was would only delay her healing. So he would keep his involvement a secret for now.

The flight attendant returned with a bottle of water and saw that Elena was sleeping.

"How is she feeling?" the flight attendant asked in Russian.

"Better, but very tired. I'm sorry we frightened you," Dimitri said. He knew it probably looked like he and Elena were having sex in the bathroom, so he'd explained that she had a terrible fear of flying and had suffered a panic attack.

"Let me know if either of you need anything."

"Thank you." Dimitri turned his gaze back to Elena. He'd pulled a few strings to get her seat changed to business class and had made sure his seat was next to hers. His foresight had been prudent. She had already needed him, and he had been there.

He curled his fingers on the lever of his seat as he remembered how soft and silky her hair had felt beneath his hand. She was beautiful inside and out. Her honey-blonde hair glowed in the soft overhead lights, and her pure green eyes had fascinated him. She was fierce and brave. Now it was his duty to protect her from harm. He had grown bored in Moscow. Fighting corruption and greed had become less and less inspiring as time had passed. Saving Elena had given him a new purpose in life.

Dimitri grasped the gold signet ring on his pinky finger and twisted the thick band, an old habit he had while thinking. On the ring's surface was the emblem of a feathered bird rising from a flame. A phoenix. Inside the band was inscribed *"Virtute et valare luceo non uro,"* which was Latin for *"By virtue and valor I shine, not burn."*

It was the motto of the White Army, a private army of men and women who still believed in protecting the memory of the dynasty of the Romanovs in Russia but also in the power of a Russia that allowed freedom and truly democratic ideas to reign. They had spent the last century fighting against the Communists and the Soviets, as well as the corruption that had thrived and now fed upon its carcass.

To live in the White Army was to live with danger. The government sought to wipe them out, but Dimitri and his closest friends were talented at playing the game of seeming corrupt when in reality they were far from it. It kept them off the Kremlin's radar.

Dimitri set the water bottle in the cupholder between his and Elena's seats and retrieved his tablet from his briefcase. The other passengers were either asleep or watching movies or reading. He'd chosen the back row of business class so he would have a large dividing wall between him and the first row of economy class. That way no one could see his tablet screen.

He turned on his computer and logged in with his fingerprint before he accessed the file he wanted and then scrolled down until he found Elena Allen's dossier. His friend Leo was the technical genius in their small cell, and he had dug up all there was to know about Elena, right down to her blood type. She was twenty years old and a junior at Pepperdine University. She had skipped a year of college by having good exam scores and taking college classes while in high school. She was a double major in anthropology and finance. Her favorite foods were pizza, lobster rolls, clam bisque soup, chocolate ice cream, and Diet Coke. She loved silly rom-coms and romance novels. She was a dreamer, but also a doer. She had been adopted at birth, taken in by an older couple in Maine who'd always wanted children.

Leo had acquired pictures of Elena's past from God knows where. There were pictures of a tiny blonde girl in a grass-stained soccer uniform grinning at the camera. There were pictures of her face bent close to birthday cakes ablaze with candles, graduation pictures, and even one of Elena standing in front of a car at sixteen as she proudly held up her driver's license. From the outside it looked like she'd had a perfect, coddled life. But Dimitri could read between the lines, she'd pushed herself at school, worked jobs during high school and college, earned a scholarship and worked hard. She was strong.

Dimitri couldn't help but smile at Elena's adorable face in the pictures. She was so vibrant, so full of life. And that roaring fire that defined her had very nearly been extinguished by Vadym. Dimitri was not going to let that happen. He felt as though he were holding that flame in his palms now, shielding it until it could return to that unstoppable inferno that only grew stronger in the wind, not weaker.

He turned off the tablet and slid it back into his brief-case before he turned off the light above him. Then he retrieved the blankets from under their seats and pressed the button to recline Elena's seat back into a bed. She didn't even stir as the seat moved. He tucked a pillow beneath her head, wrapped one of the fleece blankets around her, and then finally closed his own eyes.

These next few months were going to be the hardest. He had to find a way into Elena's life and begin the process of helping her heal. Maxim and Nicholas, his two other friends in his group, thought Elena couldn't be healed, but Leo believed it was possible. Dimitri held on to that hope with all his might.

As he slipped into a land of dreams, images from his past plagued him, ones of empty palaces and ghosts who stirred up secrets in the shadows and dust. He kept seeing a face, one in a portrait that had once hung in an imperial palace a hundred years ago and had been smuggled away, the child in that painting now long forgotten . . .

2

Elena slept all through the night and into the morning, nearly nine of the twelve hours between Moscow and Los Angeles. When she finally woke, she found herself tucked beneath blankets she didn't remember putting over herself. She sat up and hit the button to turn her bed back into a chair. The man next to her was sipping a cup of coffee and reading a newspaper. It looked like the *Wall Street Journal*.

A man who read a physical paper was kind of hot. Okay, really hot. And combine that with all the other things about him . . . she couldn't stop looking at him. She was feeling true, deep attraction to this stranger. Just as quickly as the thought hit her brain, she banished it.

"Did you sleep well?" the man asked, still perusing his paper.

"Uh . . . Yeah. Really well, actually. I don't think I've felt safe since—I mean, *slept that well* in months."

He sipped his coffee again and then handed her a bottle of water. "Drink this. You need to rehydrate. Then you can order breakfast." He passed her a slender menu, and she drank half the bottle of water before she looked at her options. By the time she was ready, the man beside her had summoned the flight attendant so she could order.

"I'll take two eggs over easy, whole wheat toast, and bacon. Thank you so much." Elena passed the menu to Dimitri, who handed it to the flight attendant. He took her order on a small electronic pad and left. Elena peeped at her seatmate, feeling suddenly shy.

"Thank you again for last night, for keeping me from . . ." She stopped just before she said "falling apart" out loud.

"You're welcome."

"I'm Elena Allen," she offered.

He held out a hand to her. "Dimitri Razin."

Elena hesitated a second before putting her hand in his. "Do you have experience with a lot of crying women?" She tried to laugh, but the sound came out rough. She hadn't felt humor, let alone joy, in months. It was one more thing Vadym had ripped away from her.

"A pleasure to meet you." Dimitri clasped her hand in his. "And I do not have a lot of experience with crying women, but I am quite capable of dealing with it." His grip was firm but not crushing, and his hand was warm, just like his body had been when he'd held her in his arms. A sudden feeling of despair came over her as she realized that she would never see this man again after the flight. Some part of her felt connected to him.

"So are you traveling to Los Angeles on business?" she asked when her food arrived. She dug into her eggs and toast, feeling hungry for the first time in a long while, and it made her weirdly relaxed and conversational. It must have been because she had slept and had a good cry. People always made fun of crying, but last night, sobbing until she had exhausted herself had made her feel lighter, as though some of Vadym's evil had bled out of her through the tears. She wasn't whole, not by a long shot, but she felt better.

"Not exactly business. There are some interests I need to oversee and protect."

She found herself lost in Dimitri's blue eyes. An ocean existed in that gaze, pulling her down beneath the surface, yet she wasn't drowning.

"And you, *kiska*? What are you going to do in Los Angeles?"

"I *was* going to college at Pepperdine, but my school has given me a semester off." A few days before she left Moscow she'd gotten the news that she'd been granted a pause in her classes to recover from what had happened. Moscow had given her class credit for the completed work and she could finish up her Russian language credits at Pepperdine.

"What will you do with your free time?" Dimitri seemed genuinely interested.

"Probably lie on the beach, see a few museums." She wanted to do normal things, *fun* things. She wanted to be a person again. As much as she loved school, she really did need time to regroup. Everything felt overwhelming now, and she was afraid trying to focus on classes would be a bad idea. Vadym had kept her locked up, shamed like an animal in that dark, enclosed space. Every minute of the day, she'd faced the possibility of death and torture. It wasn't easy to simply revert back to the old Elena who might frolic about in a park or lie on a beach and sunbathe. That Elena no longer existed.

"The beach, that sounds lovely." Dimitri smiled. "Perhaps I will see you there?"

From any other man it would have sounded like a pickup line, but with him it sounded hopeful, and that tenderness in his eyes seemed to cradle her body with invisible hands.

God, what was wrong with her? She was fixated on this man and how safe he made her feel, like some baby chick who had peeped out of her shell and latched onto the first creature she saw.

"Yeah, if you're ever near Malibu, maybe I'll see you." She laughed it off, trying to shake the sudden bout of nervous excitement at the thought of running into him on a beach.

"Passengers, please prepare for landing," one of the cabin crew announced.

Elena put up her tray table and kept silent as the plane began to descend. Her hand touched the edge of Dimitri's palm on the armrest. His skin was soft, and something seemed to jump from his skin to hers. She couldn't help but imagine what it would be like if he really touched her, put those hands on her body . . .

What was she thinking? She didn't want that. She didn't want to be touched ever again. Her stomach flipped as she felt his gaze on her. He didn't say anything, however, and after a moment, he turned his focus to stowing his briefcase below his seat.

All too soon, they were disembarking. She and Dimitri stayed close as they left the plane and headed for customs. Their paths diverged at the point where US citizens were led in one direction, while non−US citizens went the other. The thought of suddenly never seeing this man again sent a flash of panic through her.

"Dimitri," she called out as he started to walk away.

He paused and looked over his shoulder. His square jaw and high cheekbones made him look like a movie star from an old black-and-white film. He had a timeless appeal that left her near speechless every time she looked right at him.

"Thank you," she said again, but her heart wanted to say so much more than that. A storm of emotions flashed across his features before that tranquility returned.

"I am always happy to help you, *kiska*." He turned and walked away.

Elena carried her backpack and got in the line for US citizens. When she got up to the front of her line, a female customs officer waved her forward, and she presented her passport. The officer scanned it and frowned.

"You were in Russia for several months. Is that correct?"

"Yes. I went there for a study abroad semester, but . . ."

The officer waited for her to continue. Lord, she was going to tell this woman what had happened. If only she'd just kept her answer limited to school and hadn't said 'but'.

"I am . . . was kidnapped at a bar and held captive for two months."

The officer's lips parted, and her eyes widened. "Oh my God, I'm so sorry."

"It's okay," Elena reassured the other woman. "I'm free now, and I'm here."

"That you are. Welcome home." The custom's officer handed her back her passport, and she was waved through.

Elena cringed as she realized that she would have to explain her situation like this again and again. It was unavoidable. And everyone was going to react just like that, and she was going to hate it. At this point, Elena considered just living on the beach and avoiding everyone like a hermit.

After she picked up her luggage, she called for a taxi to

take her to where she would stay for the next few months. She'd lost her spot in the Pepperdine dorms a long time ago, but Royce Devereaux, the professor who had helped save her, apparently owned a Malibu beach house. He'd insisted that she stay there for the rest of the semester until housing opened back up at the university. She called her parents while she sat in traffic. She'd spoken to them nearly a hundred times since she'd reached the embassy in Ulaanbaatar, but this was, in a way, the most important call she would make because now she was on US soil.

"Honey!" Her mother's relieved voice came through the line. "Did you get through customs okay?"

"Hey, Mom. Yeah, I got through okay."

"So now you're safe in LA, right?" Her mother's tone turned sharp with worry. "Your father and I should be there in a few days. We wanted to come right away, but all the flights were booked up."

"I'll be fine until you get here. I'm almost at Dr. Devereaux's house. I'm just stuck in traffic."

"Good. Your father and I can't wait to see you. He'll be sad he missed you. He's just run to the store for a few things."

"I'll send him a text when I get to the house," she promised. Elena couldn't imagine how terrified her parents must have been when she'd gone missing. They'd tried to act all calm, but when she'd first seen them on the computer at the embassy in Ulaanbaatar, her mother had burst into tears.

"You know, I really like that man, Dr. Devereaux."

"Me too," Elena admitted. She'd had to tell her parents all the details of what had happened to her—how could she not?—and she'd told them about Royce and his grad student assistant, Kenzie, and how they had saved her. Royce and Kenzie had flown back to the States earlier and had made the trip to Maine to personally introduce themselves to her parents and tell them that Elena was alive and well.

For the most part.

"You know, he said you can transfer to his university on Long Island anytime."

"I know. I've been thinking about it." But the truth was, right now she just needed to find herself again. She couldn't make another big life change until she felt more secure.

"Call me when you get there. Text me Dr. Deveraux's address so your father and I will have it for when we come."

"I will," Elena promised, and hung up.

The driver stopped at the gatehouse and helped Elena with her suitcase, then drove off. Elena approached the gate and checked her email for the gate code. She pressed the five-digit code on the keypad, and the white wall of the gate slid open silently.

Elena's jaw hit the ground as she saw the house in front of her. She had expected a cozy beach house, but what she was looking at was no quaint cottage. It was a *mansion.* Something her Malibu Barbie would have had when Elena was a child. The front of the house looked like an Italian villa, and there was a lush garden between her and the front door. Beyond it was an endless expanse of blue water.

Elena rolled her suitcase down the stone walkway to the front door. The same code unlocked that door as well. She stepped into the house, and her heart leapt with quiet joy. It was even more beautiful inside, with modern décor that was light and airy, yet the furniture looked comfortable and lived in. She could stay in a place like this and just feel safe and calm forever. It was paradise. She closed the front door behind her and left her suitcase by the spiral staircase that led up to the second floor.

"Oh, wow . . ." Ahead of her was a huge living room with a large leather sectional sofa and a massive eighty-five-inch TV. Beyond that was a kitchen that was bigger than her dorm room at Pepperdine. Elena kept walking until she reached the outdoor deck, and then she froze.

She wasn't alone. A man stood at the balcony's edge, hands braced on the railing, his face hidden from her as he stared at the sea. He wore khaki shorts, a pair of athletic shoes, and a loose black T-shirt that clung to his broad shoulders as the breeze plastered it against his skin.

That wasn't Royce . . .

Fear spiked within her. She stumbled back and tripped over the rug and fell to the ground with a crash. Her head glanced off the island counter, and she cried out in pain.

The man on the porch turned to face her, and Elena flinched, her eyes closing as she waited for whatever awful thing would come next. His footfalls were quick as he rushed toward her.

"Please, please, don't hurt me," she begged, and held her hands and arms above her face to shield herself.

"*Kiska?*" a familiar, rich deep voice said to her.

Slowly, she forced her eyes open and lowered her hands from her face.

Dimitri Razin, the man who'd been so kind, so helpful on the flight from Moscow, was crouching over her inside Royce Devereaux's Malibu house.

"Dimitri?" she gasped. "Wh—what are you doing here?" It couldn't be a coincidence he was here. This had to be a trap. He was one of Vadym's men, come to take her back.

"My old friend owns this house. He heard I was to be staying in Los Angeles for a few months, and he told me I could stay here rather than at a hotel. What are you doing here?" he aske as she got to her feet.

She looked at him, uncertain. She made sure she kept her distance from him, enough room to run if he made any sudden moves, but she tried to look as if she were calmer now. "Uh . . . the same thing. I lost my dorm at Pepperdine, and since I'm not taking classes, a friend offered to let me stay here for the semester."

"Ah . . ." Understanding lit Dimitri's eyes. "You are a friend of Royce Devereaux?"

Elena nodded. "You as well?" Why hadn't Royce warned her that he was going to let some random stranger —a Russian, no less—stay here while she was here? As soon as she had a moment alone, she was going to call him and demand answers.

"We've known each other a long time. He is a good man."

"On that we agree." She started to sit up and groaned as pain swamped her. She reached up to touch her head, and blood came away on her fingertips.

"Here, let me."

He tried to reach for her, and she flinched back. Then the reality of what she'd done swamped her, and she forced herself to relax as he again gently reached for her, this time lifting her up. He gripped her by her waist and set her on top of the kitchen island. She started to slide off, to get far away from him, until she understood exactly *why* he was here.

"Stay, *kiska*, I won't hurt you," he said. The order was gentle but firm and absolute. The old Elena would have shivered in delight and excitement, but right now her body and mind were at war over how to react.

Dimitri returned with a first aid kit and set it on the counter by her hip. He opened the case and dug through the contents, removing an antiseptic cloth, a tube of antibacterial cream, and a small Band-Aid.

Elena stared at him as he ripped open the packet containing the antiseptic cloth. Then he cupped her chin with one hand and tilted her head to the side. Their faces were close enough that she noticed a hint of stubble on his jaw, creating an enticing shadow. God, he was a beautiful man, masculine in all the right ways— even his smell, which was natural and woodsy. Vadym had always worn too much expensive cologne that made her gag.

Dimitri dabbed at her forehead. "It does not appear deep."

Pain flared at the spot, but she didn't react. If she had learned anything while being held captive, it was never to show you were in pain, especially to those who thrived on it.

Dimitri rubbed the antibacterial cream on the small cut and then placed the Band-Aid on it.

"You are very strong." He set a hand on her shoulder, squeezing gently.

"No, I'm not," she muttered as he walked away to throw the bloodied cloth in the trash. He had no idea what she'd been through and how very weak she'd felt for the last two months. The old Elena had been strong, but who she was now? She felt as delicate as spun glass.

"So, *kiska* . . . it seems we are both staying here. Is that all right with you?"

"You're asking me?" She was surprised. "I . . ." She paused to think it over. Could she relax with him here under the same roof? He kept his distance, not crowding her, and it gave her a chance to think with a clear head. "If

Royce invited you, I wouldn't want to be rude or anything by asking you to leave."

"No, *kiska*. I can only stay if you are comfortable. Forget about Royce. What do *you* feel about me staying?"

She was quiet a long moment. Her first instinct was to say no, but she was tired of being afraid, tired of letting that fear control her life. It didn't mean she needed to go skydiving tomorrow, but she needed and wanted to start taking steps toward being her old self again if she was to eventually get past her trauma. That meant she could agree to him staying here. It wasn't like they would be sharing a bed or anything. Just housemates.

"I'm okay with it," she replied with more confidence.

The tension inside her suddenly ebbed away, like the tide of the ocean pulling it farther out to sea.

"Very well. I'll stay. Do you wish to choose which bedroom you prefer to sleep in? He has several. I am fine with any of them, so you choose where you want to sleep, and I will take one of the other rooms."

"Really? Okay, thanks." She slid off the counter and wobbled a bit. He caught her around the waist, steadying her with his muscled body. Elena leaned into him a little longer than was prudent, but he exuded such warmth and safety that she was drawn to him like a moth fluttering toward his flame.

"This way." He released her, and she followed him on steadier legs as they climbed the stairs. There were four bedrooms in the house, two of which faced the sea. One of them had a bed that directly faced the ocean. The blue walls and the gray carpeted floors worked well with the private balcony, which offered her a place to stay alone when she needed it. "Can I have this one?"

"It's yours. I will retrieve your suitcase."

"Oh—you don't—need to—" She spun around, but he was already gone. She slid the clear glass balcony door open and walked over to the lounge chair that faced the water and lay down on it. The dark-blue waves crashed upon the shore in a white froth. Lines of dark-green-and-black seaweed wavered and rippled on the surface. It hypnotized Elena, and before she could help it, she was slipping into sleep. It was a deep, dreamless, restorative sleep without nightmares.

It was well into the early evening when she woke. Without the sun burning overhead, the cold sea air had chilled her, but a warm blanket was wrapped around her body. Dimitri must have done that. She blinked and stared at the sky. The sun was a red ball dipping halfway below the horizon. She'd slept most of the day away. Elena climbed off the chair and walked into the bedroom. Her suitcase rested on the luggage rack, and a handwritten note was propped on top of it.

ELENA,

Please shower if you wish and come down when you're ready. I will have dinner for you.

Dimitri

SHE PLACED THE NOTE ON THE BED AND DUG THROUGH her suitcase until she found her toiletry kit. There was a massive bathroom connected to her bedroom. After she tested the door, she locked herself in and stripped out of her clothes.

She made the mistake of glancing over her shoulder at her back in the mirror. A pattern of knotted flesh formed dozens of crisscrossed scars on her back.

This would be with her forever, Vadym's mark of ownership. No matter how much she healed, it would always be there to remind her that she had once been broken. Elena's lips trembled, and she bit her bottom lip as she turned away from the sight in the mirror. *No.* Vadym couldn't find her here. She was safe in America. She had to move forward.

She stepped into the large glass shower and sighed at the sight of the ocean through the chest-high window. So often when she had been in that dark chamber in Vadym's office she'd wanted to be anywhere else, even in the middle of the ocean with no chance of seeing land ever again.

Elena placed her palms against the shower wall and let the hot water cascade down her body. This was land. She was safe. No more endless darkness, no more suffocation, starvation, no more drowning in her own head.

It was a long while later when she turned the water off and left the shower. She toweled dry her hair and braided it over one shoulder before she changed into jeans and a light sweater. It was wonderfully warm in California, even in the winter. After the wintry climate of Moscow, she could almost wear shorts, but she had packed only winter outfits for her time in Russia. Her parents had cleaned out her dorm at Pepperdine after she'd gone missing, and all of her summer clothes were now back in Maine. She would have to go shopping, but first, she had to figure out if she could live with a stranger under the same roof.

She found Dimitri in the kitchen, setting plates and silverware on an informal, small dining table that overlooked the patio and the sea. The lightly tanned golden skin on his forearms showed a hint of veins in the defined muscles. Many men didn't look good in shorts, but Dimitri's sculpted calves with just a light dusting of hair were well suited for them. Everything about him was athletic, a honed physical perfection that no woman could easily ignore.

"Did you have a good shower, *kiska?*" he asked. Heavenly smells wafted toward her from the stove and the oven.

"Yes. Why do you keep calling me *kiska?* It means *kitten*, doesn't it?"

His full lips curved into a soft smile that only enhanced the natural seduction of his features. "Yes. It is a common endearment in Russia. Does it offend you?"

She hadn't expected that question. "No, but you don't know me enough to have an endearment for me."

"I know that something has happened to you, something that has left you hurt and afraid. I admit, I am overly protective by nature. Your pain . . ." He paused as though choosing his words carefully. "It calls to me. I want to protect you, as I did on the plane."

"I . . ." Elena didn't know what to say at first. "I don't *need* protection."

Again that soft smile confused and frustrated her. "You don't need anyone, *kiska*. You're strong, so very strong. But I'm here if you ever want me." He nodded at one of the chairs at the table he'd set for dinner.

Elena didn't move at first. Why did this stranger think he could come into her life and just tell her all this? What she needed was to be left alone. She finally sat, and he returned to the kitchen and prepared two plates, setting one down in front of her.

She stared at the meat, potatoes, and carrots. "Pot roast?"

"You are too thin," was his only reply before he sat down across from her.

She couldn't argue with that. Her clothes were almost hanging off her. She had lost so much weight when Vadym had begun starving her. She'd gone down three sizes, and it hadn't been healthy. Starvation could rob a person of their hair, their healthy immune system, and their muscle. Fat was the last thing to go. During her captivity, she'd been weak, barely able to walk some days, which only gave Vadym an excuse to beat her more.

She'd been free from her prison for more than a week now, and she'd realized that putting weight back on wasn't going to be easy because she'd lost her appetite as well. It would take time to reach her healthy weight again. Now, though, her stomach felt like an empty pit, and smelling the pot roast caused her stomach to grumble.

"Please, eat," Dimitri encouraged.

She dug in, finishing all that he had put on her plate.

"Would you like some more?" He stood and took her plate before she could argue and filled it with a second serving.

When she was halfway through that, he finally spoke. "On the plane, you said you were terrified that we wouldn't leave Moscow. Why was that?"

She froze, her fork halfway to her mouth. She'd forgotten she'd said that. "Uh . . . I was there to study at Moscow State University for a semester and really didn't want to stay."

He took a sip of water, and his eyes fixed on her. It wasn't a threatening look, but there was something more to it than just curiosity. He knew something terrible had happened to her, not that she had any idea how he could know.

Her hand trembled as she reached for her glass of water. "I'm sorry, but I just don't want to talk about it, okay?"

He nodded. "I understand, *kiska*. But sometimes when you put words to your pain, it can help you overcome it. We are always more afraid of what we do not speak of than what we face directly." He stood and carried his plate into the kitchen to wash it.

She expected him to come back to the table and pressure her with more questions. He didn't. And that made her feel lonelier than she ever had in her life.

3

Dimitri paused just inside his bedchamber, his eyes fixated on the sea just a short way away from the house. He needed to clear his head, get some air, so he changed into a swimsuit. Elena's pain was strong enough that it threatened to strangle him. As long as she bottled it up, she would never be free of its weight. In the end, it would drown her. Frustration made his hands twitch. This wasn't something he could fight with his hands. It was something he had to confront with gentleness. It was the opposite of everything he was used to doing. He wanted to slay her dragons, kill the man who'd hurt her, but Vadym was already dead, and now she needed gentleness and support from him.

He tucked his cell phone into his board shorts before coming back downstairs. He saw Elena in the kitchen clearing away her dishes. As much as he wanted to pamper her, these normal tasks would help her settle back into a sense of normalcy. Dimitri had already opened the back door when he heard the soft patter of bare feet behind him.

"Um . . . are you going somewhere?" she asked shyly.

He glanced over his shoulder. "I'm going down to the beach. You are welcome to come. There is a path down the back steps, and there's a towel rack down there." He pointed to a shelf that held plush pale-blue beach towels. He left her alone again, hating every second of it, but she should only come to him when she wanted him. Forcing his presence on her was not going to establish trust between them. He was not here to force her to do anything. He simply wanted to help in whatever way she needed.

The sand of the beach was warm despite it being winter. He always marveled at how lovely the weather was here year-round. He'd visited LA a dozen times in the last five years, and each time he had enjoyed it. He gazed at the horizon. The sky above was a deep gold, but the light on dark water turned almost purple with golden flashes on the surface.

"That's beautiful," Elena said.

If Dimitri hadn't been trained not to flinch at unexpected sounds, he would have just then. He'd been so lost staring at the sunset that he had not heard her come down.

"It is," he agreed.

"People always say sunsets and sunrises are too cliché to enjoy, you know? But they really are the most beautiful things in the world." Her voice was soft, wistful, and it tugged at his heart.

How many nights had she lain in captivity wondering when she would see another sunrise or sunset? In that moment, Dimitri wished Vadym was alive just so he could kill him all over again. His biggest regret was that he hadn't been able to do the deed himself.

His friends had seen to it while he'd been watching over Elena. They had poisoned him while he ate at a restaurant, then they'd broken into his home and office. Leo had used Vadym's computer to trace every woman he had ever taken, hurt, and killed. Interpol had received the information anonymously, and the families of those other young women had been notified. Elena had been the last woman Vadym had gotten his hands on. She was the only one who had survived.

His hands curled into fists as the last rays of light began to fade. It was the best way to tamp down the fury that rose whenever he thought of Vadym and others like him.

A hand touched his bare back. "Are you okay?" He tensed, then forced himself to relax, his hands unclenching.

"Yes. It's been a trying day," he murmured.

"Tell me about it. By the way, *how* did you beat me

here after we got off the plane? I saw the line for non–US citizens. You should have been there for hours."

She was observant as well as intelligent. He smiled a little, relaxing. "I have a special passport that allows me to go into most countries in an expedited manner. It is a perk of my business." He retrieved his towel and rolled it out.

She joined him on the sand with her own towel. "And what business is that, exactly?" At first her body was balled up tight, her knees tucked up close to her chin, but as the silence settled between them she relaxed and stretched out.

"It varies. I have real estate interests, tech company interests, and other things."

"So how does that get you a special passport?"

He couldn't help but grin. She didn't relent. This was the real Elena, the one not afraid to seek answers.

"I may have some contacts in various governments." He glanced at her, and she was studying him intently.

One brow rose. "You're still not answering my question."

"Tell me what happened to you in Moscow, and I will answer your question."

She rolled her eyes. "Touché." She smiled a little, a sweet fire burning in her green eyes.

Dimitri took that as a small victory. He was digging the old Elena out of the dark abyss she had been tossed into.

"So . . . will you be going to work every day while

you're here or something?" She asked this casually, but he detected a dozen fears beneath that single simple query.

"Or something," he replied, then chuckled at her responding frown.

"My parents may come to visit."

He knew for a fact that they were coming out in a few days, but for some reason she didn't want to scare him off. She also didn't seem sure she wanted him near her. It was confusing to see someone want something and be afraid of it at the same time.

"I can stay somewhere else, if you wish, when they arrive," he said, keeping his tone gentle.

"It's not that, it's just . . . there might be some questions that could be awkward."

He lay back on the sand, propping himself up on his elbows. "Questions?"

"Yeah. They might get the wrong idea if they see you here. I mean . . . it's not like we're together."

"We are two people staying at the house of a mutual friend at the same time." He said it so normally that he could practically feel her relaxing again.

"Right. Of course." She lay back on her towel, and he did the same. The night sky darkened, a few bright stars flickering above.

"*Kiska*," he whispered.

She didn't respond. He looked over and found her asleep again, curled up on her side, blonde hair spilling across the towel into the sand. He hated to wake her, but she needed to rest in her bed where it was safe.

He gently brushed her hair back from her face and tucked it behind her ear. "*Kiska*, wake up."

She stirred a little.

"*Kiska*, wake up," he commanded more firmly.

Elena rolled onto her back and yawned. "God, how long did I sleep?"

"Not long, but it will be cold out here soon. You should go inside and sleep."

She sat up and ran her hands through her hair before she picked up her towel, and he followed suit. They were both silent as he let her into the house first, then locked the door to the patio behind him. They should be safe here, but he'd been trained never to take a chance with an unlocked door.

"See you tomorrow?" she asked from the top of the stairs.

He looked up at her from the bottom. "I'll be here," he promised.

He waited until he heard the door click before he pulled his phone out and dialed a private secure line.

"Dimitri, I was worried you might have fallen into the ocean," Nicholas teased.

"Yeah, how are the beaches?" Leo cut in dryly.

"The three of us are freezing our asses off, and here he is suntanning," Maxim grumbled.

It was good to hear their voices again.

"I haven't fallen into the ocean. The beaches are nice; no, and I'm sorry you're freezing, Maxim," he answered them with a chuckle.

"Maybe she needs three more bodyguards," Nicholas volunteered.

"Yeah, I'd like in on that assignment. I've been pulling more of her records. Do you know she's got ancient Russian DNA?" Leo asked.

Dimitri walked to the living room and sat down on the sectional. "What? That wasn't in the dossier you sent."

"Well, I just hacked into her ancestry account an hour ago. Do you think you could get me a DNA sample? I'd like to run one in our databases. I can't pull certain info off the basic records they run on these civilian DNA sites."

"What, like blood?"

"Or saliva. It's a lot better than a hair sample," Leo said.

"I swear you get hard when you talk about that science shit," Maxim grumbled in the background.

"I have blood. I'll have it overnighted to you." Dimitri headed into the guest bathroom and retrieved the bloody cloth from earlier when he'd cleaned the cut on Elena's head. He put the cloth into a clear sandwich bag and tucked it into his briefcase.

"Can you tell me anything about her profile?" he asked Leo.

"Well, she has some interesting matches. You know

there's a lot of DNA that our government has removed from all public databases except for ours, and they don't know we have it. She has a few common ancestors that make me wonder . . ."

"Wonder what?" Dimitri asked, the hair on the back of his neck rising.

"I can't say for sure. Just get me that DNA and I think I can get answers."

"How is she doing?" Maxim asked. Of their quartet, Maxim was the most serious. Nicholas was a charming player, and Leo was their technical genius. Maxim had been the one to poison Vadym and send Dimitri proof of his death.

"She is badly hurt, but not broken. Her fire is still there, just very weak." Dimitri would never have been able to talk to anyone else about Elena and the way he'd felt that first time he'd seen her. It had been difficult enough to explain to Royce Devereaux that he had this unexplainable need to be near her, to protect and heal her. But these three men understood.

"When she's ready to hear who you really are, you must show her that *he* is dead," Maxim said.

Vadym had taken one of Maxim's sisters. They never found her body, didn't even know if she was alive or dead, and the trauma had broken his family apart. Killing Vadym had been Maxim's right, and he had succeeded where so many others had failed.

"I will, but I'm still a stranger to her. She doesn't know

I was there at the embassy in Ulaanbaatar the day she was rescued. I need to keep it that way, at least for now. She doesn't need any reminders of what happened, not until she's ready to talk about it."

"How are you going to go about this?" Nicholas asked. "I mean, I'm no psychologist, but you need to be careful with her . . ."

"I'm not sure. I will have to let her guide me as to what she wants and needs."

"Call us if you need us," Maxim said. "Seriously, I want to be on a beach right now."

Dimitri hung up and stared out the window at the front gardens for a long while before going to bed. He stripped out of his clothes and changed into a light pair of cotton pajama bottoms and lay back in the king-size bed. Next door was the room Elena had chosen. He gazed at the ceiling. His eyes had just started to close when he heard a strangled scream. Dimitri was on his feet in an instant, rushing into her room.

Elena was on the floor, her sheets tangled around her body as she writhed and screamed. He knelt and tried to free her, but her fist hit his jaw with an unexpectedly strong blow.

"Fuck," he muttered as he blocked the second punch while she thrashed beneath him. "Elena!" He barked out her name, and her movements stilled. He had a firm grip around one of her wrists, and he could feel the frantic beat of her pulse beneath his fingertips.

"Please don't hurt me. I'll do anything," she whimpered. Her eyes were clamped shut, and she had angled her body away from his as much as possible.

"Elena," he said gently. "You were dreaming. It's over now. Open your eyes."

She gave a childlike shake of her head, and he realized that she was still locked in whatever nightmare she'd been having.

"*Kiska*," he said even more softly as he released her wrists. She curled herself into a tight ball inside the tangled blankets on the floor. Her entire body was shaking. He stroked her hair back from her face. "Did you fall out of the bed?"

"No—no. I can't sleep on beds. Too soft. I . . ." She almost said something more, but before she could, she seemed to wake enough to realize that she was talking and stopped.

Dimitri understood. Vadym would have kept her in a cell on a hard floor with perhaps only a dirty blanket to cover herself. He wouldn't have let her use a bed. This was not uncommon with soldiers who returned from war. They were used to hard bunks in military barracks, and when they reentered the civilian world, plush California king mattresses were simply too much. Well, this was stopping tonight. He was not letting her spend one more minute on the floor.

He wrapped his arms around her blanketed body and lifted her up. Then he set her down on her bed again, but he didn't leave. He pulled the light comforter over his body as he lay down beside her, and then he pulled her into his arms. She was still shaking, but he absorbed her trembling within his own body and held her until she finally stilled.

"*Kiska*, you will sleep in a bed from now on, do you understand?" he whispered in her ear. She wasn't asleep, her pulse was still too rapid, but she didn't argue with him. "And I will hold you like this until whatever haunts your dreams fades away."

Again she did not argue, but slowly, inch by inch, her body loosened. After what felt like an eternity, her breath slowed and the beat of her heart steadied.

Dimitri lay awake for several long hours. Holding her in his arms like this had awakened something inside him. He'd always been a protective dominant, but how he felt about Elena went *beyond* lust and desire. It was something deeper, something in her blood that called to his.

When he'd been at the US embassy in Ulaanbaatar, helping Royce and Kenzie get medical care, he'd seen this wisp of a blonde beauty carried to another medical exam room. She had been in shock, her green eyes glazed over with terror and exhaustion.

He had gone unseen, fading into the crowd and shadows as chaos filled the embassy hallways. Later, he'd visited Kenzie while Royce was sleeping off his wounds and heavily sedated. Dimitri had met Kenzie for coffee at the embassy, and they both sat silently for a long moment.

"Kenzie, who is the girl?"

Kenzie's brown eyes rose warily to his. "Girl?"

"The blonde one who came in with you."

"That's Elena Allen." Kenzie let out a bone-deep sigh and rubbed her closed eyes with her thumb and forefinger. "Vadym abducted her from the very bar you, Royce, and I went to. Held her captive for at least a couple of months." She met his gaze. "She was raped, tortured, and starved."

"Vadym did this to her?" Dimitri clarified.

Kenzie nodded.

"Then he is a dead man," Dimitri promised.

Kenzie's eyes turned hard. "That's one promise you had better keep. The world doesn't need a man like that in it. He's evil. Even poison is too good for him."

Dimitri had reached across the table and closed his fingers around Kenzie's. "He will be erased. I vow it." Shortly after that conversation, Kenzie, Royce, and Elena had all been transferred to the US embassy in Moscow to make preparations for their return to the States.

Kenzie had no idea how deeply he'd meant that vow. As a member of the White Army, a descendant of those who had once guarded the Romanovs, he lived by his honor, and he would not fail in his promise.

He had been haunted by Elena's face every moment since. As soon as he had heard that the US embassy in Moscow was ready to return Elena to the States, he had called Royce and set his plan in motion. He would be her shadow, help her heal and move on from the darkness of her past. He was needed back in Russia, but now that he had Elena in his arms, he wasn't about to let her go, even if that meant turning his back on his life's work.

As much as he missed his father, he was relieved his father was dead; otherwise, they would have disagreed about this. He would have ordered Dimitri to return to his duties, but Dimitri would have refused. His place in the world was now tied to wherever Elena was.

He was her man until the end, whatever end that may be.

❧ 4 ❧

Elena's face was warmed by sunlight, and a cozy feeling of security wrapped around her. She lay there a long while half-asleep, hearing the waves crash upon the sandy shore. The bed beneath her was soft, almost too soft, and she rubbed her cheek against the pillow, breathing in the heavenly scent of a man.

Every bone in her body went still. Her breath halted halfway between her lungs and her lips. Where was she? She cautiously peeped an eye open and found herself in the middle of a California king bed with a fluffy white comforter tucked up to her chin.

Bits and pieces of last night came back to her. She had balled up her bedding on the floor to sleep, and when the nightmares had started, she'd screamed, and then *he* had come into the room. Dimitri.

He had picked her up and put her on the bed. He had

slept with her. She threw back the covers and frantically searched her body. Her T-shirt, cotton shorts, and underwear were all still on. She didn't feel like she'd been violated. She was positive. After all that Vadym had done to her, she'd become hyperaware of when she had been used. But Dimitri hadn't used her. His scent clung to the sheets, and after a moment she rubbed her cheek against the pillows as her heart calmed, wanting to imprint that scent deep within her.

Part of her was tempted to lounge about all day, but that wasn't like her. She retrieved her phone from the nightstand and checked her messages. There was one from Kenzie, reminding her that they needed to video chat when she woke up. She checked that the door to the hall was closed, then called. The other woman answered almost immediately.

"Hey!" Kenzie grinned, but Elena could see the worry in her friend's eyes.

"Hey, Kenzie." Elena went out onto the balcony and curled up in a chair facing the sea. She held up her phone to an appropriate angle.

"You got into Royce's house okay yesterday?"

"Yeah, but . . . Kenzie, you didn't tell me I would have a roommate."

Her friend's face paled. "A what?"

"Some guy named Dimitri Razin. I actually met him on the flight over. He's nice, but it freaked me out to find he was staying here too. He said he's a friend of Royce's?"

Kenzie's brows drew together. "Royce!" she hollered away from the screen. "Just a second, Elena." Kenzie set her phone down, and Elena got a view of the marble ceiling. She could just barely hear a conversation in the background.

"You let Dimitri go and stay with her? What the *hell* were you thinking?"

"He's a good man. You *know* that," Royce countered.

"A good man with a serious kink . . . and you know what he's like . . . possessive, all alpha male—"

"I didn't hear you complaining when I shared you with him."

Elena's lips parted in shock. Royce and Dimitri had been with Kenzie at the same time? Vadym had never shared her, and that was the one thing she was grateful for. His greed had kept her safe from the added abuse of others.

There was a heartbeat of silence, and Kenzie growled, "I consented to that. Elena is a victim, Royce. You just fed her to a wolf."

"He won't touch her, not unless she asks him to, and maybe not even then," Royce shot back, his voice fading as they moved farther away.

The rest of the conversation wasn't audible and soon dissolved into angry whispers. Then the phone moved, and Kenzie's face was visible again, her cheeks red.

"Hey," she said again, far too casually.

Elena was tempted to pretend she hadn't heard that argument, but she had and now she had questions.

"Kenzie, who the hell is this guy? You just said he has a serious kink. What did you mean? Can I trust this guy?"

"Yeah, so Dimitri is a friend of Royce's. He's really powerful in Russia—we're talking a ridiculous amount of money and influence—but he's not like Vadym. He's a good guy, I swear."

"You trust him?" Elena asked.

"Yes. With my life," Kenzie replied without hesitation. "Royce is right. He won't do anything to you, not unless you ask him to."

Elena was silent a moment. "And the kink?"

"BDSM," Kenzie replied. "Like Royce. No sadism, just domination, sometimes bondage and discipline. You aren't into that, are you? I mean . . . after everything I don't think anyone could be."

"I was a little bit," Elena admitted quietly. "Before Vadym." It was the first time she'd said his name without it causing her physical pain and anxiety.

Kenzie didn't respond.

"Why is he here? He fed me a line about being here for work."

"Royce said he is looking to protect some valuable assets or something. If I can find out more, I'll let you know. And you let me know if I need to give Dimitri the boot. The whole point was for you to have a safe place to relax and pull yourself together, you know?"

Elena turned her gaze away from the sea and back toward the bed where she had slept through the night—unharmed in Dimitri's arms.

"I think I'm okay for now," she finally said.

"Well, you call me immediately if that changes, okay?"

"Okay." Elena ended the call and watched the waves roll in for a long time. There was a peace to be had in watching the blue water fall in on itself and transform into pale foaming tides that drifted in and out from the shore.

It was nearly noon when her stomach grumbled and she checked the time on her phone. She used to have a pretty silver watch, one her father had given her for her eighteenth birthday. But Vadym's henchman, Jov Tomenko, had stolen it and then lost it in some card game. The memory of that night made her fresh hunger briefly fade.

After a quick shower and a change of clothes, she decided she couldn't avoid seeing Dimitri again. She came downstairs, her steps quiet on the marble floor. She padded through room after room.

He wasn't *here* . . .

The thought that he'd left, that he hadn't said a word about leaving, left her feeling shaken. He'd promised to be here . . . She started to tremble.

She heard the front door click open. She tensed, suddenly rooted to the ground where she stood. Her stomach seized and her hands clenched as she readied herself for fight or flight. A moment later, Dimitri came inside and closed the door; the tension inside her bled away.

"Ah, good, you're awake. Do you want lunch?" He held up a bag of Mexican fast food.

"Tacos?" Her mouth immediately watered. After pizza, tacos were her favorite food.

"Yes, I hoped you would like them." He nodded toward the kitchen, and she joined him. He looked more intense today somehow. Perhaps it was the darker clothing he wore, dark-blue jeans and a black T-shirt and boots. Yesterday he'd seemed almost serene, but now she realized he was letting her see a new side to him, perhaps the *real* side. The old Elena would have been hooked on him like catnip.

"I, uh, do . . ." She wasn't sure what was making her mouth water more, the sight of the taco bag or the sight of *him*.

"Please sit. I'll get our plates."

His gentle but commanding tone had her instantly responding by dropping into the nearest chair at the table. She frowned at her own response.

"Dimitri, last night . . . ," she started uncertainly. "You came into my room."

"I did." He set a plate of three tacos in front of her.

"You touched me."

"I picked you up while you were enduring a nightmare. You were on the floor."

She shook her head in frustration, not even sure what she was trying to say. "You stayed in my bed."

"You needed to be held, *kiska*. Whatever happened to you, it was bad, perhaps the worst thing a person can endure. I knew only what I could offer you last night would help you. If you let me, I can be a good friend to you."

"I'm not going to just *let* you in my bed. We will never have sex. That's off the table."

She had to make this man understand. She couldn't have some casual hookup or fling. Even if she wanted him in that way, it wouldn't be possible. Her body couldn't handle being touched like that ever again.

"I am only a friend," Dimitri said. "You needed someone to help keep you grounded last night. That is all I did, and I do not expect anything from you." He pointed at her plate. "Now, please eat."

Still scowling a little, she pulled her plate close and picked up one of the tacos. It tasted like the food of the gods. A moan of pleasure escaped her lips. When she glanced at Dimitri, he was staring at her.

She swallowed audibly. He'd said he would only be a friend . . . but a man who looked like him didn't live as a monk, and apparently he'd been involved in a three-way with her friends Kenzie and Royce. She made a mental note not to let herself be attracted to him. She couldn't handle it if he changed his mind and wanted more.

"I thought you might want to shop for clothes,"

Dimitri said. "I imagine you had only winter clothes in Moscow?"

"Yeah, I could do with some shopping." She finished her tacos and put the plate in the dishwasher. He joined her, his hard body warm next to hers as he stood so close. She waited for the inevitable wave of panic, but it didn't come. He placed a hand on her arm, and she turned to look up at him.

"Would you mind if I go with you? I could use some distraction and activity."

"I . . ." She had every right to say no, but she didn't want to. While she might not know him well, she had two friends who could vouch for him, and she wanted to trust them and her own gut, which told her he was safe. "Okay. Could you be ready to leave in ten minutes?"

"Yes." He put his dishes away. "I'll drive."

"Wait, you have a car?"

"A rental. You asked how I got here before you did. Cabs often take a longer route to make their fares higher."

It made sense; her cab fare had been steep.

"I'll be back down in a bit." She raced upstairs and retrieved her purse, plus her new driver's license. Vadym had burned all the documents in her purse. Her passport had been in her Moscow apartment and left untouched, but everything else had been destroyed. She'd gotten some cash from the embassy, but it would be a few days before her replacement credit and debit cards would arrive. She would have to shop at a thrift store.

Dimitri was waiting for her by the front door. He held up a set of car keys.

"Ready?"

She nodded and put a hand on her purse, which was slung over one shoulder. The moment she got outside, she halted at the sight of the car waiting in front of her.

"Is that . . . ?"

"It is," Dimitri replied casually. He opened the passenger door of the Aston Martin for her. It was a sleek silver-gray sports car with ice-blue headlights.

"Where did you rent a car like this? You couldn't have gotten it from the airport." The sudden implausibility of his story raised more warning bells. Dimitri gunned the engine to life, and the initial rumble softened to a seductive purr.

"You're right. This is an Aston Martin One-77, worth about 1.4 million. I borrowed it from a friend. He dropped it off for me in short-term parking at the airport. All I had to do was pick it up."

"So you're like crazy rich or something, aren't you?" She relaxed her death grip on her purse a little.

Dimitri chuckled as they backed out of the driveway. "Or *something*."

"I'm beginning to think you like being an a mystery man," she muttered. "Just promise me you aren't some Russian spy, okay? I really can't handle that right now."

Dimitri let out a deep laugh full of genuine delight.

"*Kiska*, you are too much. No, I am no spy." He grew a

little more serious when he said that. He shifted gears, and the car shot down the street.

She changed the subject. "So, if you can find the nearest thrift store, that would be great."

He arched a dark brow and shot her a glance. "Thrift store?"

"Yeah, I'm on a budget. I lost all my credit cards and stuff in Moscow." Elena fiddled with the buckle on her purse strap, too embarrassed to meet his eyes. It was pathetic that she would rather have him assume she was the type of person to lose things than tell him the truth.

"No thrift stores," Dimitri said.

"But I can't—"

He lifted up his wallet and waved it. "Please. Consider it a gift from a friend."

"No, no, thank you. I really can't." This time she looked at his face. That was a mistake. There was such a harsh beauty to his features.

"No, you *can* do this. You will allow me to buy your clothes." It was in order, not a request. A strange flutter in her belly confused her. It was almost like she was nervous, but her chest wasn't tight with anxiety.

They parked in front of a store called AllSaints. It was a clothing store she loved, but it was usually out of her price range. She opened her mouth to protest, but one look from Dimitri quelled any further resistance. It was scary how much she responded to his commands, but he was into BDSM, so clearly he got off on bossing people around . . . just like she used to enjoy being bossed around, at least in the bedroom.

Fine, she'd let him have his way, this time. But she wasn't going to let him pick her clothes. She drew the line at letting a man tell her what to wear.

DIMITRI KEPT HIS DISTANCE AS ELENA SHOPPED. HE HAD seen at once that she was a woman who desperately needed to control something in her life. He had insisted they shop here, but that was the only thing that he would make her do. As much as he enjoyed buying clothing for a woman and seeing her wear it, he knew that even most submissives needed to choose their own clothes when not in the bedroom.

Dimitri cursed inwardly. He had to stop thinking of Elena as his submissive. She wasn't and could never be. He had to content himself with only fantasies of what he and Elena could do, but even those left a bitter taste in his mouth. After everything she had been through, even if she healed, she wouldn't want the kind of physical relationship he needed.

Elena pulled several silk blouses and some button-up shirts off a few racks and glanced at him. "I'm going to try these on."

"I'll be here." He kept an eye on her, making sure she went into the changing room alone. He wasn't sure why, but he'd woken this morning on edge. His intuition had warned him something was wrong, and the niggling worry at the back of his mind wouldn't go away. Something about what Leo had said . . .

He pulled his cell phone out of his pocket and dialed Leo on the secure line.

Leo answered almost right away. "Dimitri." Leo was the most reliable of his three friends when it came to phone calls. Nicholas was usually busy bedding any pretty woman he could find, and Maxim went dark sometimes— not even Leo could track him down during those black periods.

"I mailed that blood sample. It should be to you within twenty-four hours."

"Good, I'll run it through our database and prepare a full profile—" Leo suddenly went quiet. There was a beeping sound in the background.

"What is it, Leo?" Dimitri asked.

"Sorry, it's an alert. Viktor Ivanoff is in Los Angeles. He triggered the facial recognition software I have running in the TSA's system. He is using a fake passport, of course, but I still found him." Leo snorted. "These Russian agents never learn. You must use prosthetics for your nose and ears—that's the only way to fool my software."

"Why is he here?" Dimitri asked.

Viktor Ivanoff was one of the Kremlin's top agents, assigned to track down White Army operatives. But as far as Dimitri knew, his cover was intact. He given money he had stolen from the Russian party leaders back to them as donations, and therefore he stayed under the government's radar. Ivanoff had been chosen by Putin to continue to resist the development of a democratic system in Russia, and he was also involved in jailing Putin's political opponents, including the free press. Russia hadn't had a fair and free election in twenty years. If Ivanoff was in Los Angeles, it was for a very serious reason.

"I don't know yet, but I'll find out," Leo promised. If anyone could discover what the man was here for, it was Leo.

"Tell me the moment you do." It wasn't unusual for Russian agents to come to the United States, but Dimitri didn't like the timing of this. "Leo, make sure you scrub my activity again."

"Do you think you might be compromised?" There was the sound of typing on Leo's end of the line.

"It's always possible. He's exactly the sort of bastard who would be sent after me if the Kremlin believed I was part of the White Army."

"I'll scrub everything by tonight. I'll put an alert on my hacked feeds and the CCTV in your area as well. You will get a text alert immediately when he's sighted and where."

"Thanks, Leo."

Leo hesitated. "Dimitri . . ."

"Yes?"

His friend cleared his throat. "It may be possible that you need backup."

"You mean the three of you coming to LA?"

"Yes."

Dimitri's gaze roamed around the shop. He spotted Elena emerging from the dressing room. He would feel better having his brothers-in-arms with him, but could she handle four Russians under her roof?

"Let me think on it a day or two."

"Very well. That will give me a chance to run Elena's blood first."

Dimitri mumbled his thanks before he hung up and waited for Elena to approach him.

"I thought these were nice." She held up several lovely blouses and colorful cotton tops, along with a few pairs of shorts. "What should I choose?"

"You like all of them?" he asked.

"Yes, but I can't—"

"You can." He waved a clerk over, and the young woman rushed to collect the clothes from Elena's arms.

"Did you get a swimsuit?" he asked.

"No, why would I?"

He gave her a bemused look at her failing to see the obvious. "Because there is a beautiful ocean a few hundred feet from our patio."

She blushed, the delicate pink in her cheeks utterly bewitching him. "I'm not sure if I feel like swimming . . ."

"Go on," he encouraged. He put a hand on her lower

back to give her a gentle nudge toward the swimsuit section. She didn't panic, nor did she acknowledge the touch. She simply walked away toward the rack of suits. Given that it was winter, there wasn't much in the way of choices and styles, and the water was honestly probably a little too cold to actually swim. He hoped the thought of buying a suit and lying in the sun on the balcony outside her room or on the beach on the warm sand sounded tempting. He wanted her to relax, to let her tension fade a little.

Dimitri handed the clerk his credit card and chose a pair of sunglasses he was certain would look good on her and added them to the stack of clothes. Elena joined him and shyly put a modest one-piece suit on the counter.

"You really need to let me pay for something," she began. He shot her a quelling look. "Fine." She exhaled dramatically, and he sensed she was going to try to figure out a way to pay him back. That almost made him smile. When they got into the car, she was silent a long moment.

"What's wrong?" he asked.

"You. *This*." She waved a hand all around her. "Something's off. I just can't figure out what."

Dimitri started the engine and headed for the house. He needed to think. Maybe he could tell her that Royce wanted someone to look after her; he didn't have to go into more detail than that. He just hoped whatever he said wouldn't destroy that tiny bit of trust he had won from her.

❄

V<small>IKTOR</small> I<small>VANOFF</small> <small>CLIMBED</small> <small>INTO</small> <small>A</small> <small>GRAY</small> <small>FOUR-DOOR</small>
Honda Civic in the parking lot at LAX and opened the
glove compartment. A manila envelope and a black case
were inside. He went for the case first, setting it on his lap
and unfastening the hard plastic clasps. Inside was a basic
Ruger SR9. Not his usual style. He preferred a Makarov or
a Beretta, but this trip had been planned on short notice,
and his handler in LA hadn't had time to set up the opera-
tion the way Viktor liked.

He put the case back in the glove box and opened the
manila envelope. Inside were new identity documents, a
California driver's license, car insurance, car registration,
and a new US passport so detailed that it even had a few
falsified stamps indicating he'd been to France, Canada,
and Mexico. There was an address and a picture of the
apartment he'd be living in while he was here.

The last set of documents in the folder were the most
important. The name of the person to be disposed of,
along with every bit of personal information his government could find on the target. At the bottom was a series
of pictures. He frowned in confusion. He had expected a
challenge, something worthy of his skills. The person he'd
been sent after was a woman barely over twenty.

He pulled out the new burner phone in the envelope
and dialed.

"Yes?" the person on the other end answered in Russian.

"What is this bullshit?" Viktor demanded. "I'm here to kill some girl? You could have had anyone do this."

"No. We need to make sure this one is handled properly," the man said in a low tone.

"Why? Who is she?" Viktor had killed women before; he'd become a master of using ricin. A bump in an elevator, a nudge on the street while waiting for a light to change. A light prick on someone's skin, easily unnoticed. Then a day or two later, the target died. But the gun case meant he wasn't expected to use poison.

"That is not something you need to know. Make sure it's done, a head shot. Then dispose of the body so it can never be recovered."

The call disconnected.

Viktor cursed and threw the cell phone on the seat as he stared at the pictures of his target.

Elena Allen.

She was pretty in a soft, sweet sort of way, nothing like the beautiful women he used when he desired to fuck something. But there was something about her, something in her face that tugged at his memory. She was important, and he would figure out why before he killed her.

5

Elena could tell she had caught Dimitri off guard with her guess. She didn't take her eyes off him as he parked the car in the driveway and made sure the gate closed behind them before he let them get out of the car. He was being cautious; he wasn't letting her out of his sight. It was clear this wasn't about the kindness of a random stranger. He had said he was a friend of Royce Devereaux, and Royce was not someone you messed with. Just because he was a professor who dug up dinosaur bones didn't mean he wasn't able to take care of himself. She'd seen him handle a gun and keep cool under pressure. It was too much of a coincidence for her to share a house and a flight back to the States with this man. She'd been trying to ignore the thought, but now she couldn't.

"You're here to babysit me, aren't you? Royce called in a favor to get you to come all this way and watch me. Well, it's not necessary." She delivered this quietly, but inside she was screaming at the thought that the two men were trying to treat her like a child. She just wanted to be free of the control of men.

She left the bags of new clothes in the trunk of Dimitri's car and barely stopped herself from slamming the door of the house once she got inside. She tossed her purse on the kitchen table before going down the stone stairs that led to the beach. She kicked off her sandals and stepped ankle-deep into the surf.

The chilly water woke her up like an electric shock, making everything clearer. Dimitri had been shadowing her from the start. She'd been bumped up into a business-class seat on purpose. And when she had panicked in the plane bathroom, he had been calm and had come right after her. At that time, he really had been a stranger to her, but if she had been a stranger to him, there was no way he would have come to her rescue. She saw that now. He knew enough about her situation to know she had suffered. How much had Royce told him?

God, I'm such an idiot . . .

Turning back toward the house, she saw him standing above her on the patio balcony. He leaned over the railing, hands braced apart, watching her. He looked more dangerous than ever, and beautiful. How could Royce do this to her? Had Kenzie known? If she had . . . Elena clenched her hands and faced the ocean again. Without a word she began to walk deeper into the waves until they were crashing into her hard enough that she nearly lost her footing. She needed to be out in the water, to float away . . .

Eventually, the water reached her neck, and she leapt up and toward the next cresting wall of water. Suddenly strong arms pulled her back. Air whooshed from her lungs as she was pressed into a massive hard body.

"Are you trying to kill yourself?" an angry voice growled a second before she was hauled back, away from deeper water.

"Let go." She thrashed, but he held fast to her as he carried her to the shore.

When he released her, she stumbled back on the wet sand, her feet sliding in the coarse grains. She glared at him, and he glared back. He was soaked down to his bones, just like her, and his shirt clung to his upper body. His chest rose and fell as he breathed hard. He must have sprinted down the stairs to reach her as quickly as he had.

"Deny it," she yelled.

"Deny what?" he shot back.

"You're just here to babysit me. I'm just some *pathetic* creature that Royce asked you to look after."

"No, *kiska*, that is not the truth." He stepped closer and she stepped away until they were almost circling each other.

"I trusted you, Dimitri. I know I shouldn't have. You're a stranger. But I just wanted to feel safe, and you . . ." She was torn between shouting and crying. "You lied to me."

"I never lied, Elena. Never. But you are right, I didn't tell you everything."

"That's the same thing!" she gasped. He came at her quickly, giving her no chance to evade him this time as he caught her waist and held kept her from retreating. Rather than be frightened, she was something else...something that she hadn't felt in a long time.

Before she could understand what was happening, she was reaching up to grab his neck and pulling his face down to hers. He seemed to understand what she was wanted the second their lips connected. His mouth was slanted over hers in a raw, silencing kiss. She went rigid in his hold, more startled at the fact that she'd begun this, than from fear. When he *only* kissed her and didn't try anything else, that fear that held her still as marble began to fade. She pushed against his chest, not to make it stop but because her hands were trapped, and she had the desperate urge to touch him just to feel like a woman with healthy desires . . .

As quickly as he had swept her against him, he released her and tore himself away, putting his back to her. He raked his hands through his hair, muttering to himself in Russian. She caught a few words she understood: *stupid, idiot, mistake* . . .

Elena's eyes filled with tears. It was her first kiss since

Vadym, and she had just started to enjoy it and Dimitri thought it was a mistake.

Because he doesn't want to be here—he doesn't want to babysit me.

She'd never been one to feel self-pity, but in that moment, she felt truly wretched. Dimitri would never put up with someone damaged like her. All of her fears, her panic, which shut her down again and again—no man would want to deal with that. He would want the perfect woman, free of scars and issues.

"You're wrong," Dimitri said.

For a brief moment, she thought she'd spoken her fears aloud. "What?"

"I'm not here to babysit you, and you are not some pathetic creature." He faced her again, and she held her breath. "Royce did not ask me to do anything. *I* asked him. I'm here by my own choice. It was *my* idea, not his."

His words didn't make sense. "Wait . . . Just wait." She needed to understand. Maybe it was a language barrier issue. "What do you mean, you asked him?"

Dimitri was silent a moment before he said, "I know what happened in Moscow—with Vadym Andreikiv. I know all of it, Elena."

His words echoed in her head, and suddenly the world was spinning and everything tunneled into darkness.

When Elena came to her senses, she was no longer on the beach. She was on her bed back in the house. Her wet clothes were gone, and a large T-shirt covered her body. A

Sherpa blanket was cocooned around her, keeping her warm.

My clothes . . .

Dimitri had undressed her, had seen her body. She felt violated for all of a few seconds before she realized the necessity of him getting her out of her wet clothes. She could have gotten sick otherwise. She burrowed deeper into the blankets, and her nose brushed against the sleeve of the shirt she wore. Dimitri's smell was there in the fabric, that hint of him that was too enticing. She was wearing one of *his* shirts. That should have freaked her out, made her feel like he was possessive, which Kenzie had said he was, but wearing his shirt right in that moment? She felt . . . safe.

How messed up was that? God, she'd definitely have to cover that in her next therapy session.

Elena didn't want to think about what had happened on the beach, at least not about what she'd learned. What he'd said still made her stomach churn. He knew about Vadym, but he couldn't know everything. She hadn't told anyone *everything*. Her mind replayed the kiss, how she'd been the one to reach for him, to start something and how he'd met her equally in that moment, but hadn't pushed for more. It was...unexpected, and again, she felt that same strange safety knowing he hadn't demanded more like some men might have.

She moved on the bed and heard a crinkle of paper

near her shoulder. She shifted on the sheets and found a note like the one he'd left earlier.

ELENA,

Please come down when you have rested.

SHE LAY BACK IN BED AND STARED UP AT THE CEILING for a long time. Her therapist had warned her this might happen, that she would feel overwhelmed at times and faint, but it felt like she was overwhelmed *all* the time. She'd been told to find someone here, someone who specifically treated sexual assault victims to help her cope with what she'd been through. She remembered what her therapist in Moscow had said.

"Whatever you feel . . . that's okay. There's no timeline for when you should feel better. Everyone's experience is unique."

Shame, guilt, confusion, fear—those were all emotions she experienced daily. She was beginning to fear that her timeline of healing would take several years.

Unable to lie in bed any longer, she got up and removed Dimitri's shirt and changed into her new clothes. She was going to pay him back for the stuff he'd purchased today, but not until she figured out how to do it sneakily.

She found him downstairs, lounging on the leather couch, one arm draped over the back of the sectional as he watched the local news. He was utterly still as she came around to stand in front of the TV to block his view.

For a second she was distracted by the things she knew about him now, the things she shouldn't know—how it felt to be in his arms, his lips pressed to hers, the energy of his kiss and the sweet desperation of how he'd needed to show her he was protecting her, shielding her from the things in the world that would hurt her, just like a Dom would his submissive.

No, she couldn't go there, couldn't let herself get distracted by such dangerous thoughts. That was a life she would never have, a relationship she would never have.

"We have to talk," she said.

He muted the TV, his eyes never leaving her face. "Come. Sit." He patted the chaise longue part of the sectional beside him, but she shook her head. She needed to stand, needed to feel some power while she said what she had to say.

"I deserve the truth."

"The truth," he echoed softly.

"Yes. Who the hell are you, and why do you care about me if you aren't here because Royce asked you to be? If you know about Vadym, what's your connection to him?"

He leaned forward, his forearms braced on his knees. His pose seemed almost penitent. He threaded his fingers together.

"My name is Dimitri Razin—that wasn't a lie. I know about Vadym because he has is well known in some circles for what he does to young women. I've been working with my friends to stop him. I care about you because of who you are. You deserve happiness. You need to have someone with you who understands at least in some small way what you've endured." His accent was slightly thicker now and rough with seriousness.

Her heart fluttered with dread and sudden realization. Vadym probably already had another girl by now, someone new to torture and hurt. Her stomach knotted, and she fought the urge to throw up.

"He might already have someone else. Didn't you think about that? Forget me. You need to go back to Moscow and stop him."

Why hadn't she thought of this before? Why? She'd been so buried in her own wallowing pity she hadn't thought of the victims who would come after she'd escaped.

Dimitri held up a hand, silencing her panicked words.

"There will not be another girl for him ever again." The hardness of his eyes confused her. How could Dimitri possibly know that? Vadym was addicted to pain and death. He wouldn't stop hurting and killing girls.

"I wasn't his first, and I know I won't be his last."

"You are the last, because Vadym is dead."

Vadym is dead.

The words rattled around inside her head, which had suddenly emptied of all other thoughts but that one. Vadym . . . was dead.

"You can't know . . . can you?"

He stood up and pulled his cell phone out of his pocket and dialed a number. Then he spoke softly in Russian before he put the phone on speaker.

"Leo, she is listening. Please give me access to the video feed and morgue photos."

"Just a moment," a deep, masculine Russian-accented voice said.

Dimitri motioned for her to come into the kitchen. He removed his laptop from his briefcase and turned it on. While he logged on to a secure website, she hovered beside him, shock still clouding her mind.

"You have access," the man on the phone said.

"Thank you, Leo." Dimitri ended the call, then pulled up a new screen. There were a few pictures and a video file. He clicked on the video, and the screen was filled with a black-and-white but crystal-clear recording.

Vadym was eating at a restaurant with two of his men when suddenly he clutched at his throat and toppled out of his chair. He writhed in agony for nearly a full minute before he went still. The men who'd rushed toward him finally stopped trying to help him. He appeared unresponsive. The video ended, and Dimitri opened up each of the pictures, which showed a pale, lifeless Vadym on a mortuary slab. The pictures had been taken at various angles, allowing for a detailed look at his body. There was a deep red wound in his chest that had no blood around it. She'd watched enough true-crime shows to know that the wound had been inflicted postmortem.

"What is that?" she whispered and pointed at the spot.

"That is where Maxim drove a seven-inch blade into the bastard just to be sure he was dead."

"Who is Maxim?"

"Someone who is like a brother to me. Vadym took Maxim's little sister two years ago, and we don't know if she's dead or alive. *That* is why I care. That is why I'm here. And that is why he is dead."

"You couldn't help her, but you thought you could help me?" She trembled as the reality of Vadym being dead created an equally violent reaction inside her as it had when Dimitri had shown her the photos.

"Yes," he said. "I was in the embassy in Ulaanbaatar that day you, Royce, and Kenzie were saved. Once I learned what happened to you, I told Royce I needed to help you."

"How can you help me?" Tears started to burn her eyes. "No one helps this sort of thing. It's all just so fucked up. *I'm* fucked up." She covered her face with her hands. It was all too much.

He pulled her against his chest. She didn't cry this time. She just leaned into him, drawing on his heat, his strength, as though he were a brilliant sun and she a frost-bitten flower desperate for heat and light.

"You can't help me," she whispered against his chest. His heartbeat was steady against her cheek, and her heart's own frantic beat settled until they seemed to breathe and beat as one.

Dimitri cradled the back of her head, his strong fingers rubbing at the taut tendons that extended from her neck to her skull until the tension inside her ebbed away. "Tell me what you want from me. Tell me what *you* need."

"I want to live again. I want to be able to love and trust again."

"You never lost the ability to love, *kiska*. You love your parents, don't you?"

"Yes, but I mean *romantically*. I want it so badly, but I'm so afraid."

Dimitri lifted her face up so that she could see his. "You will love again and trust again."

"How can you be sure?" She wanted to believe the sincerity in his eyes, but how she felt wasn't going away overnight.

"Because I kissed you on the beach and you are letting me hold you now without fear, yes?"

"Yes . . ." She bit her bottom lip. He was right. She wasn't afraid, and she wasn't freaking out.

He slowly smiled, and tiny lines formed at the corners of his eyes . . . laugh lines. She thought of him laughing in the car earlier, the wonderful sound making her want to join in.

A wild fluttering in her belly made her knees quake, so she held on to him a little tighter.

"That is trust, *kiska*. Perhaps only a little, but it is trust all the same."

When he'd kissed her on the beach, she'd only felt a brief spike of panic before it had faded, just like it had when he'd grabbed her in the bathroom on the plane. This man was different. Her body reacted unpredictably, or so she thought, but now she saw a pattern. Dimitri was incredibly attractive, a naturally dominant man who was a master of the very sensual bed play she had once been interested in, and his touch didn't repulse or terrorize her. In fact, it was quite the opposite. He soothed and excited her at the same time. He was exactly the sort of man Elena would've been obsessed with before she'd been abducted.

But was she too broken to ever feel the way she needed to feel to be whole again?

"Dimitri . . ." It was one of the few times she had said his name. She lifted her face up to his.

"Yes, *kiska?*"

His accent made her shiver. With Vadym, his accent had left her on edge. But when Dimitri spoke, it was soft and seductive. It made her think of roaring fires, warm brandy swirling in clear stemless glasses, and bare skin sliding against fur rugs.

"Please hold very still. I want to try something." She placed her hands on his face, feeling the light scrape of stubble on her palms. Every sense was heightened, and she took in his scent, letting it fill her head as she rocked up on her tiptoes and pulled his face down to hers. Their lips brushed so lightly at first; it was almost a dream more than reality. Then she moved her mouth more insistently against his.

His breath fanned her face as he parted his lips and welcomed her timid tongue to play with his. While a sense of urgency pressed her closer to him, she dared not do more than kiss him. A tingle grew in her lower belly, and she continued to move her mouth against his, exploring him. He moved ever so slightly, and her pulse quickened as the barest brush of his fingers touched her lower back. Her lips broke from his, and her hand slid from his face down to his neck. She closed her eyes, breathing slowly. A moment later, she opened her eyes to look up at him.

"I wasn't afraid," she whispered.

"No, you weren't," Dimitri agreed. His muscles tensed as he put his hands on her waist. "Is this okay?" he asked her.

She closed her eyes again, sudden flashes of Vadym grabbing her hips, shoving her over a bed . . .

"*Kiska*, open your eyes." The command was easily obeyed, and she met his gaze. "You cannot see him or feel him if you are looking at me. Now, how does this feel?" His hands tightened slightly on her waist, calling her attention back to his touch. This time she did not close her eyes. She fixed on his blue gaze, the way his eyes were so unbelievably pure in color, yet gentle and steadfast in their intensity. His face, like the rest of him, seemed to be forged by destiny to make her dizzy with desire.

"It feels okay," she admitted. "Do you feel okay?" she asked, then felt like an idiot. They weren't two high school virgins in the back of a car.

"Holding you is one of the best pleasures and all my life," he replied.

Elena's lips parted as she stared up at him, stunned. "Me? Why?"

"There is nothing more intoxicating to me than a brave woman, and you are the bravest woman I have ever met."

"I'm not brave. I'm scared all the time."

His lips curved into a smile. "Courage is not the same thing as the absence of fear. Courage means facing one's fears. It means that you get up when someone knocks you down. You keep fighting to live."

"Dimitri, do you think . . . That is . . . I mean . . ." Her face was suddenly so hot she felt feverish.

He said nothing, his blue eyes holding her in place.

"I want to be brave. I want to be myself again, but I don't know if I can trust anyone else. Would you help me?" She clenched her jaw, waiting to hear him deny her what she needed, a man to trust, a man to explore her limits with.

The thick dark lashes framing his eyes flew up in surprise. "Elena, you aren't ready."

Her eyes narrowed. "I can be. It's *my* timeline, isn't it?

My choice of how and when I'll get back into this." She nodded at their bodies, which were still pressed against each other.

"You are right, it is your choice, but I do not want you to feel you have to push this. I didn't come here for that. I came to watch over you. To help you heal. After what happened to Maxim's sister, I cannot let you go. Not alone. Not yet." He cupped her face, his thumb stroking her cheek.

Elena leaned into the touch and let out a sigh. "Is it true that you participate in BDSM? Kenzie said you did."

His eyes searched hers a long moment. "I do enjoy the bondage and dominance, but I have no interest in sadism or masochism. But none of that will come into this if you want me."

"No . . . No, I want . . . I wanted that before Moscow. I liked it, liked what little I had experimented with. I don't want to be afraid of all that because he stole it from me. I think I'd want that, to experience dominance and submission again. Would you do that with me?"

Dimitri's lips firmed into a hard line. He stepped away from her, dropping his hands.

"*Kiska*, you offer me too much."

Elena's eyes filled with tears. She turned away, wiping at them. Of course. It was too much. No man would want to be saddled with her. She was broken, bruised, scarred, and scared. There was no way she could ever seem sexy or arousing when he would have to worry about every little thing setting her off.

"I'm sorry, let's just forget this, okay?" She turned and fled, racing back up to her room.

"Stop." He ordered in that commanding tone and she halted, her body already responding to his with submission. She stiffened her spine. If he didn't want to be her dominant, then she didn't have to listen to him. She started to move again.

But before she reached her doorway, she was suddenly grabbed, spun, and pinned against the wall by Dimitri's hard, imposing body. He caged her in his arms, eyes scorching as they held her own. Fear only captured her for a split second before she realized he wasn't going to hurt her.

"You offer me something I do not deserve, Elena. I want you desperately, I have since the moment I laid eyes on you. But that doesn't mean my desires are more important than yours. If you were a submissive, you would know that it is *you* who has the true power over your master. I feel no pleasure unless you do. That is why you asked too much. I would want you in many wicked ways, ways I fear you would be afraid of, and I cannot hurt you like that." He pressed his forehead to hers, his eyes closing as he drew in several breaths, as though to regain control.

Elena trembled, but not from fear. There were other emotions, other sensations, ones she'd believed she would never feel again. Yet they were here, coming slowly to life like a small match lit and cast upon a dry field as the winds fed the flame. She slid her hands up his chest, raking her nails into the fabric of his shirt and into his skin. He tensed, and his grip on her tightened.

She tilted her head up, her mouth a breath away from his.

"I'm not afraid." She kissed him a second time. But unlike downstairs, this was raw, hard, and it was how she wanted him. Just like it had been on the beach.

This man was the only one she could trust. Her heart and mind agreed with her body. He would be the one to pull her away from the dangerous edge of the cliff she had felt like throwing herself off of.

He buried his hands in her hair and held her captive. His mouth ravaged hers, and she moaned, going utterly boneless in his arms. He destroyed her damaged soul with his lips and built a new one for her, one stronger than the last. One that would not shatter, not this time. His kiss was more than hope. It was a vow.

6

This was a terrible fucking idea. The moment he told Royce, the man would be on the first flight to LA to beat him up, and he would deserve every blow.

Dimitri stepped back from Elena, his blood roaring in his ears and desire burning inside him like he held the heat of a star within his chest.

"We need to do this," Elena said. Her lips were swollen from his rough kisses, and her hair was tousled from his hands. Her face was flushed with color.

It was the most alive he had ever seen her, at least since first spotting her at the embassy in Mongolia. This must be how the old Elena had looked, the one unafraid to live out in the world.

"*I* need to," she corrected. She held out a hand to him, palm turned up. "Please . . ."

Her plea left him undone. He couldn't deny her this. He couldn't deny her anything. As he looked at her, he saw what he'd always dreamed of in a woman—she was perfection, inside and out. The room suddenly seemed hot. He curled his hands into fists to keep from reaching for her. If he didn't control himself, he'd try to touch her, and he wouldn't do that until they'd established rules and boundaries. He was a Dom, but the last thing he wanted to do was scare her.

"If we do this, I have rules," he warned.

She nodded and waited patiently for him to continue.

"You do *anything* I ask. Most commands will be for your safety and not for the purpose of intimacy. You will use the green, yellow, and red system with me, and it will be respected by me. We will start slow. I will not let you rush anything because it might set you back. Do you agree?"

She nodded. Only then did he take her hand in his. This was it. He had surrendered to her in more ways than she would ever surrender to him, and she would never know. He pulled her slowly toward him, and when she was flush against his body, he pressed a kiss to her forehead.

"Are we starting n—now?" She didn't sound afraid, but he heard the apprehension in her voice.

"We start tonight, and the first step is easy. You will sleep in my bed."

"Just sleep? But we've already done that. It was . . ."

"Easy?" he finished for her. "You may think so, but in

many ways sleep is more intimate than sex. It is the time when you are most vulnerable to another person."

Her brows drew together as she started to understand what he was telling her.

"You won't . . . do something to me while I'm asleep, will you?"

The hesitancy of her quiet voice pierced through to his heart. "No," he said in a breathless reply. "I would *never.*"

She seemed satisfied with that response, her chin raised slightly and her shoulders unhunched.

"But," he continued before she could interject with more reasons why they should jump to intimacy, "your lesson will be to trust me. To sleep beside me and know that trust could be broken, but trusting me anyway."

Her face flushed a deep scarlet. He let her think that over before continuing.

"We've slept together before and I did not harm you, which I hope will make this easier." Easier for her, of course. Sleeping so close to her would be a challenge for him. He wanted to touch her, to pleasure her, to make her forget all the pain, but that would come later, and only if she continued to progress and trust him. She had been right—the timeline of her healing was up to her, and there was no right or wrong speed at which she should heal. He just hoped this bargain they had made wasn't a mistake.

"It's too early for bed, and we haven't had dinner," she pointed out.

"You're right. I should cook something." He put some

distance between them again. Touching her tended to cloud his mind, and he needed to think clearly, at least for the next few hours.

"Actually, I was thinking maybe we could go out? As much as I like the quiet here, it would be nice to be around people for a bit."

He agreed. He was usually a solitary person himself, but being out on the town, so to speak, would be a nice distraction for him so he wouldn't overthink tonight's new sleeping arrangements.

"Go change. I will see you downstairs in half an hour."

She touched her lips with her fingertips, her gaze sweeping over his body in a way that she had to know was playing with fire, then she stepped into her bedroom and closed the door.

Dimitri went to his own room and stopped at the sink in his bathroom. He turned on the water, cupped one hand under the cold spray, and splashed it on his face.

What was he thinking? Agreeing to this was dangerous for them both. Now that he'd had a taste of her, he wasn't sure he could keep his promise to go slow. He stared at his face in the mirror, but he wasn't really looking at himself. He had known the moment he'd gone after her in the Moscow airport that this was a possibility, but it had seemed infinitesimal at the time. Now it was a certainty.

He was in danger of breaking his vows, of putting a single person above the cause of the White Army. For once, he was glad his father wasn't alive. His parents had put duty and honor above all else, even their love for each other. He had been raised to be the same, but somewhere along the way he had found a new purpose, one that he straddled along with the path he had been born into. It had been easy when those roads had traveled parallel to each other, but if they were to diverge? He'd choose Elena and he feared it might cost him dearly.

Meeting Wes Thorne, a man he'd met while getting into the Parisian art markets, and Royce Devereaux, the charismatic college professor, had changed him. They had shown him a side of life that a part of him had always longed for. A life with love and independence. He fought for the freedom of his people, but he rarely ever felt free himself. He wanted to be the master of his own fate, not a pawn in a larger battle. But that could never be. It would mean abandoning Leo, Maxim, and Nicholas, and he couldn't abandon the brothers of his heart.

Dimitri changed into a pair of jeans and a white button-up shirt that he left untucked and the sleeves rolled up. Then he headed downstairs and retrieved his wallet and keys. He paused, listening to the sound of water running above him. Assured he had a moment to himself, he opened the hall closet and retrieved a slim black case. Royce had told him where to find this before Dimitri had left Moscow. Inside was a simple sidearm. Nothing fancy, but it would do for now. He hadn't brought anything through customs, so this would be, for the moment, his only weapon.

It was a CZ 75 B, a handgun made in the Czech Republic. The model was well tuned and had slide rails on the inside of the frame, which made it incredibly accurate when firing shots in rapid succession. It was a favorite firearm for many European military and police forces. Dimitri loaded it and then tested the weight in each hand. He tucked the gun into his jeans and pulled his shirt down over it, then closed the case and put it back into the coat closet. He'd need to get a concealed-carry holster soon since Royce didn't have one at the house for him to borrow.

He returned to the entryway just as he heard Elena's steps on the stairs, and his heart skipped a beat as he saw her. She had combed out the loose waves of her blonde hair, letting it tumble past her shoulders. She wore a pair of seersucker shorts that stopped midway down her thighs and a white blouse that had long sleeves that gathered at her elbows. She wore navy-blue cork wedge sandals. It was one of the outfits she had purchased at the store today.

"How do I look?" she asked and bit her bottom lip as she reached the bottom stair. "I still don't feel comfortable wearing dresses," she added a bit more quietly.

He understood. Vadym would have kept her in revealing dresses or practically naked for easy access to her body. The thought sickened Dimitri, and he tried to banish it from his mind.

"You look beautiful," he told her. Too beautiful, if he was honest with himself.

She brightened at that. "So, where are we going?"

He opened the door and gestured for her to go ahead of him. "There is a food truck near the Los Angeles County Museum of Art that has a rather interesting reputation."

"Oh?" Curiosity illuminated her green eyes, and he smiled back at her.

"I'll tell you when we get there."

IT WAS DUSK WHEN THEY ARRIVED AT THE ROW OF FOOD trucks. People were already lining up and ordering dinner.

"Are we going to get tacos again? If so, I'm not complaining." Elena focused on the three Mexican food trucks nearby and almost missed Dimitri's bemused smile.

They stopped in front of a dark-blue truck with a green, white, and red Italian flag arching over part of the back.

"The Prince of Venice?" Elena read the name and looked at Dimitri.

"You see the man there?" He pointed to an attractive guy with sandy-brown hair who was cooking over a stove by the truck's open windows as he spoke with customers.

"Yeah . . ."

"That is Emanuele Filberto di Savoia. He is the grandson of King Umberto II, the last reigning king of

Italy. He is of the royal Savoy dynasty that has existed since 1003 in the Savoy region of Italy."

Elena studied the prince more closely. "I didn't know the Italians had a king so recently."

"After Mussolini's regime ended, King Victor Emmanuel III was temporarily in charge of Italy, but in 1944 he handed his powers over to his son, Umberto, hoping to bolster the monarchy. But Umberto only ruled for thirty-four days, from May 1946 to June 1946. He was called the Re di Maggio, the May King. Now his grandson, a true prince, runs this food truck. This is the most authentic Italian food you will find in Los Angeles."

"Wow . . ." Elena's lips parted as she simply stared at the food truck. "A real prince."

Dimitri put a hand on her back, his touch gentle as he guided her to the line in front of the prince's food truck.

"What would you like?" Emanuele asked as they stepped up to the window.

Dimitri looked to Elena, who scanned the menu before she ordered. "I would like the orecchiette al pesto."

"And I would like the lemon bucatini," Dimitri added, then slipped Emanuele his credit card.

Their pasta was soon ready, and they took their carryout boxes to a park nearby that had some comfortable picnic tables.

"It's crazy to be wearing shorts in the middle of winter," Elena said as she took her first bite of pasta. It was so creamy, so decadent, the flavors so rich and savory, that she barely stopped herself from moaning.

"You and I both come from cold places. Maine and Russia." Dimitri chuckled and raised his bottled water in salute.

Elena smiled. After a few more bites, she realized she had at least a dozen questions that still needed answering. "Dimitri, if we do this, I need to know who you are." She'd sensed from the beginning that he wasn't just some beautiful badass dominant. Something about him was filled with an almost heartbreaking tenderness, which seemed to be at constant war with the darker side of him. He wasn't just any man. He was someone powerful, but in what way she didn't have a clue.

His blue eyes softened, and he looked away for the briefest second. "*Kiska*, there are some things that I cannot tell you, things that only my family or my wife could be told."

"You're married?" she gasped.

"No, no, I am not," he rushed to reassure her. "But someday, if I married, those deeper truths would be explained to my wife."

His wife . . . For some reason, the thought of him marrying someone sent a pang of desperate longing through her that echoed like a church bell. But she couldn't think about marriage, or even Dimitri marrying; that was a muddled mess of thoughts and emotions she wasn't ready to untangle, so she forced herself back to her line of questions.

"What can you tell me? I need something, Dimitri."

He reached across the table to take one of her hands and hold it between his own. He gazed deeply into her eyes in a way she was beginning to suspect mesmerized her.

"My name is real. I have not hidden that from you. What I will tell you now is known only to a few, and I hope you will respect my confidence in sharing it with you."

She nodded.

"My mother died when I was four, murdered by agents of the Kremlin. My father raised me, but I wasn't alone. He gave me brothers in the life he chose for me. That life is what I must keep hidden, but the brothers of my heart, I can tell you a little about them."

"You aren't like Vadym, are you? Into mobster stuff and hurting people for the pleasure of it . . ."

"No, I am the opposite of that bastard. My brothers and I fight against everything men like him represent." Dimitri rubbed gentle patterns over her palm with his fingers. Such a simple thing, to be caressed, and so inno-cent a location, yet somehow it touched her to her very core.

"Good, because I can't do that ever again. I can't be under the power of someone like that." She'd felt silly for even asking, since every instinct inside her told her he wasn't like Vadym, but she liked him too much to trust her instincts.

Dimitri continued to caress her palm in that easy way. "Ask me anything, and I will do my best to tell you the truth when I can."

"You mentioned brothers, but not blood relations?"

"Yes, I called them the brothers of my heart. We first met when we were eight years old, and since then we have been inseparable. Leo is a technical specialist, Maxim a security expert, and Nicholas, well, I suppose you could say he's a diplomat of sorts." His affection for these brothers was so clear in his voice.

"What is it you really do?" she asked more quietly.

His eyes darkened. "All I can tell you is that my life is devoted to stopping men like Vadym." That was all he would say, and for now it would have to be enough. "And what of you, *kiska*? Why did you want to go to Moscow?"

It was a personal question, but he couldn't have known that. But he was being honest, so she would have to be as well.

"I was adopted when I was a baby. Last year I did one of those DNA tests. It came back as fully Russian. I don't even know my mother or father's names or anything about them. I guess I wanted to feel closer to them, to know them. My mother died right after I was born. She bled out —that was the only thing the hospital could tell the adoption agency and she was alone, there was no sign of my father. I decided to take a year of Russian language at

Pepperdine and they had a semester long abroad program to Moscow. I thought it would be good to go there and see where she'd come from."

"You're Russian," Dimitri mused. His gaze turned distant, and she wished she knew what he was thinking.

They finished their pasta and the bottles of water, and then, without a word, Dimitri held out his hand and they walked toward the Los Angeles County Art Museum. Several dozen white-painted streetlamps from the 1920s and 1930s had been installed in a tight pattern in rows. The streetlamps' rounded globes were pearly white and gave off a shimmer like moonlight upon fresh snow. It was an indescribable sight. Music played from some distant park, a single violin's song wavering upon the evening air.

Elena stopped walking as she reached the middle of the posts and touched one of the metal columns, tilting her head back to gaze at the lights above and the darkening sky beyond.

"I was without light so many times," she said.

Dimitri cupped her face and turned her toward him. "You are never without light."

He pulled one of her hands to his chest and pressed her palm flat above his heart. She could feel the faint but steady beat beneath her palm. "Light comes from within, and you *always* shine." His deep voice and the gentle rumble of his accent was slowly becoming enjoyable to hear rather than unsettling.

She leaned back against the lamppost and stared at

Dimitri's mouth. The sudden hunger for his kiss left her dizzy and confused. Her hand was still on his chest, and she curled her fingers slightly, fighting the urge to grab his shoulders and cling to him.

"Would you kiss me?" she finally asked.

He cupped the back of her head as he leaned in. "I can ask for no greater gift than that," he said as he lowered his head to hers.

That touch of lips was fire and light, banishing the shadows that slithered within her, threatening to hold her back from life. The healing presence of this man was so potent, it was as though she had discovered a miracle drug that could cure her, and she was desperate to bottle it. Memories of other hands, another body hurting her, pressed against the mental box she'd locked them in. But they had no power over her when she was in Dimitri's arms.

He deepened the kiss, her lips parted, and she curled an arm around his neck, holding herself close to him as he conquered her fears with her. As long as she was with him, she had hope that she could heal.

VIKTOR LINGERED BY A PICNIC TABLE, EATING A BURRITO from one of the food trucks. As he finished his meal, he walked toward the Urban Light display in front of the Los Angeles County Art Museum. Straight ahead of him, two hundred yards away, was his target. He had tailed her movements to a house in Malibu that evening and had waited for the car to leave. He was good at tailing without being seen, but he'd almost lost the car twice. He hadn't expected her to be with someone, however. Not that it mattered. It was just one more body to handle when the time came. All he had to do was wait for the right opportunity.

He meandered closer to the glowing lampposts where the girl stood. She pulled her companion toward her, and the two began to kiss.

Viktor snorted. This was almost too easy.

The man's shirt tightened on his back as he leaned in, and the hint of a blocky shape at his lower back made Viktor freeze. The woman's date was carrying a gun. This complicated matters.

Moving again, but slower, Viktor removed his phone from his pocket and began to take pictures of the light display, acting like any of the dozens of tourists lingering nearby. He kept changing his position over and over, taking pictures each time until he was able to zoom in on the face of the man with Elena Allen. There was something familiar about him, but he couldn't place the man's face. He sent the photo to his contacts back in Moscow, asking them to run a facial recognition. He would go after the girl soon, but he needed to know what he was up against first. It might not be as easy to kill the girl as he'd first believed.

7

Elena was more than nervous when she and Dimitri drove back to Royce's house. It didn't help that she was wide awake now. Sleeping at odd times throughout the day had left her feeling that sleep for now was impossible.

"I think I am going for a walk on the beach," she said as they entered the home. Dimitri set his keys down in a glass bowl by the door and looked at her, an unreadable expression in his eyes that she didn't really like.

"Stay within sight of the patio," he said, and it was clear that was an order.

"I'm not challenging you, but why? If Vadym is dead, I shouldn't be in danger, right?"

For a long moment, he didn't speak. "Vadym is dead, but I don't trust anyone or anything when it comes to your safety."

"That's being a little paranoid."

He stared at her, his lips thin. "If you had grown up the way I did, seen the things I have seen, you would know that danger can be anywhere."

"I do know," Elena reminded him. "And nothing is worse than what Vadym put me through, not even death." She walked past him and out onto the patio, where she removed her shoes and descended the stone stairs to the beach below. The light from the house cascaded down onto the beach, casting everything in monochrome.

The briny sea breeze cleared her head and let her think. She was going to sleep with Dimitri tonight. *Just sleep.* Would it build trust the way she hoped? It had to. She had already drifted off to sleep in his presence a few times. Something about him calmed her enough to trust him, but now she would be trying to do it on purpose. That changed things.

She cast her gaze out across the water and gasped when she saw a fin breach the surface. A moment later a second one followed. *Dolphins!* She stepped into the shallows, watching the dolphins fifty yards away as they played in the moonlit water. Something about them filled her with peace. They were pure creatures, full of heart and driven to protect those they loved, even the occasional human. It reminded her that there was good in the world. Not everything was darkness and suffering. Elena remained on the beach for another fifteen minutes before making the climb back up to the house.

Dimitri was in the office that Elena assumed was Royce's, given that the bookshelves along one wall had a collection of fossilized leaves. Dimitri didn't react as she put her head just inside the door. He was focused on his computer, reading something.

"I'm going up to bed. If you still want to . . . do what we talked about, you can join me whenever you wish." She said this so confidently, but inside her soul was quaking with the thought. This was insane. Part of her knew that this whole idea that a complete stranger could heal her was madness. It was even more insane that she should trust him enough to sleep with him. But at this point she was desperate to feel something, anything but fear, and Dimitri summoned a dozen emotions within her whenever he walked into a room. Not one of them was fear.

He lifted his gaze to hers, their eyes locking.

"Sweet dreams, *kiska*. I will come to you soon."

If that didn't just make her melt, something so sweet that the old Elena would have laughed at it, but right now she loved that someone wanted to wish her sweet dreams. Not to mention the promise he'd left hanging that he would come to her. *Just to sleep,* she had to remind herself, but still, her imagination, the part of her that wanted love and passion, was waking up from its long slumber.

She stopped just inside her bedroom and stood for a long moment, uncertain. Vadym had forced her to sleep naked on the floor, and she had been conditioned to obey that rule, but that wasn't something she had to deal with anymore. Yet part of her still needed a set of rules to follow. Rules were almost always safe. When she obeyed, nothing too bad happened to her, at least not immediately. Elena didn't want to feel that way, but the need for rules was still there, like an anxious hum at the back of her mind.

Shaking off the flutter of thoughts in her head, she changed into a pair of jersey cotton shorts and an over-large T-shirt. It wasn't sexy—she didn't want sexy. Comfort was what mattered. Then she pulled back the covers and climbed in. The bed was still way too soft, but she remembered Dimitri saying she couldn't sleep on the floor. *A rule.* It made it easier. She wriggled a bit, trying to get comfortable, but it wasn't easy when she wasn't dead on her feet.

She was nearly asleep by the time Dimitri opened her bedroom door and stepped quietly into the room. The bright moonlight illuminated him as he stopped beside her bed. He unbuttoned his shirt, and her eyes fixed on the movement, fascinated.

"You aren't asleep," he said softly.

She shook her head. "I'm still not used to the bed." She rolled on her back to stare at the ceiling. She wasn't sure how much clothing he was going to remove, and she felt bad for wanting to watch him when nothing would come of it. The covers shifted on the bed, and he eased down beside her on the mattress. There was plenty of space for them both, even when she stretched out in the middle of the bed.

"Do you want a certain side, or—?"

A chuckle rumbled through him and made the bed quiver ever so slightly. Then he rolled on his side to face her. "*Kiska*, you are adorable."

They were a foot apart, yet it felt like a wide chasm existed between them. She wanted to be closer. He propped his head on one hand, and the sheets pooled low around his waist, letting her eyes have their fill of his bare upper body. He was built for strength, built for power, and it should have terrified her, but it didn't.

"What's this?" She pointed to a knotted scar on his left shoulder.

"A bullet wound. An old one."

"A wound there would do major damage, wouldn't it? What happened?" She stared at the spot, wondering what horrific circumstance had caused that wound.

"It did. I underwent two separate surgeries to fix the nerve damage. It's back to about ninety-five percent of its strength now."

"How did it happen? Can you tell me?"

Dimitri took her hand and held it in his own. He then placed her hand on his chest in silent encouragement to touch him.

"It's a long story and a rather grim one. Are you sure you want to hear it?"

"Yes." Strangely, she wasn't put off by the idea of a

story that possibly didn't have a happy ending. She had suffered so much that she felt she could take a little more, even if it was hearing someone else's painful story.

"I was young when my mother died, as I told you, but what I didn't tell you was that I was there when she was killed . . ."

Elena's stomach knotted. Maybe she wasn't ready to hear this.

"My mother didn't believe in the Soviet government."

"She was against the Communist Party, you mean."

"Yes. She was devoted to the people of Russia, and to a way of life lost to us. She . . ." He hesitated. "She performed tasks, delivered things, if you understand what I mean."

Elena was pretty sure she did. His mother had been a spy.

"One night, as my mother brought me home from the market . . ." His blue eyes darkened. "We'd spent hours in a line for food. The old days were tough. Times are still difficult now, in fact in many ways worse. I remember the smell of the bread. It was so enticing, and my stomach wouldn't stop growling. My eyes were closed. I heard the rush of footsteps coming toward us, and then my mother made a sound, a soft groan as she slumped to the ground beside me. It was dark, just after dusk, and I remember looking back, seeing a man in a dark coat rushing away. At first, I didn't understand what had happened. I turned to my mother. She lay facedown on the concrete, the tips of her fingers on one hand touching the back tire of our car. I dropped the bag of groceries so that I could kneel down beside her. I remember that so vividly still . . ."

Elena couldn't breathe. She was there with him, trapped in the slowly building nightmare of his past.

"Her throat had been slit. Blood pooled out, thick and dark, staining the tips of my shoes." Dimitri's voice didn't waver, it was as though he had told this story a thousand times, yet she wondered if he really had or not. From the open, raw look in his eyes, she wondered if maybe this was the first time he'd actually said the words to someone other than himself.

"I ran after the man . . . I'm not sure why. Most children at my age would have stayed by their mother. But I barreled after him and latched onto his leg as he reached his car. He spun on me, stunned to look down and find a child was holding him back. He slapped me, but I didn't let go. That's when he pulled a handgun with a silencer out of his coat and pressed it against my shoulder and fired."

"He shot a child?" Elena nearly sat up as a fresh wave of horror washed over her.

"It hurt like hell. I passed out and came to an hour later in a hospital. It took my father nearly half a day to find me. My mother's murder was buried in bureaucracy, and even my hospital records were edited to say that the cause of my injury was unknown."

"What? Why would they change something like that?"

Dimitri still held her hand, and he continued to hold it

against his chest. "When a government wishes to control people, they do not only silence the voices of the opposition—they *erase* them. The Russian government is a master of painting the erasing of truths in a positive light, calling it social and political progress, when in fact erasing history is the very opposite of progress. Even though it puts the ones I love in danger, I stand against that ideology every day." He let out a weary sigh. "Even now, such ideas spread beyond the borders of Russia . . . even here . . ." He didn't say any more, but she understood. The world had started to change in the last few years and not for the better.

To know that Dimitri wasn't afraid to fight, even if it was a fight he would probably lose, told her something important about him. He was loyal to people and causes he believed in.

"What happened after she died?" Elena moved her fingertips over his chest, and he let her explore him. There was a sense of security in him, and the way she could talk about hard things while having the ability to comfort him with her touch.

"Losing my mother nearly broke my father. He spent ten years trying to find the man who killed my mother and almost killed me. But the deeper he sank into his grief and lust for revenge, the more he forgot that I was still alive, that I still needed a father." There was pain hidden in his voice, but he couldn't hide it in his eyes.

"Is he . . .?"

"Alive? No, he was killed in a car bomb explosion when he tracked down my mother's murderer. From what others have told me, he had one chance to take the man out, and the bomb's remote trigger failed. He chose to set it off manually. He hid in the back of the target's car and waited."

Elena didn't want to picture it, yet somehow she could. He would have looked like an older version of Dimitri as he stayed hidden in the back of the car, waiting, heart pounding as he made the choice to die to avenge his wife's murder rather than stay alive for his son.

"This is why I am afraid to try to give you what you ask," Dimitri said.

"What do you mean?"

His eyes closed, and she lost herself counting his long lashes fanned out on his cheeks.

"There's a darkness inside me, *kiska*. My life has been full of pain. It has shaped me in part to need things I cannot ask of you. You aren't made for my darkness."

"Don't you think I have darkness in me?" she asked quietly. Her hand had traveled to his lower stomach and paused, resting against the steel-hard perfection of his abdomen.

"You are light, pure and bright. There is no darkness in you." Dimitri said this with such conviction that it surprised her.

"You're wrong. Let me prove it to you." She sat up in bed. "Before Vadym . . . before he took me, I was not some sheltered virgin who dreamt of fairy-tale princes. I had hungers, Dimitri, ones that align closely with your own."

At this he sat up as well. "No, *kiska*. You don't have to prove anything to me." He growled the words as his dominant side began to emerge.

Elena controlled her suddenly fast breathing. "Maybe I need to prove it to myself." She slipped out of bed and left the room. She went into his room next door, and she found what she was looking for before she returned to him. He had gotten out of bed too and was standing in her doorway. His eyes fell to what she held in her hand, a gray silk tie. She extended her hand, offering it to him.

"*Kiska* . . . ," he warned in that addictive voice.

"I just want to try it. Just the restraint . . ." She wanted him to be the one who held her down, who controlled her. If she could trust him and trust the experience, it would be a huge leap forward for her.

She pressed the tie to his chest. Then she skirted around him and walked back to the bed. She climbed in and lay on her back, waiting. He turned around slowly, the silk tie glowing pale and silver in the moonlight from the wall of windows that faced the sea.

Dimitri coiled the tie around his hand, pulling the fabric taut. It was similar to what Vadym had used to do with a leather belt. Her heart slammed against her rib cage, but she didn't take her eyes off Dimitri. He wasn't Vadym, and when he was near her, she felt the way a woman was supposed to feel when she was with a man she desired.

He approached the bed, storm clouds still hovering in his eyes. Even in this simple action, she was mesmerized by his raw, commanding power.

"Come here." He pointed to the side of the bed. Elena sat up and moved to the edge and let her legs drop off the side.

"Hands." His tone was gentle but brooked no argument, just the way a Dom in her deepest, most secret fantasies would sound.

Elena extended her wrists out to him, and he pulled the tie from around his clenched fist. Then he began to wrap the silk around her wrists, binding them together. He pulled the tie tight enough to trap her hands together, but when he was finished knotting the silk, she could feel proper blood flow. Vadym had never . . . She shook herself free of any more thoughts of that man. She was with Dimitri now, and that was all that mattered.

"How do you feel?" he asked. "Red, yellow, or green?"

Those words were far easier to use while her mind was flooded with thoughts and reactions. "Green . . ."

"You don't sound sure." He sat beside her on the bed.

"Green with a hint of yellow," she clarified. "Could we . . . try more?" Her heart was racing as her mind caught up to what her body wanted.

"How much more?"

She bit her lip. It was so embarrassing to explain what

she wanted. A good Dom would have been able to just act and let her slow things down when she got to a point she wasn't ready for. But these were far from normal circumstances for them both.

"Um, what if we just sort of keep going and I'll tell you when it's too much?"

Dimitri's brows pulled together into a scowl. He looked like he hated the sound of it, but Elena didn't want to stop. In the light of day, she would never be able to ask him to do this, but the night had given her some power back, and she didn't want to waste it.

"Please, Dimitri."

He held her bound hands and stroked the backs of her knuckles in light little caresses.

"I shouldn't agree to this," he murmured, more to himself than to her.

"I need to see how far I can go."

He finally answered with a slow nod and got up from the bed.

"Where are you going?"

He was at the door when he spoke. "To get more ties."

❧ 8 ❧

Elena held her breath as Dimitri stepped back into her bedroom with more silk ties. He tossed them onto the bed before he bent in front of her and lifted her to her feet by tugging gently on her bound wrists. He walked her to the glass windows facing the sea.

"Watch the ocean," he commanded, then stepped behind her. Little apprehensive tremors moved through her. She didn't like her back exposed.

"Dimitri . . ."

"*Kiska*, you will use red, yellow, or green when I do something you have a strong reaction to, good or bad, do you understand?"

She nodded.

He curled a hand around her waist. "Did Vadym order you to call him *master*?"

She flinched at the vile, debasing memories that resurfaced.

"What would you prefer to call me when we play this game?" Dimitri's words were as silken as the ties binding her wrists.

"Sir," Elena said. She had always liked that. It was respectful and yet still playful.

"Then from now until we are finished tonight, you call me *sir*." The hand on her waist held her still. His long, strong fingers held her as he stepped closer to her from behind. The heat of his bare chest warmed her back through the T-shirt she wore, making her feel naked.

"Now, watch the ocean and tell me how you feel." That was her only warning before he pressed his lips to her ear in a light, sensual kiss.

"G—green," she whispered. His mouth moved lower to the sensitive spot just behind her ear. She jolted as a bolt of arousal ripped through her. That spot had always been her biggest weakness.

"*Kiska?*" he growled before nipping that spot and flicking his tongue against it. Waves of sensual hunger surged through her, unstoppable, making her desperate for more.

"Green, green, green . . . ," she panted so fast it sounded like a wild chant.

Dimitri chuckled. His hand on her waist moved so that he now held her bound hands by encircling her wrists with his fingers.

"You are under *my* power now, *kiska*. I hold you in my hands." The words should have terrified her, but they didn't.

He waited for her response, and she whispered, "Green." Only then did he continue. He pressed her more firmly against the window, his body covering hers from behind, caging her. She felt his arousal dig into the cleft of her ass. They both wore clothes there, her shorts and his briefs, but it didn't matter—she swore she could feel every inch of that most masculine part of him. Would he go too far and take her? The thought scared her, but not as much as she expected it to.

"Do you like knowing that you belong to me? That you are safe in my arms?"

"Yes, sir." She did feel safe, and it made no logical sense. After the hell she had endured, she should be too afraid to want this again. But didn't she deserve to have her life back? Didn't that include her physical desires as well? She shouldn't let Vadym destroy what she'd loved about sex, about the domination without pain, the gentle guidance a good and caring Dom could give her, so she didn't overthink sex the way she was doing right now . . .

He kissed her neck again. "You are thinking too hard. There are only two of us in this room, do you understand?"

She bit her lip and nodded. That's what she needed. He could help her focus on what she wanted . . . just this, just the two of them. He rewarded her by turning her away enough from the window to claim her lips with his. His mouth worked magic, that slow, playful, teasing kiss sending all other thoughts far away. There was only this man, this room, this kiss. But she needed more, she needed to feel what she hadn't felt in more than two months.

She wriggled, tugging on her wrists, and he tightened his grip, silently reminding her who was in charge of her body. "Please, sir, I need . . ."

"Yes, *kiska*, what do you need?"

"I need to come, please . . ." It was so easy, so natural to ask him, and if she had been thinking more clearly, she would have been wondering why that was, but she was too lost in her desires at the moment.

"Please what?" He bit gently into the sensitive spot between her neck and shoulder, like a wolf pinning his mate in place. The wild thought only heightened the sharp pangs of her arousal. She clenched her thighs together, but it wasn't enough.

"Please, sir, please use your hand to make me come." She wasn't ready for anything but that, but it would still be a victory she never thought she would have again.

Dimitri's sensual chuckle almost made her smile as well. "Because you asked so sweetly, I cannot deny you." He made this darkly erotic game sweet and *safe*. He made it exactly what she needed most.

He continued to kiss her neck as he pushed one of his feet between hers, forcing her to step wider apart. Then he trailed a large palm down her body, skimming over her collarbones, then her breasts, down to her soft belly. His fingers snaked beneath the waistband of the shorts and panties she wore. While his hand was gentle, she felt the rough scrape of his fingers over her skin. His hands were so strong, a testament to a life lived fully. It felt amazing. When his fingers reached the top of her mound, the hand that grasped her bound wrists shifted slightly and adjusted its grip.

"And now, *kiska*?"

"Green," she whispered, then held her breath as he moved his fingers down her folds, which were already slick with her desire.

"Good. You will tell me if that changes."

"Yes, sir." Elena wished there was a color better than green as he parted her folds and traced the sensitive skin with his fingers. Her legs trembled, and she whimpered.

"Are you ready for me to touch you?" he asked.

She nodded frantically. She needed his touch to erase the memories of all others who had come before. She wanted only him to ever touch her again.

"Yes . . . Oh God, please . . ." She threw her head back as he slid a finger inside her. She tensed, but he murmured soft words of comfort in her ears, praising her bravery, her courage, her beauty, and how she pleased him. He thrust his finger in and out slowly at first, allowing her to get accustomed to the feel of him.

"Please, sir, harder." She wasn't afraid. She wanted him

to send her over the edge, and she didn't need gentleness just then.

"Such a bad girl, *kiska*," he teased her. Rather than frighten her with the threat of punishment, he rewarded her with pleasure. He added a second finger, stretching her, and then he moved his hand faster, his long fingers sinking deep into her aching wetness.

So close . . . So close . . . She was almost there. Tears of frustration clouded her eyes as she suddenly feared she might never climax again.

"You are mine, forever, *kiska*. Bound to me always," Dimitri growled.

It was that possessive promise that sent her over the edge. She gasped, too overcome to scream as a tidal wave of ecstasy ripped through her, devastating her. Her legs gave out, and she collapsed against the glass of the window. Dimitri held her up, his fingers still inside her, but gentle now as he drew out her orgasm, encouraging little aftershocks that made her body twitch with pleasure until she sagged in his hold. Then she was lifted up in his arms and carried to the bed. Dazed, she lay still as he unbound her hands and massaged her wrists.

He pulled back the comforter and tucked her beneath the blankets. She was cocooned in heat and decadent softness, and suddenly it was too much. She began to cry in great, choking sobs. He joined her in the bed, curling her body into his, holding her as she rode the roller coaster of emotions until she was too tired to do anything more than peek up a few times and nuzzle her face against his chest.

"You've been very brave tonight, *kiska*. Those are tears of joy. You have regained your desire and pleasure tonight. *You* did that. Do you understand?"

She nodded, too tired to speak, but he was right. Her tears *were* ones of relief and joy. She was no longer Vadym's captive. Her body was becoming her own again.

VIKTOR IVANOFF CHECKED THE ZIPPERS OF HIS BLACK wet suit. He sat on the edge of a small motorboat that was anchored half a mile out to sea from the shore that faced a row of expensive Malibu beach houses. He checked his watch. It was nearly midnight. He would wait a little longer and then go ashore.

His burner phone vibrated on the seat beside him. He picked it up.

"Yes?"

"The photo you sent didn't come back with any matches."

"You're sure?"

"Positive. The woman must have met him in Moscow. She was one of Vadym Andreikiv's little whores. You know how those women are. She probably moved on to the next man after Vadym was killed."

Viktor was familiar with Vadym's file. After his mysterious poisoning, the Kremlin had wondered if it might be related to a string of disappearances of several Russian mob bosses in the last six months. The only thing that set Vadym apart was the public nature of his death. The other men had simply vanished, leaving their operations in disarray. His right-hand man, Jov Tomenko, had gone mad and shot at some Americans as they fled toward the US embassy in Mongolia, which had in turn gotten him shot by US Marines. But Vadym had other underlings who would have taken Elena Allen and killed her when they were done with her. Yet somehow, she had escaped and left the country. Was this why she was Viktor's new target? Had she seen or heard something she shouldn't have while sleeping with Vadym?

Viktor had been trained never to ask questions, but this mission bothered him. He had no qualms about killing the woman, but he didn't like it when he sensed a bigger issue was at play and he wasn't informed about it.

"Finish her and send a report, then return to Moscow."

Viktor hung up, placed the phone inside his wet suit in a waterproof pocket, then picked up his air tank, scuba mask, and fins. When he was ready, he fell backward over the side of his boat and sank into the dark water and headed for shore.

Dimitri held Elena in his arms for a long while. She slept as though she would rest for a thousand years, and for that, he was glad. Tonight she had proven she had a soul that darkness could not conquer. The small flame had grown to a healthy fire, but there was still a long road ahead to bring back her inferno.

Yet he had hope. She had come so far in only a few days, farther than he'd imagined. However, he would have to be careful not to push her too hard or too fast. Any misstep had the possibility of sending her crashing back down. That was the last thing either of them wanted.

He pressed his lips to her cheek and closed his eyes. He tried not to think about his own reaction tonight. He had claimed her, she was his forever, but could she handle forever with a man like him? Playing these games to become comfortable in her own skin again was one thing, but sharing her life with a man who had dark desires and a darker future . . . that would be too much for any woman. It was why he had never settled down. If he dared to love a woman enough to marry her, to build a life with her, he would only ever subject her to a life of lies and danger. She would never truly be safe. This life had killed his parents. He couldn't let it claim the life of a woman he loved. Yet, even knowing that, he couldn't help but crave a different life, one he could share with Elena.

It was well past midnight when he felt the urge to relieve himself. He kissed Elena on the forehead and slipped out of bed. After using the restroom, he walked back into the room and stared for a moment at the moonlit sea. He couldn't shake the restless feeling inside him. Was he being paranoid? Maybe it was only because someone like Viktor Ivanoff was here. He didn't believe in coincidences. Too much had happened in his life to make believe that things like this just happened.

He turned back toward the bed where Elena slept, and his heart clenched in his chest. It was madness to want her, to crave all of her the way he did. He knew so much about her, but those were facts sorted into a dossier. He wanted to know all the things his network would never know. What did she dream about when those dreams weren't tainted by nightmares? What inspired her as she lived day to day? What were her favorite books? What side of the bed did she actually prefer? Did she like to exercise? Did she enjoy the beach as much as he did? He felt like a foolish teenager, wanting to know everything, and that was exactly his problem. He should be keeping his head on straight and not acting like a lovestruck fool.

The temptation to return to her in bed was almost overpowering. He opened the balcony door instead and stepped out onto the stone balcony. It was bright enough that he could see the sand clearly on the ground below. It was pristine, untouched as the tide came in . . . almost. He leaned farther over the balcony railing to get a better look. His blood chilled in his veins. A set of footprints led out of the water toward their beach house.

❄

LEO ANTONOV LEANED BACK IN HIS CHAIR, FEET BRACED
on the edge of his desk as he held a baseball in one hand.
The screens of his computer displayed the progress of a
deep analysis of Elena Allen's blood, which had arrived by
private courier an hour ago. All he had to do now was wait
for the tests to finish.

Nicholas called out from behind him, "Toss it here!"

Leo tossed the baseball over his shoulder without
looking, and he heard Nicholas chuckle. "How is the
science coming?"

Leo dropped his legs from his desk and spun around.
"The DNA analysis should be done soon. So, when did
you get back?"

Nicholas shrugged. "Just now."

Leo, Maxim, and Nicholas had lived in the small
manor house outside St. Petersburg for the last ten years,
ever since the old palace near the lake had been abandoned and the remnants of the White Army had been
sent into hiding. Dimitri also lived with them when he was
in town, but he was usually in Paris or Moscow for most of
his missions. They used to joke that they were the four
musketeers, like the heroes in Alexandre Dumas's book.

Nicholas threw himself onto a couch and tossed the
ball into the air. It was one of Leo's favorite possessions.
He had caught a foul ball at Wrigley Field when he went

to a Chicago Cubs game one day while he was in the United States on assignment for a year.

"Where is Maxim?" Leo asked.

Again, Nicholas shrugged. "Out."

Leo's lips turned down. "Call him. We need him back here."

"Why? He'll only be all doom and gloom." Nicholas put his feet up on the ottoman. This was Leo's office, but for as long as they had lived here, his office had become a place for Maxim and Nicholas to relax. Leo usually didn't mind, but tonight he was concerned.

"Nick, I'm serious—" The chime of his computer cut him off, and he turned back to his desk to analyze the results. There were dozens of matches filling the screen, but several were highlighted in red by the analyzing software.

Leo stared at the screen, his jaw dropping as he forgot to breathe.

"Leo?" Nicholas's voice began to cut through the sudden ringing in Leo's ears.

"Nick, call Dimitri now!" He could barely get the words out.

"You're scaring me." Nicholas was suddenly behind him, peering over his shoulder. "What is that?"

Leo pointed to one particular line on the screen in red.

"Twelve point five percent match," Nicholas said. "Match to whom?"

"Nick, call Dimitri. This is an emergency."

Nicholas pulled his cell out of his pocket and dialed Dimitri, put it on speaker. It went to voice mail.

"Dimitri, call us back. Code 78," Leo said, then nodded at Nicholas, who ended the call.

"Are you going to tell me who Elena Allen's blood matches?" Nicholas asked.

Leo shook his head. "You won't believe it. I'm afraid even to tell Dimitri over the phone."

Nicholas dialed Maxim's number and left the same message with the Code 78 for him.

"We have to get to Los Angeles now. Pack a bag." Leo coded the DNA file analysis of Elena's blood so deep only he would ever be able to decode it again.

"That serious? What about Maxim?"

Leo shut his computers down and removed the portable hard drive. "He can meet us at the airport." He secured the drives in the dining room under a floorboard up against the wall. The entire room had metal plates throughout the floor to give off false readings if anyone swept the room with any detection devices. They couldn't take any chances.

Dimitri was guarding a ticking time bomb. If they couldn't get there in time, everything they had been raised to fight for would be in vain.

ELENA WOKE WHEN SHE STRETCHED OUT AND FELT ONLY the empty bed. Dimitri had gone . . . so soon after she had opened herself up to him. Her heart clenched, and she curled in on herself in deep pain. She lay there a long moment, trying to focus on breathing. That was when the lightest of sea breezes tickled her face.

She sat up and stared at the open balcony door. She pushed back the covers and slipped out of bed to go check the deck. It was empty. She shivered and closed the door, flicking the lock into place. Why had Dimitri left the door open?

Something crashed downstairs, and she jerked toward the door, intending to go see who it was. But she froze. A man stood in the doorway, a gun pointed at her. He was tall like Dimitri but older, in his forties, perhaps. He had an unremarkable face that would blend easily into a crowd and cold, dark eyes. She pressed herself against the glass of the closed balcony door.

"Who are you?" the man whispered in a Russian-accented voice. "What makes you so special?"

Another Russian. Another man like Vadym. He took two steps into the room. There was another distant sound of shattering glass. Elena's eyes darted toward the door.

"Your boyfriend was hard to put down, but those bullets in his chest will catch up to him eventually." The man laughed at his own joke. Elena's stomach turned.

No . . . Please no . . . Dimitri was hurt. Dying. And she was alone. The living nightmare had returned.

The man stalked toward her, and before she could run, he had her by the throat.

"*What* makes you so special?" he demanded again, tightening his grip on her throat and using his other hand to dig the barrel of his gun into her stomach.

Tears blurred her eyes as she tried to claw at his throat. "I'm not special," she gasped. "I'm nobody."

"Then why does my government want you dead?" He shook her like a rag doll, and her head smacked against the thick glass of the balcony door behind her. Pain exploded through the back of her skull, and white stars dotted her vision. It was getting harder to breathe. The man pointed the gun at her temple as he leaned over her. She gazed up at him, her body losing its strength. His eyes bored into hers but suddenly widened, his brows lifting.

"You look . . . No . . . That is impossible . . ."

Elena's hands dropped and fell against her sides. When her fingers collided with the glass of the patio door, she had one last idea. She flipped the lock behind her and began to slide the door open.

For a moment, she and the Russian man were free-falling. Then he caught himself, but he had to release her to do so. She fell onto her back, the air rushing out of her lungs, and he loomed, glaring down at her.

"Stupid bitch," he muttered as he raised his gun again.

"Actually, she's rather clever," someone said behind him. He started to turn, but then half a dozen bullets ripped through him, the sound deafening. Elena clutched her ears and curled into a ball.

A second later, the man stumbled and collapsed to the ground. His gun clattered to the floor, just out of reach. Elena scrambled to grab it and pick it up, afraid he might get up again. Dimitri emerged out of the shadows of her bedroom, a gun in his hand. His other hand gripped his side, and blood was trickling down the side of his face.

"Dimitri," Elena gasped. He winced as he stepped over the dead man's body to take the gun from her trembling hand. He tossed it onto the bed and then held out his hand to her and pulled her to her feet.

"Did he hurt you?" Dimitri pulled her closer, wrapping an arm around her in a fierce embrace while he kept his other hand ready to fire.

"Not much. But you . . . he shot you."

Dimitri pulled back and opened the buttons on his shirt to reveal a bulletproof vest underneath. "Yes, but I was prepared."

"When did you—?"

"I will explain everything, *kiska*, but first we must clean the scene and go. Someone might have heard my gun firing."

"Go?" She stared numbly at the body lying on the balcony floor. What would they do with him?

"Yes. Get dressed and put on your running shoes and some comfortable jeans. Pack your suitcase." Dimitri released her and grabbed the man's limp arms, dragging him through the room and into the hall.

"*Kiska*, now!" Dimitri's tone jerked her focus back. Within fifteen minutes, she was dressed and packed, her bag standing up by the door. He came down the stairs ten minutes after her, his bloody face cleaned and his clothing changed.

"Where did you . . . ?"

"The basement."

"But won't someone . . . ?"

Dimitri shook his head. "I have friends who will take care of the matter."

Elena cut herself off before she even tried to ask a question. He had friends who would dispose of a body and clean a crime scene?

"We must go."

He ushered her out the door. She got into the car, feeling even more uncertain about her future than before. She heard the words that Russian man had spoken echoing in her head.

Why are you so special? Why does my government want you dead?

9

Dimitri's hands shook as he gunned the engine of the Aston Martin. They would have to abandon it soon, but he needed to call a few people to help since he hadn't planned on running like this.

Viktor Ivanoff was dead. That was the only good thing to come from all of this. Dimitri glanced over at Elena. She was quiet, her eyes focused on the road straight ahead. He clenched his fingers tight on the steering wheel as he saw the angry red marks of Viktor's handiwork on her throat.

I almost lost her. The thought made him sick. She was supposed to be safe, and he had brought danger to her door.

"What did he mean?" she asked, finally turning to him.

"What?"

"He said, 'Why does my government want you dead?'"

"What?" The man had told Elena his government wanted *her* dead? Shock ricocheted through him, but it explained so much. Dimitri had let the man think him mortally wounded after he'd unloaded two shots into his chest. Viktor should have tried to finish him off with a shot to the head, something Dimitri was ready for, but instead, he'd gone straight up the stairs. Dimitri had tried to break a few things to draw him back down, but Viktor had been focused on finding his target.

Dimitri turned down a darkened side street and stopped the car. "*You* were the target?"

"Yes. But why? Why would he . . .? I'm not . . . Is this because of Vadym? I knew he had friends in high places, but I didn't think they would come after me here in the States."

"It's possible. Maybe the government assumes you overheard or saw something that could hurt them."

"But I didn't," she insisted.

"It does not matter, so long as they believe you did. It would be safer for them to kill you."

"Oh God . . . My parents! Are they in danger? They were coming to visit me in a few days."

"Call them now, and then we have to ditch your phone. Tell them to cancel their visit."

She pulled out her cell and left her parents a voice mail, and then he took the phone from her. After removing the SIM card, he tossed it and her phone out the car window.

"Wait—"

"I promise I will get you a new one, *kiska*." He caught her chin and turned her to face him. "You need to trust me. Do you understand?"

He waited for her to nod. Then he pulled his cell out of his pocket. He had missed a call from Leo, and there was a voice mail. His heart stuttered to a stop as the first words he heard were *Code 78*.

"What's a Code 78?" Elena asked. She was sitting close enough that she had heard the message.

"It is need-to-know."

"Does it have to do with me?" Her voice was pitched sharply.

"Yes."

"Then I need to know!"

He really couldn't argue with that, but now was not the time. He needed a minute to process what that meant. It was a code that he had been told would never be used. His father had only mentioned it a handful of times when Dimitri was younger. The only reason he even remembered it was because of the flights of fancy his mind would take, imagining a world where such a thing was possible.

He restarted the car engine and chose his route out of town carefully, going north on the PCH. "It's not safe to talk about it."

"We're in a car, completely alone. No one will hear."

Even though the Pacific Coast Highway tended to be crowded, it wasn't like they had the windows down.

"*Kiska*," he warned, unable to stop a bit of a growl escaping his tone.

"Please," she begged, and her hand fell on his right forearm. The touch grounded him, and he remembered that she was more than just involved in his life now—she was at the heart of it, in more ways than one. She was more precious to him than he could even rationalize, and he'd nearly lost her. Elena deserved the truth.

"Code 78 means someone like me must protect someone like you."

"But you already were . . ."

"This is different. This is the reason I am what I am. It means you *are* special."

She tightened her hold on his arm. "Special how?"

"It's your blood. Something in your blood makes you special. I can't say how until I speak to Leo. He tested the sample I sent, and—"

"What?" Elena gasped. "*My* blood? How . . . ?"

"When you cut your head that first day at the house. I sent him the cloth I used to clean your wound."

"You just mailed someone halfway around the world a sample of my blood to run *tests* on? That's not okay, Dimitri." She let go of his arm. "That's pretty damn far from okay."

"I know you deserve your privacy, but this . . . this is bigger than your privacy."

"What could possibly be bigger than my privacy?"

He glanced her way with a grim look. "The very fate of Russia."

She was silent a moment, biting her bottom lip. She had no idea what he meant when he said that, but she would soon enough.

"So it's really not about Vadym?" She looked like a small, frightened child. He wanted more than ever to pull over on the side of the road and tug her onto his lap and soothe her.

"No, I thought it was, until Code 78."

She was silent a long while. The miles flew past as he got them onto the open road.

"Where are we going?" she finally asked.

"Colorado."

"Why there?"

"It's ski season. We need crowds. Other agents will expect us to go into hiding somewhere small. We won't."

"Won't we be at risk of being seen? We could be in the background of hundreds of vacation photos. I mean, don't they have image-recognition software?"

"You are right."

"So why there?"

"Leo's software acts faster than Russia's. It will find any photos online of our faces and delete them before they are found by the enemy."

"The enemy," she said, her tone heavy with disbelief.

Dimitri hated that she was going through this now, and

it was only going to get worse. Once Viktor failed to report to his handler, the Russians would know Elena had protection. The Kremlin would soon know him for what he was, a guard in the White Army. He would be looking over his shoulder for the rest of his life, and so would Elena.

She yawned and cradled her head in her arm as she rested against the passenger-side window. "Are we stopping soon?"

"In half an hour. I will need coffee so I can drive another few hours."

She lifted her head to stare at him. "Dimitri, you can't keep driving that long. You didn't get any sleep. We should stop at a motel or something."

"It's about three and a half hours to Vegas. We will stay there and then keep going."

"Vegas . . . ," Elena sighed, half listening, putting her head back in the crook of her arm.

"Vegas indeed," he echoed with a heavy sigh. It was going to be a long four hours.

ELENA GOT OUT OF THE CAR TO STRETCH HER LEGS three hours later. Dimitri parked their car in the back of a very clean little motel with a small flashing sign that said "Aces Wild."

"What? We aren't going to stay at the Bellagio?" she

teased. The stress and exhaustion were starting to make her feel rather slaphappy.

"No. We can't be around cameras yet. Leo will have dropped everything to leave Russia for a Code 78. He won't be able to help us until he's here on US soil."

"Leo's coming here?"

"And he will most likely bring Maxim and Nicholas."

"So I get to meet your family, I guess?" She was strangely excited, but also intimidated at the thought of meeting three more men like Dimitri.

He chuckled, but his face was still weary. "Yes, my family." He motioned for her to follow him into the office of the motel.

The attendant, perhaps close to her age, was watching a TV show on his laptop as they entered the office and stopped at the front desk.

"We would like a room, please," Dimitri said in a flawless American accent. He removed a wad of cash from his wallet.

"Sure thing, no problem," the young man said. "All we have left are king-size beds. Is that okay?"

"King-size is fine," Dimitri replied. "If number six on the back side is available, we'd like it."

"Sure. You guys newlyweds?"

"We are." Dimitri wrapped an arm around her waist, pulled her into his side, and pressed a kiss to her temple. Elena wanted to melt into him. In the last several hours, she had felt lost all over again, tired and defeated by the world, but his touch, his kiss, even so innocent a one, was like a strong rainfall after months of drought. She soaked him up, clinging to him in return.

"Congratulations! You guys look like you're really in love." The young man handed Dimitri a room key. "What name should I put down?"

"John St. Michael."

"No problem. Have a great night." The clerk waved at them as they left. She and Dimitri walked to the room near the car and let themselves in.

"You should rest for a bit. I will bring in our suitcases." His accent was back. She'd actually missed it.

Elena wanted to help him, but the exhaustion was catching up to her again. She lay down on the bed and closed her eyes, but when she heard the door click shut and Dimitri moving about the room, she forced herself to sit up.

"Here, change into these." Dimitri placed her pajamas in her arms, and on top was her toothbrush and toothpaste. He always thought of everything.

"Thanks." She shut herself inside the small bathroom, changed, and brushed her teeth, then headed straight to bed. He had already pulled the covers back for her. The inviting nature of so small a thing made her throat tighten. He truly did care about her.

"Go to sleep, *kiska*. I'll wake you in the morning," he said.

"You'll sleep with me tonight?" she asked as she buried her face in the pillow.

"Of course." He bent over and pressed a light kiss to her cheek. "As long as I am with you, and you wish it, you will never sleep alone."

DIMITRI WASHED HIS FACE IN THE BATHROOM AND stripped out of his clothes before he checked on the small cut on his head. The liquid stitches were holding well. He tried to distract himself from thinking about Leo's message and to focus on what to do when they reached Colorado. But every one of his thoughts came back to *Code 78.*

He hadn't been able to tell Elena everything. He could barely believe it himself. He had been telling the truth when he had said that her blood, her very DNA, was special. The code was reserved only for close relatives of the Romanov family. Leo must have found some matching genetic code to one of the relatives of the imperial family. She wouldn't be the only one. There were dozens of minor relatives who had escaped Russia. The question was, which one was Elena connected to? And why was the government coming after her and not the others?

He retrieved his phone from the small desk in the bedroom and left Leo a voice mail. "Twenty-three, nine, eight, four, sixty-seven." The code would allow Leo to know that Dimitri was on the move with Elena after having put down a threat, and they were headed northeast from Vegas through Utah and then to Colorado. He would leave another message soon, but there was no point until he decided where in Utah they would stop for the night. Leo wouldn't bother with commercial airlines—he would use the private jet so they wouldn't be stuck waiting on flight times. But that still left somewhere between 6 and twelve hours before he would be set up in the United States. Dimitri would have to give him a heads-up on where to rendezvous.

Dimitri peeked through the curtain to check the parking lot, and then re-locked the front door before he retrieved his gun and sat down on the edge of the bed by Elena. She was already fast asleep. He marveled at the amount of trust that had to involve. He scraped a hand over his jaw as he realized he had one more call to make. He dialed Royce on a secure line.

A sleepy voice answered after half a dozen rings. "Dimitri?"

"We had to leave Malibu."

"What? Why?" Royce sounded more alert now.

"It's a long story, but there's a dead Russian agent in your basement."

"A dead Russian . . . in my basement? You know there are better gifts to give a friend. Like an expensive bottle of scotch." Royce was teasing, but Dimitri didn't miss the worry in his friend's words.

"I promise it will be handled soon. There was some damage to your place. Bullet holes, a couple of lamps . . ."

"Those are replaceable," Royce assured him. "Are you both all right?"

"Yes, thanks to you. I borrowed the Kevlar vest and the handgun. I figured you wouldn't mind."

"And to think Wes gave me hell for putting a bullet-proof vest in the closet of my beach house. Who's laughing now?" Dimitri managed a smile. Wes Thorne, their mutual friend, always believed Royce overreacted, but Royce had been right this time.

"I took two shots to the chest, so you can tell Thorne I'm on your side on that issue."

"Fuck. What about Elena?"

"He got to her. The bullets slowed me down." He winced as his cracked ribs protested. "She's alive, but . . ." Dimitri struggled to finish. The sight of her bruised neck replayed in his mind again and again. "She's shaken."

"How is she handling it? That kid has been through so much, and she's only twenty."

"I know." He kept forgetting how young Elena was. She seemed so mature, so brave, *an old soul*, as his grandmother would have said. But she really was young. He tried to remember what he had felt like at her age. That would have been nine years ago. It felt more like a century.

"She's been braver than I could have been had I gone through what she's been through," he admitted.

"You know, she should talk to Cody Larson, Emery Lockwood's tech man."

"Yes? I remember him. He was the one who helped give you a way to escape Vadym's car in Mongolia."

"Well, you recall when I told you about Emery's kidnapping? Finding his twin brother after twenty-five years?"

"Yes . . ."

"Well, when that all went down, Cody was abducted and tortured by the man behind Emery's childhood kidnapping. The bastard shattered one of his hands with an iron mallet. He isn't the same, physically or emotionally, but he survived, you know? It might be good for her to talk to him."

"I agree. Would you send him my number? Tell him why I'm asking for it?"

"Will do." Royce hesitated. "So if you left Malibu, you're somewhere . . ."

"Sinful," Dimitri replied with a grin, knowing Royce would get the reference.

"Sinful indeed." Royce chuckled. "Well, whatever you do, no drive-through weddings. Kenzie would be pissed if she missed it."

Dimitri rolled his eyes.

"Where will you end up?"

"New Orleans, I'm thinking," Dimitri replied, again using a code to see if Royce would get his meaning.

"I guess you packed your snow gear, then?" Royce said.

"I hear it's cold in New Orleans this time of year." He pronounced New Orleans as *Nawlins.*

"We did." Dimitri relaxed. The code had worked.

"Travel safe."

"We will." Dimitri ended the call.

"I thought we were going to Colorado?" Elena spoke up from behind him. He turned on the edge of the bed to face her.

"We are."

"But you said New Orleans."

"That was code."

"Code for what?" Elena sat up a little in the bed.

"Royce told me about a place in Colorado he loves called Steamboat Springs, and he talked about how Colorado isn't a place suited to having steamboats, so we both wondered how the town got the name. I said *New Orleans* because it's famous for steamboats."

"So you really are Royce's good friend."

"Yes, *kiska.*" He smiled and leaned toward her. "Now go back to sleep."

"Will you . . ." She swallowed hard enough that he heard the sound. "Will you hold me? I seem to sleep better when you do."

"As you wish." He put his gun by the nightstand, stripped down to his briefs, and turned off the light. She cuddled up against his side, and he pulled the blankets around them. His heart tightened as he held her in his arms. She was soft, small, and so perfectly feminine in all the right ways. She let out a sigh, her warm breath covering his chest, and he had to quell the rising desire in his body. Anything that happened between them must be at her request, not his.

He brushed her hair back from her face and admired her features. She was truly the loveliest woman he had ever seen. She was free of worry lines, and her petal-soft lips curved slightly, as though whatever dreams now captivated her were good ones. For that he was glad. This woman deserved no tears caused by pain. He would kill to protect her and give her the future she deserved. He only wished he knew what his role in that future would be.

❧ I0 ❧

Elena was dreaming. She had to be, because in her dream, she was bound and gagged, helpless, trapped in the dark, barely able to breathe.

Wake up! she tried to shout, but the gag prevented anything but a muffled sound from escaping. A door suddenly opened, and bright light illuminated a tall, intimidating form. She cowered, the chains rattling as she tried to curl in on herself and make herself a smaller target. The man came toward her, stepping into the darkness and crouching beside her.

"*Kiska*, you need never be in the dark again," a voice soothed her. Soon, his hands were at her wrists, unbinding the shackles and removing the gag.

"Dimitri?" She threw her arms around his neck, clinging to him. He was the only thing keeping her afloat in a black sea of despair.

She burrowed her face in the crook of his neck as he lifted her up in the cradle of his arms. "Please, never leave me."

As they stepped into the light, the Dimitri in her dreams gazed down at her. "Why are you special?"

"I'm not."

She bit her lip, and tears filled her eyes as everything, even the warm light, began to fade around her.

"I'm not special. I'm not!"

Elena jerked awake with a gasp and then a groan as her head pounded with a headache. She was back in the dark . . . No, she wasn't. It took her a moment to process her surroundings. She was lying in a hotel bed, the curtains pulled tight on the windows. Everything was calm and quiet. The shower running in the bathroom explained Dimitri's absence from the bed. She sat up and took in a deep breath, but she winced as pain clamped down around her throat. She touched the tender spot where the man had tried to strangle her. She had to be bruised there.

Had that all really happened last night? A Russian agent broke into her room and tried to kill her? Demanded to know why she was important? She remembered Dimitri firing his gun, bringing the man down. She should be more traumatized, but she wasn't, at least not as much as she thought she should be. Being Vadym's plaything, she had seen much worse. He had killed dozens of people in the two months she had been his captive, most of them so close in front of her that blood had splattered her face and she had been unable to wash it away for hours at a time. It had amused Vadym to see her suffer like that.

But Vadym was gone. She had to stop thinking about him. Her life was moving forward, not backward, even if people were trying to kill her. That was something she hadn't yet processed, the insane idea that she was somehow special enough that the Russian government wanted her dead. It was too much to take in.

She just wanted it all to stop, for life to go back to the way it had been. College classes, worrying about midterms and finals, spending hours in the library looking for resources for her class papers.

The sound of running water in the bathroom reminded her of what she would lose if she returned to her old life.

The only thing she didn't want to change was Dimitri and the way he made her feel. Her skin flushed and her toes curled as she remembered what it felt like to have his hands on her, his mouth on hers. She'd felt not only normal, but *alive*.

Flashes of him carrying her out of the darkness and into the light made her shiver. The water shut off in the bathroom, and Elena quickly lay back down and pretended to be asleep. She hadn't forgotten what they had done last night before they had been attacked. He had brought her to a blinding climax while she had been at his mercy. Even the memory of it made her blush. She held her breath as the bathroom door opened. Soft footfalls around the room teased her enough that she parted her lashes to steal a glance at him.

And what a glance it was. He wore only a tiny motel towel, barely big enough to stay on his lean hips. Dimitri had perfect slender hips that accompanied a set of broad shoulders. She had seen him in swim trunks and even briefs, but just a towel and dripping wet? That was something far more exciting. She bit her lip to hide a smile. This was good. She wanted to see him naked. She had never thought she would want to see any man naked ever again.

"I know you are awake, *kiska*," he teased. She let out her breath in a rush before opening her eyes. "Did you rest well?"

She sat up and stifled a yawn. "I did." She didn't mention the dream that had woken her up. It wasn't exactly a nightmare, but it was far too personal to share. He might not want to know just how dependent she was on him. It might scare him away, no matter what he'd vowed to her.

"How long have you been up?" She looked at the clock on the nightstand. It said 9:00 a.m.

"About an hour."

"Did you get any sleep at all?" Somehow, she pictured him standing guard all night. She hoped he hadn't done that. The last thing she needed was for him to exhaust himself protecting her. They were in this together, and she didn't want him taking all the responsibilities.

"I did."

"But not much," she guessed.

Dimitri shrugged. "I am used to working with very little sleep."

"When we get to Colorado, will you sleep then?"

He came toward her, stopping mere inches from the bed. If she wanted to, she could just reach out and pull his towel away.

"Why do you worry so much about my sleep, *kiska?*" He cupped her chin, tilting her head back so they could meet each other's eyes.

"It's just . . . I know what sleep deprivation can do to someone." When she admitted this, her voice was barely above a whisper.

Dimitri leaned over the bed and cupped the back of her head. "You kill me." Then he was kissing her. The magic of his mouth on hers chased away the bad thoughts and memories. This man was a light-bringer, the hero she had always wanted who would carry her out of the darkness.

She moved closer, her legs getting tangled in the sheets, and she heard him laugh against her lips. It was the most wonderful thing, to feel such tender joy with a man like this, where passion was not a punishment but a pleasure.

"Please never stop," she begged as he started to pull back from her.

"If I don't stop now, I will go too far, and neither of us is ready. We need to keep moving. When it's safe, you and I will take our time and explore this." He traced her lips with the pad of his thumb and pressed his forehead against hers, holding her close, their breath mingling as he slowly reined in his control.

"Shower and dress. I need to change cars and fetch us breakfast."

"Okay." She freed herself from the blankets and got out of bed.

"Keep this door locked. When I return, only open the door if I say the word *phoenix* to you. Do you understand?"

Elena nodded, then collected her clothes and shower kit before heading into the bathroom.

Phoenix . . . it reminded her of the gold signet ring he wore on his pinky finger on his left hand. She hadn't gotten a full, detailed look at it, but from what she had seen, it might have been a phoenix. She wished she had a cell phone. She wanted to look it up, see if any secret organizations had members who used a phoenix symbol. The Masons had their Square and Compasses, the Templars had the red cross, and the Illuminati had the Eye of Providence. She wasn't an expert on symbols in secret societies. She had read *The Da Vinci Code*, and that was pretty much her only experience.

She showered and put on a pair of jeans and a loose

white blouse that had a cute little blue whale pattern embroidered on it. Then she put on her running shoes.

As she finished packing her bag back up, she realized that Dimitri had left his phone behind. On purpose? She turned on the screen and swiped. It required a ten-digit code.

"Of course." She put the phone back and tried to lose herself in the news on the TV.

There was a large event for the United Nations coming up soon. A dinner to honor the recipients of the humanitarian awards. Ambassadors from all over the world planned to attend, and security was heightened all over New York. The second news story focused on local news, the weather, and the latest shows in the major casinos. She scanned another channel and another until there was a knock on the door.

"It's me," Dimitri said.

She started to unlock the door, then froze. "What's the password?" She felt like a silly kid, but he had warned her to do this, and she trusted him. He had kept her alive and safe so far.

"Phoenix," he said.

With a sigh of relief, she undid the locks and let him in.

"You almost unlocked the door," he said, a dark brow raised in challenge.

"Yeah. I'm sorry. This whole *Spy vs. Spy* thing isn't easy to get used to."

He tilted his head slightly. "Spy versus spy?"

"Yeah, you know, those cartoon characters with big hats and triangle faces, one all white, one all black. Always running around and trying to kill each other in espionage games?"

Dimitri shook his head in disbelief. "You Americans with your cartoons."

"It was more of a comic strip." She felt oddly compelled to defend her childhood. She actually liked comics. *Sabrina the Teenage Witch* and *Wonder Woman* had been her favorites.

He chuckled and retrieved his phone and suitcase. "You are sweet, *kiska*. Never change. Are you ready to leave?"

"Yep. You already switched cars?" She grabbed her suitcase and followed him to the door.

"Yes. I found something more appropriate."

Waiting for them outside was a black Range Rover.

"Not exactly inconspicuous," she pointed out.

Dimitri frowned, not following. "It is very inconspicuous."

"Sure, but, you know, in that trying-too-hard kind of way." He still didn't understand, so she added, "Like you're expecting people with dark sunglasses and suits carrying concealed guns to pop out of it?"

He shrugged. "You watch too many movies."

"I suppose you just had another friend willing to lend you a car like you did the Aston Martin?"

"I do, and I asked him for this one because it has bulletproof glass."

At this, her eyes widened. "Are we expecting to get shot at? I was only kidding about the men with guns popping out."

"Under the circumstances, it is safer to plan for all scenarios."

"I don't think I want to know what the scenarios are."

Dimitri lifted her suitcase into the back alongside his. "No, you do not."

She climbed into the passenger side, and sweet heavenly smells hit her.

"Oh my God . . . Where did you get these?" She practically pounced on the cinnamon roll box between the seats. The bun inside was still warm, and the frosting was still gooey. A cup of coffee, steaming hot, was in the cup holder next to the box.

"I snuck into the Bellagio breakfast buffet." He laughed at the look of shock he saw on her face.

"Seriously?"

"Why not? We are pressed for time." He grinned, and the boyish mischief on his face was so appealing that Elena had to remind herself that this man was some sort of secret agent and not just a harmless, sexy Russian billionaire.

"You told me back in LA that you aren't a spy."

"I'm not. I just happen to have the same skills."

"Tomato, toh-mah-toe," she muttered.

"Sorry?"

"Never mind. So how long is the drive to Colorado?"

"Depending on the weather, it will be around ten hours. Though if we were going to cut straight through Utah, we could take a day to relax. I trust open land more than cities, and no one would expect us to stay overnight on parkland."

"Parkland? Like camping?" Elena wrinkled her nose at the thought. She was definitely not a camper. Glamping, maybe, but definitely not roughing it.

Dimitri grinned as he pulled a lock of her hair. "Not a camper, little *kiska*?"

"Not exactly. I like hot showers and a door I can close against bugs."

He laughed and shook his head. "A true *printcessa*."

"Did you just call me a princess in Russian?" She scoffed, but only to hide a giggle. "Okay, I might be a bit of a princess. You know, when I was a kid my dad took me to this group of young scouts, called Indian Princesses. Totally un-PC, name-wise, I know, but it was fun. It was just dads and daughters. I loved all the adventures, but camping in tents with mosquitos was *really* not my thing. So Dad would flatten out the seats in our SUV, and we slept in sleeping bags in the car. One year there was a massive thunderstorm, and I was damn glad he and I were in the car when it hit. The rest of the girls and their dads got flooded out of their tents." The memory warmed her, and she couldn't help but smile as she watched the road ahead.

"You have a beautiful smile, Elena," Dimitri said. "You must smile more."

"You can't say that here."

"What?"

"Never tell a woman she should smile more. Trust me." The frown on Dimitri's face was one of puzzlement and disappointment, so she tried to explain. "The kind of men who say that tend to be creeps. They always say, 'You should smile more, it makes you pretty.'"

Dimitri nodded. "Ah, I understand. They objectify the women, correct?"

"Something like that."

"I did not mean it that way. Smiling can make you feel better. That is why I suggested it." He offered his own smile, the gentle one that melted her inside out like a popsicle on a sunny day.

"I know," she sighed, and her attempt at a smile faltered. The therapist at the US embassy in Moscow had told her that the act of smiling could often trigger feelings of genuine happiness. It was just so hard to think of smiling, let alone being happy, most of the time. But smiling, even laughing, was becoming easier and easier with Dimitri around.

"Why don't you eat your breakfast and then try to sleep a bit more?" he suggested. "Sleep is nature's way of healing, both emotionally and physically. I want you to feel your best. You deserve that."

He was bossy, but in a sweet way, and she kind of loved him for it. It had been disorienting after two months in captivity, unable to make any choices about her own life, to be suddenly thrust back into full control. She had been conditioned to follow orders without question. While she desperately craved her own life back and control of her own decisions, she was relieved that Dimitri could offer her some sort of structure until she was comfortable enough to control her life again.

She turned her gaze to the road, taking in the glittery, flashing world of Las Vegas before they passed through to the open road again. The bright sun illuminated the highway in front of them, and the strangest feeling came over Elena. She looked at Dimitri discretely from beneath her lashes as she recalled him in her dream carrying her into the light.

This man was her destiny. As wild and unexplainable as it was, she could feel it. Fate had driven her into his life, and he had welcomed her, scars and all. Elena reached across the console between them and placed her hand on top of his. He turned his hand over, and their palms connected. His fingers curled around hers, and it felt as though the seismic plates deep within her soul shifted, sinking into place. She was home, only now *home* was no longer a little house in Maine with a white picket fence.

It was this man, her beautiful, scary, Russian protector.

❄

MAXIM KAMENEV ENTERED THE MALIBU BEACH HOUSE address Leo had given him. The door code worked at the gate as expected, and he slipped into the house with the stealth of a leopard on the hunt.

Leo followed right behind him. "What do you see?"

Maxim didn't answer. He had his gun out at the ready. Glass shards and blood littered the kitchen and family room.

The sight made him tense. He was so close to Dimitri, Nicholas, and Leo that when one of them was hurt, he practically felt the pain in his own body.

"Are we on body removal?" Nicholas asked as he came up behind Maxim and Leo. "Because that is my least favorite part of the job."

At this, Maxim and Leo turned to stare at him.

Nicholas gave his devil-may-care smile. "What? You can't say you enjoy it."

Maxim shrugged. "It's like laundry. Boring but necessary." He turned his focus back to the house, moving from room to room. He noticed that only one bed was unmade.

"Dimitri is sleeping with her," Maxim said to the other two men as they joined him in one of the rooms that faced the sea.

Nicholas's eyes widened. "You're sure?"

"Only one bed was unmade. They had no time to tidy up."

"But he . . . he doesn't know who she is. If he did, he would never have . . ."

"He knows enough. He knows she has Romanov blood," Leo said.

"But so do a lot of people," Maxim countered. "You couldn't tell him her true ancestry over the phone. He's just following his desires now. The moment he learns that she's not just any Romanov descendant, he will let go and step back."

"I hope so," Leo murmured. "We took a vow."

"A vow to protect," Maxim said as he knelt by the pool of blood on the balcony.

"We vowed that we would protect, and we can't do that if we are emotionally attached. It makes us vulnerable," Leo reminded him.

Maxim believed in the rules, but this was one that made him conflicted. Sometimes a person was braver, faster, more alert, when defending the life of someone they deeply cared about. It was why the four of them worked so well together even after all these years. They loved each other like brothers, and that made the fight in them that much stronger.

"Where's the body?" Maxim asked Leo.

"Basement."

"You two handle the blood and anything broken. I'll handle the body."

The three of them split up, and Maxim located the door to the basement. It wasn't some creepy dark lair—no, it was a casual family room complete with a flat-screen TV, sectional sofa, and in the corner, well, damn . . . a spanking bench, a Saint Andrew's cross, and a wall of fun little toys.

Maxim whistled softly. A Dom definitely lived here, one who knew where to purchase the best toys, not the crap most men bought for their private playrooms. No, these were quality BDSM products. It was no wonder Dimitri and Royce got along. The rest of them were into the lifestyle a little too, but not as much as Dimitri.

Turning his focus from the play area, Maxim found the body of the Russian agent who had attacked Dimitri and Elena. He frowned as he recognized Viktor Ivanoff. He'd never tangled with Viktor personally, but he'd cleaned up a lot of situations Viktor had been involved in. Most Kremlin agents these days focused on subtle deaths, making it hard to prove who committed the crime. For Viktor to attack so openly like this . . . it was unusual. Whoever sent him here believed blunt action, something not survivable like a gunshot, was necessary, but that raised a whole new question. Who was the target? Dimitri or Elena?

Maxim guest Elena, simply because of what he knew about her bloodline, and Dimitri's cover had always been the most inconspicuous of the four of them. The Kremlin believed Dimitri to be a rich playboy who liked to visit Paris and Long Island and blow his money on women and indulge in BDSM. The Russian government thought him a fool who would support the men in power without question. That meant it was more likely Elena was the target, and that meant the job of protecting her had become that much more difficult.

With a heavy sigh, Maxim focused on the body he was meant to dispose of. It was going to be an unpleasant couple of hours, and all he wanted to do was lie on the damn beach in the sun.

❧ 11 ❧

Dimitri took a turn off the highway down to a small country road.

"Where are we going?" It was late in the afternoon. Elena sat forward in her seat, eyes glued to the red-and-gold landscape of the craggy desert terrain of Utah.

"Dead Horse Point State Park."

"That name sounds foreboding." Elena bit her lip, more than a little worried that there were no signs of life anywhere. It was barren. Beautiful, but barren.

"It will be fine, *kiska*. You are with me."

"So not only are you an actual mystery man, you also are a wilderness survivor type?" She was only half joking.

"Yes and no. I can promise you we will be fine, but we won't be out in the wild—at least, not the way you think."

She sat back, arms crossed. "Russians and their riddles . . ."

He laughed. "See, we are already here." In the distance, beside a lazy brown river, was a large lodge, a smaller building, and a huge set of solar panels.

"This is the base camp adventure lodge. I booked the entire building, all seven bedrooms, just for us. It isn't fancy, but it's well above a tent on a patch of hard rock."

"You had me at *lodge*." She relaxed as he parked the Range Rover in front of the building. A man in his late fifties came out to meet them.

"Ah, Mr. and Mrs. Smith?"

"That's us," Dimitri said in that perfect American TV accent.

"Congrats on your wedding. This is a perfect place to have a honeymoon. The skies will be clear tonight, and the stars will be magnificent. I left you some directions on the kitchen table as to where the best stargazing spots are." He shook Dimitri's hand. "Name's Walter. If you need anything while you're here, just use the walkie-talkie. Channel 8."

"Thank you," Dimitri said, then turned to Elena. "Honey, I'll get our bags. You go on inside."

That American accent made her shiver, but not in a good way. He so easily morphed into a man who wasn't him. Did she even know the real Dimitri? There was still a lot she didn't know. While they were here, she was determined to find out as much about him as she could.

She stepped into the lodge and was definitely pleased with what she saw. There was heat, which was crucial given that it was winter. They were lucky they didn't have any snow on the ground yet. Plus, there was electricity and indoor plumbing—all the hallmarks of civilization and what she needed to function. The bedrooms were all cozy and cute. She chose the master bedroom, which had a queen-size bed. If Dimitri kept his promise, they would be sleeping nice and snug together in that bed. She stared at it, imagining being held close in his arms.

"Well, *kiska*, what do you think?" Dimitri's Russian accent was back.

"So we're the Smiths?"

He nodded. "For today."

"You do realize that *Mr. & Mrs. Smith* was a movie about a couple of spies on opposites sides who married each other? You're not exactly disproving my theory that you're some kind of spy."

Dimitri grinned and pulled her body back against his. He wrapped his arms around her and kissed the shell of her ear.

"Be a good *kiska* and I will *show* you what I am tonight."

The way he spoke, teasing her to be a good kitten, sent shivers of desire through her so strong that she almost gasped. Being with him had made it so easy to find the old Elena, the one who had craved passion and romance. The one who'd wanted to find a Dom of her very own someday.

She had spent two months believing that Elena was dead, but she wasn't. It was as though part of her had been trapped in a deep slumber, like Snow White frozen beneath a glass coffin. Now, after Dimitri's kiss, she was coming back to life. She closed her eyes and embraced the heady sensation of his mouth as it explored her neck.

"How does one become a good *kiska?*" she asked between sighs.

"A good *kiska* will eat dinner with me and then sit beneath the stars . . . After that, she will tell me one fantasy she's had about sex."

"Just one?" She was somewhat disappointed at the thought of only sharing one fantasy with him.

"For tonight." He nibbled her earlobe and she moaned, helpless to stop the wetness growing between her thighs.

For the first time in what felt like forever, her fantasies seemed like just that, a beautiful fantasy and not a distorted nightmare that would leave her screaming herself hoarse.

"Now, if you want to shower, go ahead. I will prepare dinner."

"What are we having?"

He trailed a fingertip down the length of her nose. "It's a surprise."

Her heart swelled with a flood of warmth that was too wonderful to name.

He left her alone and headed toward the kitchen. Elena sank onto the bed and took a few deep breaths.

Ever since the attack in Malibu, she had been coiled tight like a spring, almost crushed to the point where she might snap rather than spring back. But now they were far away from that house and the dead body. They were in a state park, with their path almost untraceable —at least she hoped it was. Dimitri seemed to have relaxed as well, and that made her feel even more safe. They had escaped. They were on the run, yes, but it was okay, at least for now, and now was all she could focus on.

After she freshened up in the shower and changed into some warm clothes, she followed the delicious smells to the kitchen. Dimitri was removing something from the oven, and she had a moment to admire his backside in the jeans he wore. He had donned a fisherman's sweater and now looked like he belonged in Maine. The thought of him looking so like he belonged where she'd grown up made something stir inside her.

A deep longing for a quiet life by the sea washed over her, with endless sunsets on a rocking sailboat, or snowy winters and warm fires. It was a life she'd never truly considered before. She'd been so focused on exploring the world, but in just a few months, all of that had changed. *She'd* changed. Elena wanted what her parents had. She wanted a future with Dimitri. That realization stunned her. It took her a moment to gather her thoughts, and she swallowed past the sudden lump in her throat.

"What's for dinner?" She used her most casual voice as

she sat on a stool facing the bar that overlooked the kitchen.

He shot her a sexy look that flared with such intensity that she felt like she was standing in front of an open oven.

"Lasagna. One of my specialties."

"A Russian who likes Italian food?"

"You like pizza. That's Italian." He winked at her, and she laughed.

"You got me there." She loved the way the loose sweater hung off his muscled form. She fantasized slowly pulling that soft sweater off his body, making love to him, and then wearing it and nothing else . . .

Elena jerked her thoughts back. Damn, the man was dangerous.

"Wait, how did you make lasagna? There's not exactly a grocery store nearby."

"I purchased groceries this morning right before I snuck into the Bellagio and got you a cinnamon roll. I stored them in the large cooler in the back of the Range Rover."

"Oh . . ." She had totally missed the cooler. Well, she had seen it, but she hadn't given it any thought.

"You are still too skinny. Meat and carbs are what you need." He set the pan on the kitchen island to let it cool, then turned back to the oven and pulled out a bit of wrapped foil.

"Garlic bread?" she asked. The smell made her mouth water.

He grinned and gave her a wink.

"You are some sort of evil genius. Garlic bread is one of my weaknesses."

"I know," he chuckled.

She froze. "What do you mean, you know?"

Dimitri removed the oven mitts and retrieved his briefcase from the kitchen table. He pulled out his tablet, logged on, and then opened something up on the screen and handed it to her.

"We have traveled too far together for this to be a secret." He let her turn the tablet around so she could see what was on the screen.

She stared at the dozens of photos of herself at various ages. Everything about her life was there—down to her favorite foods and even her grade school report cards. "This . . . this is my life . . ."

"This is only a piece of you," Dimitri said, as if it absolved him.

She could barely breathe. It felt like a betrayal. "Why do you have this?"

"When I learned of your escape from Vadym, I told Leo to work up a dossier on you. That was when I knew I wanted to take care of you. I wanted to know everything about you so that I can give you what you need."

It took a long moment for her to process that. He'd

been keeping a file of everything about her? Was she okay with this?

"These are only simple facts, *kiska*. They don't tell me who you really are."

"They don't?"

He smiled, but it was a sorrowful expression. "Childhood report cards don't tell me anything. I would rather have you tell me what subjects you loved, who your favorite teacher was—the things that matter." He nodded at the tablet. "The things that define you aren't in there."

The old Elena would not have listened to this, but the person she was now had aged a century in the last two months. She could see his side as to why he'd wanted this information and how it wasn't enough to truly know someone. It was so clear that he was from a vastly different world than she was, where invasions of privacy were seemingly commonplace. She was going to have to get used to that.

"Would you give me one of these dossiers about you?" she asked after a moment.

That mischievous twinkle was back in his blue eyes. "You would like one?"

"Seems only fair. Text that Leo guy and have him make one of you for me."

"Consider it done. Now, sit and we'll eat." He gestured to the table, and she waited for him to bring her a plate. She realized that despite him being a Dom in the bedroom, he loved to serve and care for her. She certainly didn't mind if a man opened the door for her or brought her food. It was Dimitri's way of showing respect and affection. That only made him infinitely more irresistible.

She thought back to the dossier, and what he knew about her, while they ate the perfectly cooked lasagna.

"What is your favorite color?" she asked. "And your favorite foods?"

"Orange, the color of a burning flame. And my favorite food is beef stroganoff."

The mention of the flame reminded her about his ring.

"And the bird on your ring? It looks like a phoenix. Is it?" she asked.

He leaned back in his chair, his hand raised above the table as he stared at the gold signet ring on his finger. He removed it and leaned forward, handing it to her. It was heavier than she expected as it landed in her palm, and she closed her fingers around it protectively. The gold was warm to the touch, and when she opened her hand again, the phoenix emblem seemed almost alive. A hint of letters carved on the inside of the band caught her attention.

"What does it say?" She angled the ring to better read the words. It wasn't written in Cyrillic, but she didn't recognize the language, either.

"*Luceo non uro.* It's Latin for 'I shine, not burn.'"

"What does that mean?"

"It means that I do not let the fires of tribulation burn all-consuming—I shine through. And if I must burn, I become reborn into the flames."

The hair on the back of her neck rose, and Elena shivered as she handed it back to him. "So it is a phoenix. Is that a family motto?"

"In a way," he replied.

"One of those things you can't tell me?"

"I'm sorry, *kiska*." He pointed at her plate. "Finish, so we can go stargazing."

"Stargazing?"

He smiled. "It's part of why I chose this place. It is a remote location, but this state park is also designated an International Dark Sky Park. The high plateau and the distance from city light pollution makes it an ideal place to view the celestial sphere."

Elena had never stargazed before, but it sounded fun.

"Dress warmly. Meet me at the front door in a few minutes." Dimitri collected their plates and headed back to the kitchen.

She retrieved a dark-blue peacoat, mittens, and a white knit cap, then met Dimitri at the door. He carried a thick picnic blanket under one arm and two pillows under the other. He was dressed in a long black wool coat.

"Let me get the door for you." She opened the door, and they walked outside. She closed the door behind them, and they were swallowed up in darkness. The lights from the lodge were completely hidden by blackout curtains.

As her eyes adjusted, she saw Dimitri stride ahead of her toward a distant spot on the ground. She followed him as he unfurled the picnic blanket and laid it down. He eased onto the blanket, and she did the same. They were close, almost touching. The night air was clear and a little cold around them. Elena wanted to curl into him and absorb his warmth. After a moment he stretched out flat on his back, cushioning his head with a pillow.

She joined him. It was just the two of them now, a night sky horizon all around them and quiet stars above. It was like they were the only two people left in the universe, and the thought sent a strange wave of peace through her.

"Tell me what you see," Dimitri said as he pointed up at the night sky.

Thousands—no, hundreds of thousands, perhaps *millions* of stars covered the sky so perfectly that all she could see were celestial objects. Straight above them was a thick band of gold-and-purple clouds that seemed to glow.

"Is that the Milky Way?" she gasped. It was so clear, so visible. She had only ever seen pictures of it that looked like this in books. There was always too much light pollution where she lived. Only a fraction of these stars would have been visible, and certainly not the Milky Way. Yet here it was, far more vast, infinite, and wondrous than she could have imagined.

"They say not all wonders are endless, but I believe this one is." Dimitri's voice was so gentle that her heart quivered.

He was right—the beauty above was infinite. Her eyes burned with tears as she took in the enormity of that thought . . . a beauty that was never-ending. Stars died and new ones were born, but there would *always* be celestial objects glowing in the night sky visible from somewhere in the universe.

Her mother had said once that thinking about the stars and the universe made her feel small, that she didn't like to think about it. But for Elena, it was different. Especially tonight.

The endless beauty of the heavens made her feel like she was a part of something greater, something more powerful than anything here on earth. What Vadym had done to her, what he'd made her feel . . . none of that mattered, not when she looked up at that sky. He was a tiny, inconsequential thing. She wasn't. She was a part of the stars, a part of the mysterious beauty above her. After all, she was made of stardust, just like everything else in the universe.

She let out a sigh. So much of her fear and anger from the last few months bled away into the night. "It is endless . . ."

"Endless and precious beyond imagining," he agreed.

She turned to him and saw his gaze was on her, not the heavens. She stared back at him, aware of what he was really saying to her. She wanted more than anything to tell him that he had given her a gift. He'd helped her to see her value in the world, to feel like she belonged and that she was in charge of her fate again. Not only that, but she felt wanted and desired by a man she wanted and desired back. It left her almost dizzy with optimism.

"Dimitri . . . ," she whispered and reached out to touch him. He rolled onto his side to face her, and she slid closer to him, tugging herself into his arms.

"You *shine*, not burn, Elena. Never forget that."

The funny thing was, she *believed* him. For the first time since Vadym had taken her, she felt the power of her life was back in her hands. Even though they were on the run, she felt hope for the first time in what felt like forever.

She lifted her head a little so that it rested on his pillow beside him, then touched his full lips with her fingertips and briefly lost herself in dreams of kissing him.

"You saved me," she said as she traced a finger over his mouth and then caressed his jaw.

"You saved yourself, *kiska*." As he spoke, his voice was slightly rough with emotion.

"I didn't."

"You did. You stayed alive, lasted longer than any other woman in your situation and had the strength to get free, to fight."

"It doesn't feel like I did anything."

He placed a hand on her hip, the gentle but firm grip grounding her. "Every day you draw breath is a day you have saved yourself, a day you have won by living your life."

She sighed and closed her eyes before she kissed him.

Was it possible for a man to taste like darkness and light all at once? Because Dimitri did. He tasted like everything she'd always dreamed of in her perfect fantasies. But he wasn't a fantasy. He was real.

She rolled onto her back as he came on top of her. They continued to kiss while he captured her hands and pinned them on either side of her head. The weight of him on top of her felt so good. She had forgotten this feeling, the feeling of safety beneath a man. The only thing he would do was devastate her senses with pleasure. He owned every part of her, yet she felt strangely free at the same time. Elena trusted him with her body, and now her heart and soul were his too.

He slowed his sensual, playful kisses and looked down at her. "You're thinking too much again, *kiska*." He used that teasing Dom tone that sounded disapproving but really wasn't.

"I wasn't thinking," she argued with a smile. "I was feeling." She lifted her head up to his and bit his bottom lip. He groaned and lowered his face back down, ruthlessly claiming her mouth. She adored the way he kissed. One minute it was all sweetness and gentle courtship, and the next he was nearly savage in the way he seemed desperate to devour her. She wanted all of it, all of him.

She gasped for breath as he moved his mouth to her throat. "Dimitri."

"Yes?"

"I want it all with you." She hoped he understood. She was ready to try going all the way this time.

"Not yet. We don't need to. We have all the time we need." He kissed her throat again, pressing his teeth against her flesh in a way that sent pangs of lust through her.

She moaned. "Please, I need this. I'm ready. Be my Dom, not a gentleman."

He raised his head and looked down at her. "If I sense for one moment you aren't ready, we will stop. Understood?"

Her heart swelled. "You really are a gentleman, aren't you?"

"Only with you, *kiska*. Only with you." But as he said it, she knew that wasn't true. He was a gentleman in every sense of the word. Then he stole her lips in a kiss that seemed to send every star above them into a heavenly blaze of brilliant light.

Elena parted her thighs, wanting him to take her right there beneath the stars.

He growled, the sound encouraging rather than reprimanding. "*Kiska*."

Dimitri suddenly stiffened, his head jerking up. The soft, indulgent expression on his face vanished, and the man who had a thousand secrets was back. She heard the hum of a car engine, and the beams of headlights cut through their perfect night.

"Get up. Run. Head for the riverbank. Do not stop

until you reach that bank. Stay down, no matter what you hear, and take this." He was already off her body and had pressed a small handgun into her palms.

"Dimitri . . ."

"There's no time." He dragged her to him for one last kiss that stole the breath from her before she was pulled to her feet and shoved in the direction of the riverbank.

When she reached it, she slid off the steep ridge and down about six feet into a hollowed-out bank that hid her from view. Then she held her breath. Her blood roared in her ears as she waited for any sound, anything at all. But it was quiet and dark. She prayed that Dimitri would be okay. *If anything happened to him . . .* No, she wouldn't think that. He would be okay—he had to be.

DIMITRI TOOK SHELTER AROUND THE CORNER OF THE lodge. In a place like this, it wasn't smart to be in a dwelling you could get trapped in and your enemies could smoke you out. He held a long hunting knife.

The car in the distance finally reached the lodge. The high-beams blinded him, and he couldn't see past the glare. The lights died, and the driver killed the engine. Dimitri counted the car doors that opened and closed. Two, no, three people. His eyes were still adjusting to the darkness after the bright headlights.

He crouched down as he listened for any sound of their movements. They were very quiet, but the loose gravel made it impossible to be completely silent. As his eyes regained their night vision, he counted two men, but his gut warned him that he'd heard three doors closing. Dimitri spun just in time to deflect an attack that came from behind him.

He turned, took the man down, and rolled backward in a somersault, sending his assailant flying over the top of his head, and then he flipped up onto his feet with his dagger ready.

"Fuck, Dimitri," a voice grumbled as the man got up and dusted himself off.

"Maxim?" Dimitri exhaled, and every tensed muscle in him went lax. He turned to see Leo and Nicholas, guns in hand as they rounded the corner.

"You're here." Dimitri couldn't believe his friends had caught up so fast.

"Yeah, you'd know that if you'd answered my calls," Leo said.

"I left my phone at the house. I thought . . ." He shuddered. He hadn't thought. That was the problem. He had been so focused on taking Elena out to stargaze and having a quiet evening alone with her and not worrying about what was to come that he'd broken one of the most basic rules of protecting someone. He'd let his guard down. It was a small mercy his friends had found him before his enemies.

"How did you find me? I didn't leave instructions on how to get here."

Leo grinned smugly. "I may have put a tracker in your favorite boots some time back. The black widow model is so small, airport security misses it every time."

"So did I, apparently." Dimitri was glad his friend had kept track of him. It was a smart move, and he was mad he hadn't thought of it. Maxim looked to Leo. "Wait. You did not put one in *my* boots, did you? You know I demand my privacy."

"Of course not," said Leo. "I'd never do that to you."

Maxim turned back to Dimitri, all business. Leo grinned and nodded behind his back, indicating that he totally did.

"We handled your body," Maxim said. "Cleaned the scene for Devereaux too."

"Thank you."

Nicholas stared at Dimitri and glanced around. "Is it just me, or are we missing someone?" There was a teasing note to his tone that Dimitri had missed since he'd been away from his friends.

"Elena is hiding," he explained.

Nicholas snorted. "Where? Under a rock?"

"Almost." Dimitri led his friends toward the rocky embankment of the river. He held up his hand up to indicate they should stay back. He put his knife into his boot and called out.

"Elena, it's safe. We have company. Good company."
Then he carefully peered over the edge of the bank.

It was empty. She was gone. His stomach plummeted as he feared his friends might have been followed.

"Stay where you are!" A shout rang out. Elena stood behind them, her back to the lodge, gun aimed at Maxim, who was closest to her.

"Well now, she's a clever one," Nicholas mused in Russian.

"*Kiska*, it's safe. Phoenix . . . remember? This is Leo, Maxim, and Nicholas, the brothers of my heart." Dimitri moved toward her, hands held up.

"These guys are your friends?"

"*Kiska?*" Maxim chuckled and continued speaking in Russian. "Dimitri, you have found your kitten at last, and you had to choose the one woman you can't have."

"What?" Dimitri responded.

"Not now, Max," Leo interjected. "Let's get the gun away from her before we break the news."

Dimitri reached Elena and gently took the gun from her before he pulled her into his arms.

"Elena, this is Leo. That's Maxim, and Nicholas is over there." He pointed at all three of them. One by one, his friends put their right fists over their hearts, and each man knelt on one knee before Elena.

The next words they spoke changed his life forever.

"Klyanus' zhizn'yu tebe, poslednemu iz roda Romanovykh. Pravnuchka velikoy knyagini Anastasii."

12

Elena stepped back when the three men knelt before her and Dimitri. They all spoke in Russian, but they weren't words she had learned in her Russian language studies. She shot a glance at Dimitri, who was still as stone beside her. Whatever they'd said had swept over him like a powerful tide. Even though she couldn't understand the words, she realized that everything had changed.

"What did they say? And why are they kneeling?" she asked.

Dimitri slowly released her from his gentle hold, and he moved to stand next to his friends. Elena's stomach suddenly bottomed out. What was happening? What was he doing?

"Dimitri, what did they say?"

He cleared his throat. "They said they vow their lives

to you, the last of the Romanovs, the great-granddaughter of Grand Duchess Anastasia Nikolaevna."

There was only the glitter of stars above as Elena watched Dimitri join his brothers-in-arms by kneeling at her feet, one fist clenched over his heart.

It took a moment for what Dimitri had said to sink in. If her knees hadn't locked just then, she would have fallen down.

"I am what?"

"You are the last . . . ," Dimitri said. "The last of the direct imperial royal bloodline of the Romanovs."

"But . . ." Elena had no words. What he had just said was impossible. They all continued to stare at her expectantly, still on bended knee.

"I can't be . . . that's not possible. She died. The Russian government said they found bone remnants of hers in a shallow grave." Elena remembered that news story from when she'd been younger.

Leo spoke up. "Those findings were fabricated. They wanted to stop the rumors due to the current political unrest."

"Wait, please tell me this is a joke." She searched Dimitri's face, which had gone as pale as the starlight.

"This is no joke, Your Grace," Dimitri replied solemnly. That was when Elena realized he was serious.

No more *kiska*, no more teasing, no more sweet seductions. Some invisible barrier had just risen between them.

The freedom she had felt so sure was in her grasp had now been ripped away, tossed upon the wind.

"Please, get up. All of you." She waved at them, and they all stood. "This is ridiculous."

"Your Grace," Dimitri said uncertainly, and that was the worst part. She needed him to take charge, to be the man she'd come to rely on. But now he wanted her to be in charge? Some kind of royalty? It wasn't fair. It wasn't okay.

"Please, just all of you go inside and leave me alone for a minute."

"You cannot stay out here alone . . . ," Dimitri began.

"Then he'll stay." She pointed at Maxim. He seemed to be the quietest of the four, and she believed that he would give her some space.

"Max," Dimitri said softly to his friend.

"She'll be safe out here with me," Maxim assured him.

Desperate for a moment alone, Elena turned and strode away. She stopped as she reached the picnic blanket. Only a short time ago, she and Dimitri had been lying here beneath the stars, ready to make love. The strength in her legs gave out, and she collapsed onto the blanket and buried her face in the pillow that still carried his scent.

This was a dream . . . or a nightmare. Something her exhausted imagination had conjured up after everything she had been through in the last few months. Anastasia died in Russia more than years ago. Elena was just a girl from Maine. A girl who had been adopted and, according to her DNA profile, was part Russian on her mother's side.

But the descendent of Anastasia Romanov?

It was a fairy tale, one with blood and darkness in it. The Romanovs had been brutally murdered by Communist soldiers. The young duchesses had died slowly because of the royal jewels they had hidden in their corsets, and the soldiers had finished them off with bayonets. It had been a heartless, soulless murder of innocent people like Anastasia and her little brother Alexei, along with their three beautiful older sisters.

Elena closed her eyes, and thick tears rolled down her cheeks.

You are the last . . . Dimitri's voice echoed in her mind.

She was a Romanov.

For her entire life, she had known she was adopted, but she'd only begun to wonder about her birth parents in the last few years. She'd had a wonderful childhood growing up. She wouldn't give that up for anything. But now she had answers, terrifying ones, as to who she truly was. She thought of her mother, scared and alone as she gave birth only to die a few minutes later.

Who was she? Who was her father? The answers she had been given had only raised a dozen more questions.

She was barely aware of Maxim's presence at first, but after a moment, she forced herself to sit up and face him.

"Why . . . why did Dimitri change when you told him about my ancestry?"

Maxim did not look at her. His eyes searched for threats on the dark horizon.

"Because it is his duty, his life's greatest mission, to protect you. You are the descendent of the last emperor and empress of Russia. You will forever be out of his reach now. He knows that."

Maxim's words, intended to be kind, only cut her deeper.

"I'm not out of reach. We . . ." She blushed and was grateful for the night shielding her so that he couldn't see what was so plain on her face.

"You are drawn to each other, but that cannot continue. To be your guard, he must keep his heart out of this. If he doesn't, he could make a mistake that could get you killed."

"But he cares about all you . . ."

"True. But you are the woman he loves."

Dimitri loved her? But they had only been together a short time. All she knew was that, to her, he had become more than a life raft in a storm. He was something deeper, something more to her than any words could express.

"I need him," she told Maxim. Her words were soft, but they carried on the night air.

"You will always have him, Your Grace."

"Please, don't call me that. Titles like hers don't pass down to someone like me."

"They do according to the White Army."

"The White Army?" She stared at him. "The army that served the Romanovs? They were wiped out a hundred years ago by the Communist forces."

"The elite royal guards went underground. We had to, after the Romanovs were slain." He paused for a moment. "One of the Red Guards realized Anastasia was still breathing. He carried her to our forces, and she was smuggled away by our men. The guards who stayed in Russia never knew if she survived her wounds.

"All our lives we have grown up with the story in our hearts, but we've had no proof it was more than a child's fairy tale until tonight." Maxim smiled wryly. "You even look like her. I've studied her portrait enough to see the Romanov beauty in you."

Elena wiped tears off her cheeks with the back of one hand. Never in her life had she felt so alone. Even when she had been trapped in Vadym's dark cell, she hadn't felt like this.

"Why does it even matter who my great-grandmother was? Why would the Kremlin even care? I just want to be left alone to live my life." She sniffled. God, she hated crying, and she had done so much of it lately.

Maxim stepped closer and produced a white handkerchief. He held it out to her like some old-fashioned hero out of *Downton Abbey*. She wiped her eyes and then stared at the phoenix symbol embroidered in gold thread on the corner of the cloth.

"Nothing will ever be the same. You are a beacon of hope to many in Russia who resist the current regime. You are the living, breathing cry for change, for an end to the government that has broken the backs and souls of our people. That is why the Kremlin wants you dead."

She handed him back his handkerchief. "But how do they even know about my ancestry?"

"The DNA test you did last year. Every major government in the world can easily access those databases. The Kremlin has been on alert for years, waiting to see if direct descendants of imperial royal family are out there. They wouldn't have had access to your blood like I had to determine that you were linked to Anastasia, but they would be able to narrow it down enough to know you belong to Nicholas and Alexandra's bloodline."

"Are there more? Perhaps someone else could—?"

"It is possible, but unless we find them, you are the best we have."

"Listen, I don't want to be anything like that." She nearly told him she just wanted to go home, but Dimitri was home to her in a way no other person or place had ever been.

"Sometimes fate chooses our paths for us, and we must bear the burden of our gifts."

She laughed bitterly. "Gift? It's a curse."

"There are millions of people you could help, Elena." Maxim held out a hand to her. "The question is, will you let your past keep you a victim the rest of your life, or will you face your destiny and be a leader for those you could help?"

She flinched. He was right. She had been letting herself hide and focus on her pain. Only weak people did that. They let others define them, and they let their own selfishness corrupt them until all they did was demand things of others and blame them when things went wrong.

Her parents had raised her to be self-reliant, not destructive. She had to do the right thing, no matter how hard it was. The world had become so dark with hate and fear . . . it was time to believe in herself, time to shine through the darkness. To become a star in the empyreal wonder of the night. But that didn't mean she had to be a slave to the expectations of others, either.

She reached up and took Maxim's hand so he could help her to her feet. Then they started back to the lodge. Somehow she would convince Dimitri that her bloodline didn't matter, not when she needed him in her life.

DIMITRI PACED THE ENTRYWAY, HIS HANDS CLASPED behind his back. Every few seconds he paused to check his watch. She had been out there too long. She was going to get cold . . .

"Dimitri, stop or you'll wear a hole in the floor," Nicholas teased.

Dimitri glared at him. He and Leo watched him pace

with bemused expressions. For the last several minutes, they had been joking with him about his overprotectiveness and how his little *kiska* had managed to get around them from behind. They had been impressed. He had been relieved. He knew she was strong and could take care of herself, but he didn't want her to have to.

Yet the thought of her out in the night alone, shivering from the cold and facing the news that her life would never be the same again, was too much for him. He didn't care if she needed space—he had to make sure she was all right.

"I'm going after her." He opened the door, only to find her standing right in front of him, Maxim behind her, looking out to the road for danger. Dimitri's focus locked on her red-rimmed eyes. His *kiska* had been crying. Her face reflected the devastation he felt inside, knowing he could never hold her again, never again touch her the way he had, and never be with her in the way they'd both dreamed. It was an icy hand of grim truth that dug into his chest and fixed its claws into his heart.

"Excuse me." Elena stepped past him into the lodge, her tone emotionless.

"What did you say to her?" Dimitri growled in Russian at Maxim the second he followed her into the lodge.

Maxim lifted one dark brow. "Say?"

"She's been crying."

"She cried because of *you* and because her entire world was just turned on its head."

Dimitri shot a look at Elena again, who was watching him and Maxim argue in Russian. Her eyes, such a lovely green, were shadowed with worry. Those beautiful eyes bored into him, carving out a hole and leaving him defenseless against her.

"She cried because of me?"

"She's in love with you," Maxim snorted. "I explained to her that we have been raised to put her above all others, that you aren't good enough for her, not in that way. None of us are."

Maxim's words hit him in the gut. *Not good enough . . .* He supposed Maxim wasn't wrong. Dimitri had no business trying to carry on a relationship with a woman who was the last of the Romanov bloodline. His sacred duty was to protect her, not indulge in fantasies of taking her to bed and soothing her painful past with pleasure.

"I'm not wrong," Maxim said to Dimitri, a rare apology lingering in his tone. "But I understand what it means to want something you will never have."

"Can you guys please stop that?" Elena asked.

"Stop what?" Dimitri and Maxim spoke at the same time.

"You're talking too fast. I'm trying to follow, but I'm not fluent, so most of what you are saying is going right over my head."

Nicholas stood behind Elena and seemed to be fighting off a grin. Leo's curiosity and admiration for Elena was clear on his face.

"My apologies, Your Grace," Maxim said politely.

Elena stared expectantly at Dimitri.

"I'm sorry," he said.

She blew out a breath. "I didn't want an apology. I wanted to know what you were talking about."

"You don't need to worry about it. You should go to bed."

"Bullshit," she snapped, her eyes like jade daggers. "I do have to worry about it. This is my life, and you can't just tell me what to eat and where to sleep like some little pet."

Dimitri held his tongue. Had she not been a Romanov descendent, he might have teased her that she was a little kitten in his bed, but she wasn't. If anything, he was the one who belonged to her, who would do *anything* she commanded.

Elena turned to his friends. "Which of you is Leo and which is Nicholas?"

"I'm Leo," Leo said, raising his hand.

"Maxim," Maxim grunted.

"And I'm Nicholas, but you can call me whatever you wish, Your Grace." Nicholas bowed grandly, and Maxim elbowed him in the ribs.

Elena's eyes glinted with humor, and Dimitri's tension eased a bit. It was going to be difficult for them to adjust to the confines of their new relationship after they had become intimate with each other. He was relieved his friends were here to help provide a distraction and some distance.

"Have you all eaten?" Elena asked.

"Yes, Your Gr—"

"Please don't call me that unless I ask you to." Already her tone held a sense of confidence to it, though Dimitri doubted she had noticed it. "Well, there are plenty of rooms to choose from. Please feel free to pick one. I guess I'll see you all in the morning."

She turned and walked toward the room they had planned to share tonight. The room he'd planned to share with her, along with so much more. It left him aching in a way he'd never felt in his life, to see her walk away, forever out of reach. She got to the doorway, and he waited for her to turn to him, to cast one glance back at him so he didn't feel so alone in that moment.

She didn't, and it killed him inside.

Despite her casual manner, Dimitri had seen the tension in her face. She was still upset, and she had every right to be. He had made a vow to her to be whatever she needed, and now he was breaking it to keep the vow he'd made to his father.

"I like her," Nicholas said.

"She is rather fascinating," Leo added.

Maxim merely turned his gaze on Dimitri. "What are you going to do?"

"What do you mean?"

"About her. She has eyes only for you, just as you do for her."

A pang stung his heart. He couldn't respond right away. His emotions were too thick. He glared at his friend. "You said it yourself—I'm not good enough, nor would it be right. I made a vow."

Maxim, Nicholas, and Leo all exchanged a look that made Dimitri realize he'd been left out of whatever conversations they must have had on the way to meet him here.

"Dimitri, we all made that vow, but sometimes you have to break your word if it's more important to do what's right," Leo said. "I think I speak for all of us when I say that we would release you from your vow."

Maxim and Nicholas both nodded.

"If she wants you, she should have you," Maxim said. "With what's to come, she will need you more than ever."

Dimitri wanted to agree, to go straight to her and take her in his arms. But he'd made so many promises to his father, to the White Army, and all he could think of was that moment his mother had been killed and how it had driven his father into a death spiral of his own. If Dimitri stopped it now before he and Elena grew any more attached, that might be the safest course of action for both of them.

"I can't," Dimitri murmured. He stepped out the front door into the chilly darkness. Elena was safe for now, and he needed time to raise a wall around his heart.

He walked all the way to the riverbank and stared out at the black expanse of the plateau, drinking in the starlight. His mind replayed Elena lying beside him, her eyes reflecting the vast expanse of the Milky Way. Fate was cruel, offering him the only dream he had ever truly wanted, and then pulling it away.

13

Dimitri didn't return to the house for nearly half an hour. He stood beneath the stars near the blanket and pillows he'd brought out for him and Elena to stargaze on. It was strange to think that a mere hour before he'd believed these stars held all the answers, that he and Elena were blessed to have found each other. Now the stars were once again out of reach. He'd never imagined he'd face being torn between duty and love in this way, yet here he was, being pulled apart.

He picked up the blanket and pillows and began the walk back to the lodge. When he stepped through the doorway, he found his friends gathered in the kitchen, talking softly to one another as they drank a few beers. It seemed they had brought their own groceries. Nicholas offered him a beer. He shook his head.

"Did you handle the body?" he asked them. It was easier to focus on work than his forbidden desires.

"Yes," Maxim replied grimly. "You owe me for that."

"We found his boat anchored half a mile out to sea." Nicholas leaned back against the kitchen counter. "He must have swum to shore, which is why Leo didn't get any hits on the facial recognition software. We also found his burner phone in a waterproof pouch in his wet suit."

"Find anything on it?" Dimitri asked.

Leo nodded. "I made a call to his handler and used old voice records we had on file to simulate his voice. Told him the mission was complete. It wasn't easy, but I think the handler bought it. He was ordered to return home to Moscow. My guess is this is his usual routine for foreign missions."

"So we bought ourselves maybe two days," Dimitri guessed. Two days wasn't much, but it gave them a little time to regroup and plan how they would handle this.

"I think so, but we have to be careful. They have pictures of you kissing her, Dimitri. From what I could tell, he's already shared those pictures with his handler. They'll dive into every file they've got on you to figure out why you're here with her. They don't believe in coincidences. Once they learn their agent is dead, they'll start piecing things together. I've kept your online presence clean, but that doesn't mean they won't be watching you closely."

They were both targets now. There was no place to

hide that they would not eventually be tracked down. Dimitri dragged his hands through his hair so hard that it hurt. "She'll be on the run for the rest of her life."

"There is one option." Nicholas set his beer down, all humor gone for the moment. Leo and Maxim looked confused. Dimitri had no idea what Nicholas meant either.

"You guys are way too introverted," Nicholas muttered. He pulled his cell phone out of his pocket and tapped on his screen, then let them see.

"The United Nations is having a massive gala. It's their annual humanitarian awards. The event is coming up."

"Are you serious, Nick?" Maxim growled. "Just put a target on her forehead and feed her to the wolves?"

"No, of course not. Think about it—you bring the last true Romanov out to a United Nations event, you make her so public that she becomes—"

"Untouchable," Dimitri finished. His heart was beating harder than usual. The four of them fell into a moment of silence.

"Every leader in the world will see her, meet her, and love her," Nicholas added.

"All but one," Maxim said, his eyes dark. "And he won't be able to touch her."

"It's not the most insane plan we've ever had," Leo mused. "But we would need reinforcements. We need to light the signal fires, so to speak."

Dimitri could almost see it now. The White Army

stepping out of the darkness, shedding the ashes of the past and heralding a brighter, better future with Elena at the forefront. She could never rule Russia, nor would he want her to, but her existence and reemergence would be of huge cultural significance. She could change the world if she wanted to.

"It might be possible . . ." Dimitri reached for the nearest unopened beer, but a sudden scream shattered the quiet.

He ran up to the master bedroom to find Elena shivering in her bed, arms wrapped tight around her body. The other three men barreled into him from behind.

"Elena, are you all right?" Dimitri approached the bed, his eyes sweeping the room. There was no sign of an intruder, which meant her nightmares were back.

"I'm fine." She looked away from all of them and pulled the sheets and the comforter up to her chest.

Maxim gave Dimitri a pointed look as he left the room. "I think you can handle this."

Leo offered Elena a warm, brotherly smile before leaving as well.

Nicholas clapped a hand on Dimitri's shoulder as he joined the others and leaned in to whisper, "Stay with her."

Dimitri closed the door, and darkness descended in the room. He turned on the lamp by the bed, illuminating Elena's pale face.

"I'm sorry. I didn't mean to scare you guys. I just had a small freak-out."

He eased down on the bed beside her. "You mean a nightmare."

She nodded. "I'm okay, Dimitri. Really. You can go back to whatever you were doing—cleaning your guns and talking about assassinations or whatever you guys do." Her flippant tone didn't conceal the distress in her eyes.

"Elena . . ." Dimitri cleared his throat. "I made you a promise, one that until tonight did not go against everything I've been raised to believe."

"I know. I know you can't be with me. That's really stupid, by the way." She shot him a glare. "Letting someone tell you who you can and can't be with?"

"It is . . . but it is the truth. You are above me, Elena."

"No. I'm not," she shot back. "I haven't changed in the last day, Dimitri. I'm just me. My blood doesn't make me some fairy princess who can't be with you. So quit being stupid and kiss me."

She reached for his sweater, grabbing the collar and pulling him to her. He was startled by her bold act and moved instinctively, his hands braced on the bed frame on either side of her body as he leaned in. Her mouth was wonderfully soft, and he lost himself in the pure pleasure of kissing her. He wanted to gather her in his arms and never let go of her. She was the most exquisite thing he'd ever tasted in his life.

Elena's arms slid up and locked behind his neck. Their mouths moved in perfect harmony with each other, gentle but deepening with every bit of longing he'd ever felt in his life. The touch of her lips jolted his body with an intense awareness. He smelled the clean floral scent of her body, the soft silkiness of her hair, the smooth skin of her cheeks as he pressed light kisses down around her jaw and neck. Her pulse throbbed in her throat, and he let himself count the beats of her heart as he kissed her neck. She wore only a T-shirt, and it would be so easy to push it up and out of his way . . .

The reality of his thoughts came like a bucket of cold water over him. He pulled back. Her hands were still clasped behind his neck, preventing him from making a full retreat. He caught his breath and so did she.

"How bad was your nightmare?" he asked. His hands were still braced on the headboard on either side of her. Dimitri ached to hold her.

"Bad," she admitted. Her fingertips traced the back of his neck as though the mere act of touching him was enough to calm her.

"You know nothing will harm you, not with me here," he promised. "I would give my life for you, as would my friends."

Elena tugged on the hair at the back of his head to force him to look at her.

"Please, Dimitri. I don't need you to die for me. I need you to *be* with me. Please *choose* me, not whatever vow you made that keeps you away. If you want me to be this

Romanov descendant of the grand duchess, then you need to give me the one thing I need . . . and that's *you*. I want what you promised me. I want you." The despair and desire in her eyes were an undeniable combination. To be desired for being oneself was such a potent thing.

In that moment, Dimitri knew he would never be able to stay away from her. She was his sun, glowing in the dark universe, and he was pulled into her orbit, bound forever to the stunning force of her beautiful gravity.

"You win, *kiska*," he sighed, and that barrier he'd begun to erect around his heart earlier today came crashing down as if the trumpets of Jericho had sounded.

She cupped his face, her green eyes glowing in the dim light. "We do this only if you want me too, remember?"

He closed his eyes, savoring her touch. "I've never wanted anything more."

Her shoulders relaxed, and she traced his lips with a fingertip.

"Thank you," she whispered.

"For what?" he asked, his gaze locked on her mouth.

"For wanting me. I didn't think . . . I didn't think anyone would want me after what happened."

"Elena . . ." Her words were a knife to his heart. How could she think that?

"I know." Elena's sigh was heavier than the world itself in that moment. "The therapist said it's normal to feel that way, but there's nothing normal about feeling broken, used . . . destroyed from the inside out."

"You are none of those things. No matter what you think, you aren't. Do you understand?" He held her gaze, and she managed a nod.

She placed a hand on the bed beside her. "Will you stay?"

As if he could leave her now. As if he had ever been able to. He nearly laughed at the thought, but he didn't want her to think he was laughing at her.

"I'll stay, *kiska.*"

The smile that lit her face was brighter than any of the stars they had seen in the sky tonight. "I was starting to miss that."

Dimitri pulled his sweater over his head and let it fall to the floor. "Starting to miss what?"

"You calling me *kiska.*" She blushed a little as she pulled back the covers next to her. "It makes me feel safe."

Dimitri leaned in and cupped her chin. Her breath hitched so strongly that he felt it pull at him with her quiet desires and eager eyes. He leaned forward, and she licked her lips. He forced himself to speak the words she deserved to hear.

"A strong woman deserves a strong man. Strong women also deserve to feel safe. You have nothing to be ashamed of."

"Make me feel safe, Dimitri."

She leaned back in bed, the invitation to be with her so clear and pure. It wasn't about sex, not tonight—it was about human connection, and he would give her that. He unfastened his jeans and tugged them off. He felt her gaze on his body, and he had to work hard to keep himself from responding. Tonight was not the night for that. She still needed to process the information she'd been given. He would not let her try to use her body and his to escape thinking about that. She also needed to rest.

He slipped into bed beside her, more than pleased to feel her body warm against his. She wore only a shirt and cotton shorts. Someday he wanted them to sleep skin to skin, but not tonight. He turned off the light, cloaking them in darkness.

It was dark, but her body found its way to his. She pressed close to him. They lay in silence for a time, listening to the wind blow against the windows. There was nothing more perfect than holding this woman in a warm bed when he knew how cold it was outside.

"Tell me about something beautiful. Something wonderful. I don't want my mind to go back to that dream." She pressed her cheek to his chest, and he circled his arms around her body, hugging her to him.

"Something beautiful." As a boy, he'd loved learning about the world, about everything that was around him. That had only deepened as he'd grown up. He'd become obsessed with nature, art, and history. In every city he traveled to, he visited museums and art galleries and historic sites, soaking up the knowledge of the world. It reminded him of the beauty that the world offered.

"There is a species of jellyfish that is immortal."

She giggled at that. "What?"

"It's true. It can revert back to its child state after having become sexually mature, and therefore it never dies. It's very small and is found worldwide in temperate to tropical waters."

"Can you imagine living forever?" Elena asked.

Dimitri tangled his fingers in her hair and gently massaged. "I cannot." If he could live forever, he would only do it if he had Elena with him.

She yawned and burrowed closer. "Tell me some more interesting things."

"Hmm, let's see . . . polar bears have black skin and see-through fur."

"How is that possible? Their fur looks white."

He moved his hand to his shoulders, rubbing her soothingly. "The long, coarse guard hairs that protect the bear's undercoat are hollow and transparent. The thinner hairs of the undercoat are not hollow, but, like the guard hairs, are also colorless. They look like they do because the airspace in each hair scatters light of all colors. The color white becomes visible to our eyes when an object reflects back all the visible wavelengths, rather than absorbing some of the wavelengths. So polar bears reflect all light."

"How do you know all these things? Is that in your spy handbook?"

He chuckled. "As a child, I had many books on animals. My mother used to read me some of them. After she died, I kept reading. She taught me about learning to bring joy and pleasure."

"And your father?"

"He taught me duty." Dimitri didn't want to talk about him. He had idolized the man, but now he was realizing that he no longer wanted that life.

"I'm sorry." She pressed a kiss to his skin, and a flush of warmth filled his chest. He cradled her even closer. He tightened his hold on her, and she shifted slightly. His body responded to her pressing against him, but he ignored it and instead focused on the sound of her breathing. She would be asleep soon.

"Thank you," she said drowsily against his chest.

"For what, *kiska*?"

"For *you* . . ." He felt her body relax against his as sleep claimed her. He didn't want to move, didn't want to disturb her now that she was finally resting. The peace that filled him at holding her was almost overpowering. But if he wanted this dream to become a reality, where he could hold her for the rest of their lives, he had to figure out a way to protect her, not just now, but forever. He had a plan, and he hoped it would work.

He waited until she was deeply asleep, then slid out of bed, grabbed his cell phone, and stepped into the hall. He dialed Royce's number.

"Man, these after-midnight calls are going to kill me," Royce grumbled as he answered. "What is it? You all right? Don't tell me you're already in Colorado?"

"No, we're safe but still en route. There something I need you to do."

"Name it."

"Elena's parents were planning to visit her in California. She left them a message to stay home before I destroyed her phone. I want her to be able to contact them, but their phones are most likely being tapped by the Russian government. I need them to be given safe phones, and I need them to be moved out of their house and put under protection."

Royce sounded more alert, his tone sharp-edged with concern. "Are you going to tell me what the hell is going on? I thought she would be safe with Vadym dead."

Dimitri rubbed his eyes with his thumb and forefinger. "We tested Elena's blood."

"Okay . . ." Royce waited for him to continue.

"You remember the stories that someone escaped the Romanov massacre a hundred years ago?"

"Yeah, one of the daughters. Anastasia . . ." Royce was silent, then cursed. "No, that's impossible. Crazy."

"Not so crazy after all, it seems."

"So if that's true, how did the government find out?"

Dimitri let out a breath. "Elena knew she was adopted and decided to run a blood test on one of those ancestry websites to find out about her past. They don't know her exact connection to Anastasia, but they'll have had enough to know she's a direct descendant of the imperial royal family."

"Holy shit. Do her parents know?"

"I imagine not, but they will still have targets on their backs. The Kremlin will want to use them to get to her."

"Okay. I'll go pay a visit to them and stash them at my house on Long Island until you give the all-clear."

"Call me when you have them so we can speak to them. Elena will need to hear their voices."

"I'll let you know." Royce hesitated. "Can I tell Kenzie about this? She's worried about Elena."

"Yes, of course," Dimitri assured him. "And I have one more favor."

"I'm listening."

"Call Wes Thorne and tell him I need five tickets to the United Nations gala that's happening in New York soon. I also need a dress for her."

"A dress?"

"Yes, a very specifically designed one. I'll text you some images. Maybe you could put Kenzie on that if she wants to help."

"Sure. Send me the details."

"Thank you, Royce." He ended the call and stood still in the silent house, thinking. There was one more thing to do, and he would need to call in every favor he was owed. He checked his watch. It was after two in the morning. He dialed another number and waited.

A British-accented voice answered. "Edgeworth here."

"It's Razin," Dimitri said. "Is she awake?"

"Yes, but she is not taking calls, even from her favorites." The British Private Secretary chuckled.

Dimitri smiled a little. Edgeworth's boss did have a soft spot for him. "Please give her this message. I need access to a certain tiara."

"Which one?"

"The large diamond diadem of Alexandra Romanov."

Edgeworth drew in a deep breath. "There is only one person she would give that to."

Dimitri kept his tone quiet. "Its rightful owner."

"You can't mean . . . My God, after all this time . . . The stories are true?" Edgeworth now knew just what was at stake.

"Yes, and we need to send the Russian ambassador a message. The biggest one we can."

"Only the royal jeweler knows that she has that tiara. If she sends it to you, there could be questions about how she acquired it."

"Acquiring a piece like that at a private auction is not something to be ashamed of," Dimitri promised him. "And we need never say where it came from."

"Very well, I will convey your request to her when she wakes. If this means what I think it does, you had better be careful."

"I will."

Dimitri stood still in the hallway a long moment before he returned to bed. Then he took Elena's body in his arms and finally got some rest. Knowing Maxim, Leo,

and Nicholas were watching his back gave him a chance,
for the first time in days, to dream.

"SIR, IVANOFF HASN'T CHECKED IN."

Vladimir Andropov spun his chair to regard the man
who stood nervously at his door. Normally he didn't let
any of the lower-level intelligence agents bother him. They
knew to stay in their cubicles in the nondescript building
at the edge of Moscow's city limits, but it seemed today,
he was going to be pestered by them. He cursed his corner
office being on the same floor as these fools.

"How long has it been?" Vladimir Andropov
demanded. He didn't know the man's name. It didn't
matter. The man, like any other agent handler, could be
replaced.

Viktor's handler pushed his thick glasses back up his
nose and shifted on his feet. "It's been about six hours
since we expected him to send us flight details."

"Six hours?" Vladimir didn't yell. He didn't have to.

"We assumed he had a delay, but his last check-in said
he was on time. He didn't confirm mission completion, at
least not with the code he was assigned."

At this, Vladimir leaned forward, his chair creaking in
slight protest.

"Are you telling me *you* haven't confirmed his kill?"

By the pallor on the man's face, the handler could tell

that the answer might just get the underling killed. "We were certain when he checked in. He promised to send more with his flight details, but we haven't received anything . . . ," the man stammered.

"Bring me everything on his assignment, *now!*" Vladimir took no small amount of satisfaction in watching the man trip as he rushed away.

When Vladimir was alone, he stared at the wall of his office where his service medals awarded by the president of Russia hung in decorative window boxes. Beside one was a framed picture of him as a young man, barely twenty years old, and his partner, Viktor Ivanoff. They had both been young back then, but they'd worked well together and had taken to the grim nature of their work.

As the years had passed, Viktor had wanted to stay in the field, but Vladimir had craved the comforts of power and had worked his way up the ladder of the intelligence sector. He was officially Viktor's boss now, but he always assigned someone else to be Viktor's handler on missions. Now he sensed that had been a mistake.

The man returned in a flurry and placed a file on Vladimir's desk. "This is all we have."

Vladimir shooed the man away and began to sift through the papers. It was a new file, yet there were dozens of pieces of yellowed paper that were tucked haphazardly between crisply printed new reports. He removed all the older pieces, examining them closely. His heart stuttered to a stop as he recognized the date and the location.

Maine, the United States. Twenty years ago. He reached up to touch his neck where a jagged scar marred his skin. He and Viktor had shared an assignment in Maine to kill a woman named Tatiana Anderson.

It should have been easy. Yet it had been anything but. He and Viktor had barely escaped with their lives. The woman had help escaping them. She had been with a man who knew his way around weapons. In the end, they had killed him, but she, the actual target, had gotten away.

They had been forced to seek medical aid and had agreed to say they had killed the woman. She had been nine months pregnant and wouldn't have gotten far on foot in the winter storm she'd escaped into. Most likely, she'd died in the woods. They had been too far from any hospital for her to get help, and Vladimir had been certain her water had broken during the fight that night.

Vladimir dug through the file, his hands trembling now as he pieced together something he never could have imagined.

Tatiana Anderson *had* made it to a hospital and had given birth before dying. A child now fully grown. Vladimir examined the photos in the file. A pretty blonde woman, young, with big green eyes. Tatiana's file had resurfaced because her daughter had used a DNA profiling site. Her DNA markers had triggered an alert in their system. Vladimir's blood ran cold as he realized what that meant.

Tatiana had been a direct Romanov descendant, straight from the line of Nicholas and Alexandra. Tatiana's daughter carried that same imperial royal blood. No one had told him or Viktor this when they'd sent them after her twenty years ago. If Vladimir didn't find out what had happened to Viktor and fix this mistake, things could go badly for him.

He continued to search the file. There had to be answers somewhere in it. Viktor wouldn't go this long without reporting. Failing to report to headquarters meant Viktor was injured or dead. He had a cyanide capsule in one of his molars, so if he had been captured, he wouldn't have stayed alive long enough to betray his country.

Vladimir was going to have to handle this himself.

Vladimir slammed the file shut and put it in his attaché case. He grabbed his coat from the coatrack in the corner of his office.

The man who had told him Viktor had not checked in was lingering in the hallway. "Sir?"

"I'm leaving for a week. Report to Boris Yatvin while I'm gone."

"Yes, sir." The man ducked back into his cubicle and left Vladimir alone.

His mind was already miles away, plotting the death of a girl who should never have lived.

❧ 14 ❧

Elena wasn't sure what to think when she woke alone in the master bedroom of the lodge. For a second, she didn't remember where she was. There was no sound of the sea, no briny breeze drifting through an open balcony door. Then last night's events came screaming back, creating a dull ache behind her eyes.

She was descended from Grand Duchess Anastasia of Russia. It was like something out of a childhood fairy tale . . . except for the fact that Russian assassins were trying to kill her.

She stretched across the bed, feeling the slight indent left in the mattress where Dimitri had been beside her. Last night, he'd promised to stay with her, to *be* with her. She searched the pillow, expecting to find a little note from him, but there wasn't one. Her stomach cramped with sudden panic.

Had Dimitri already broken his promise to stay with her?

When she pushed the covers back, she suddenly heard Dimitri's delighted laugh coming from down the hall. The knot of tension inside her eased. She dressed in jeans and a sweater and padded on her bare feet toward the sound of activity. She halted at the sight of the four handsome Russians cooking up a storm in the kitchen. Dimitri was working the griddle, flipping pancakes. Maxim was slicing lemons and dropping them into a pitcher of water. Nicholas was setting the table. Leo was cooking scrambled eggs on one skillet and frying bacon on another.

"Good morning, *kiska*." Dimitri beamed at her.

"You *all* cook?" It wasn't like they were impressive chefs or anything, but she'd honestly expected to come in and see them cleaning their guns instead of doing something strangely domestic.

"Naturally," Nicholas answered with a wink. "We have *many* skills."

"Did you sleep well?" Leo asked.

"Yes, I did. I'm sorry I woke you all last night." She remembered seeing all of their faces crammed in the doorway, staring at her as she suffered a night terror.

Dimitri pointed at the kitchen table with the spatula. "Have a seat." He seemed far more relaxed now that his friends were here. She was glad. In a way, they were making her more relaxed too. It felt like she had a small but fierce army to protect her now. But she still worried that it was selfish of her to ask him to stay with her when it put his life in clear danger.

Dimitri filled up a plate with food and set it down in front of her. She was relieved to see a sensuous gaze mixed with affection in his eyes. So he hadn't changed his mind about them. He'd merely gotten up early to make breakfast. She felt like a fool for worrying.

Soon, the four men had their own plates and were seated all around her. Their plates were stacked high. She almost laughed. They definitely needed the calories, though. They were all built like Dimitri, tall, hard-muscled, with raw power emanating off them. She was glad they were on her side.

As she ate the men spoke freely, with a gentle, brotherly intimacy between them, and it filled an emptiness inside her that she had never noticed before. She was an only child, and she had never had the camaraderie of siblings before. Dimitri hadn't been wrong—these men *were* his brothers. She should have felt shy around them for any number of reasons, but they were surprisingly easy to be around and didn't expect her to join in their conversation if she didn't want to. They spoke in English and offered her brotherly smiles, which still made her blush.

"So, where in Colorado are we headed?" Maxim asked as he buttered a slice of toast.

"Steamboat Springs. There's a mountain resort that has private cabins that have plenty of bedrooms. We'll be close to civilization, but not in the middle of it."

"What about internet?" Leo asked.

"They should have it, but I imagine you'll need to enact every security protocol you have and boost the signal," Dimitri said.

"I'm sure I can," Leo agreed.

"Max, Nicholas, and I will be training Elena once we get there."

"Training?" Elena said suddenly. "What training?" She didn't like the sound of that.

Dimitri reached across the table and placed one hand over hers. The touch instantly calmed her sudden panic. "Self-defense."

"What, you mean like throat, nose, and groin punches?" she asked.

Nicholas winced at the mention of groin punching. "Yes, but more than that."

"Yes. There is more to self-defense than punching. Most often, the attack comes before you are ready. You need to learn how to react when you're already in a losing position."

A losing position. Yes, she was all too aware of that. While she was nervous about the lessons, she knew she needed them.

"Okay, I'm in." That earned a smile from Maxim, but she had a feeling he was going to be her most challenging teacher.

The more time she spent around them, the more she saw how different each of Dimitri's friends were. Nicholas and Leo were more fun, if *fun* was the right word. More relaxed, perhaps. Maxim and Dimitri were more tightly wound, but when all four were together, they interacted seamlessly. She supposed if anyone had trained together pretty much their whole lives, they would be that accustomed to each other.

After they finished breakfast, Elena returned to her room to pack her suitcase. She suddenly had that eerie feeling of not being alone. She looked over her shoulder and saw Maxim in the doorway. He stepped into the room, tension practically radiating from his dark-brown eyes.

"Your Gra—"

"Elena," she corrected firmly.

"Elena. When you were with *him* . . ." Maxim avoided saying Vadym's name, but his tone made it clear who he meant. "Did he ever mention a girl named Katya?"

Elena sat on the edge of the bed and drew a deep breath. She worked so hard to not think about those days. "Katya . . ."

A flare of hope lit Maxim's eyes. "She is my little sister."

Elena didn't give any sign that might let him know she already knew about his sister. She didn't want him to be mad at Dimitri for sharing such a personal story. "I don't think so . . ."

He pulled his wallet out of his jeans pocket, dug through the contents, and held out a photograph. It was worn at the edges, as though it had been handled frequently. A dark-haired young woman with lovely light-brown eyes grinned from the photo. A sudden, violent memory came back to her, making her gasp.

"What is it?" Maxim came closer, his voice soft and urgent.

"I . . . I didn't know her name . . ." She tried to summon up every detail of that memory. "I was in his office . . . He had left my cell door open. I thought it was a trap at first . . ."

Her cell had always been so cold, and she only ever wore a thin black shift as clothing. She had been starved for warmth, and his office had been cozy compared to her cell. "I crawled into his office. My chains had been attached to the wall. He had left me in a hurry." She continued, desperately trying to pull every detail back, knowing it was a terrible idea, but she had to tell Maxim what she had seen. Her hands tightened into fists as she delved deeper into her memory. Her skin turned clammy, and she had to swallow down bile.

"I hid in the corner of his office, and I noticed a set of files at the base of a bookshelf. They were tucked behind a couple of old books. It was not an obvious spot to hide something. I don't even know why I looked, but I hoped that whatever had driven him away from his office would keep him away long enough for me to read the files. I remember the folders were bright red. I didn't see anything in there except pictures of young women, and your sister was one of them. It looked like statistics sheets, but my written Russian is so limited I only recognized one word."

"What word?"

"*Krasnyy*. Red. It was typed at the top of every paper." She suddenly opened her eyes. "Give me a sheet of paper."

He opened the nightstand by the bed and handed her a pen and a pad of paper. She focused on the shapes of the second word that had accompanied *red* every time she had seen it.

"It looked something like this." She drew the symbols as best she could, then handed it to him. He was silent a long moment and drew a similar pattern and held it up.

"Was this what you saw?"

Elena studied the words and slowly nodded. "What does it mean?"

Maxim's eyes were stormy as he gazed at the wall behind her. "It means . . . sparrow school."

"Red sparrow school? What does that mean?"

"It is an old school from the Cold War era. We believed it had been closed." He met her gaze. "Young men and especially young women were trained to be spies there. They used manipulation, especially sexual, to gain information from their targets."

Elena couldn't hide the look of horror upon her face. Maxim's face hardened, and he cursed to himself in Russian. His hands curled into fists.

"I'm so sorry, Maxim. What will happen to her?"

He was silent a long moment. "If she is still alive, she

will be broken down and rebuilt into a heartless killer." His voice softened. "She will be a tool of the state, willing to betray anyone she loves without a second thought. A creature better off dead than alive."

Elena's throat suddenly ached as she wanted to cry for Katya, and for Maxim. She placed a hand on his arm. It was the first time she'd willingly touched a man other than Dimitri since she had been rescued. It felt good, even during such a terrible moment, to show support and affection to another.

"Thank you," he said. "At least now I have some idea of what happened to her."

"Will you go after her? Maybe it's not too late."

"The moment she arrived at the school, it would have been too late." He covered her hand with his, a sorrowful expression in his eyes that nearly broke her. "You should pack. We must leave soon." And then he was gone.

Elena collapsed onto the bed, her hands shaking. She had gone back to the dark place in her mind, but then she'd come out again and she was okay. Relief nearly overwhelmed her. Maybe it would get easier and easier to face the past. She knew it might not, but she could hope.

FIVE HOURS LATER, THE PAIR OF RANGE ROVERS PULLED into a resort's driveway. Dimitri and Leo went into the lobby to check in, while Maxim and Nicholas watched over Elena in the first car. Leo had already accessed their Wi-Fi system and set up his facial-recognition-blocking software to filter out any pictures of their group that might surface, including footage on security cameras.

Elena found the silence a little unsettling. Maxim hadn't said a single word since she had told him about his sister back at the lodge in Utah. Nicholas had tried once or twice to start a conversation before giving up. Now he was just as broody as Maxim. "So . . . What will be the first lesson in my self-defense classes?"

"Hiding," the men replied in unison.

"Hiding? Are you kidding me?" She snorted. "That's not a defense."

"Of course it is," Nicholas said. "The best defense is avoiding a fight entirely."

Elena smirked. "I thought the best defense was a good offense."

"An American attitude if there ever was one," Maxim said without inflection. "When combat is inevitable, then yes. But when the question is one of survival, avoiding contact with the enemy is always preferable. There is no shame in hiding."

Nicholas leaned around the seat to stare back at her. "Actually, you did that part pretty well in Utah with the riverbank."

"I wish I could claim credit for that. Dimitri told me where to hide."

"But you left the hiding place and managed to get

behind us before we even realized you were there."
Nicholas grinned. "You don't know us well enough yet, but
I assure you, that was impressive."

"Nick is right," Maxim said. "Now we have to teach
you to improve those skills. Hiding is not just about
staying still. Eventually, you will be found. It is about
finding an unlikely place, leaving little to no trail, and
knowing when to move to a new hiding place without
being discovered."

Elena thought back to that night. She had faced the
choice of running and hiding again, or holding the gun on
men she didn't know to help Dimitri. She would not admit
it to Maxim or Nicholas, but she knew she wouldn't run if
Dimitri was in danger.

"Okay, so what's after hiding lessons?"

"Stopping an attack in progress," Nicholas said.

"Not preventing an attack?" She had thought that
would be the next logical step.

"Normally, yes. But the threats you are facing are
above average. Chances are they will be on you before you
see them. You need to know how to escape a chokehold or
lower your body's center of gravity to throw a man off his
feet."

That was something Elena wanted to learn. There had
been so many times when she had been pinned down,
unable to get free . . .

The car door opened, giving Elena a start. Dimitri
motioned for Nicholas to return to the second car

with Leo.

"We're all checked in," he said. "You and I are still Mr. and Mrs. Smith. Maxim is Mr. Black, Leo is Mr. Brown, and Nicholas is Mr. Gray, in case anyone asks."

Elena nodded in understanding. "Eye color, got it."

"What?" Maxim turned to look at her too.

"Your aliases. Dimitri made them to match your eye colors," Elena explained. A blush crept up her cheeks.

"She's right," Dimitri chuckled. "I hadn't thought of it that way."

Maxim frowned. "My eyes are brown."

"Yes," Elena agreed. "But they are such a dark brown that in the evening they look almost black. Leo's are lighter and more clearly brown."

Maxim shrugged and fell into silence again. Dimitri drove the vehicle away from the main resort and up the hill along the side of the mountain. Every quarter of a mile, there was an entrance to a cabin. Dimitri kept passing them until they reached the eighth one. He turned up a private drive and entered a code into a gate.

Up ahead, built into the side of the mountain, was a large cabin. It was even bigger than the lodge in the park in Utah. It sat at the end of a road lined with fir trees. It was made of hand-hewn logs and reclaimed timbers. Despite its impressive build, the house was as subdued as the breeze in the treetops that towered above it.

"How many bedrooms does it have?" Elena asked.

"Only seven," Dimitri said. "It also has a hot tub, exercise room, and a few other rooms."

"Oh, is that all? As a grand duchess, I expected more," Elena joked. She was definitely overwhelmed by the epic-looking cabin that looked more the size of a manor house. She'd guessed they would be staying in some small, cozy little cabin. This looked like it should be featured in *Architectural Digest*.

Dimitri parked the car in the circle drive. Leo did the same with the second Range Rover. Everyone helped unpack and quickly moved inside.

Leo waved Elena off when she started hefting one of the suitcases deeper into the house. "Just leave the luggage in the hall—we'll see to it."

Elena set the bag down by the doorway and moved into a vast great room that was illuminated with winter sunlight through a series of high windows that offered a floor-to-ceiling view of the mountains.

She studied the massive two-story native rock fireplace that overlooked the central seating area. The collected stones had been placed so perfectly that they looked as though the fireplace had tumbled down from a mountainside into a perfectly flat wall of rocks.

"Whoa . . ." Elena walked deeper into the living room and ran her palm over the buttery-soft leather sofa and chairs. Buckskin-colored plaster walls warmed the room with earth tones. Despite the snow outside, this vast cabin felt warm and homey.

Dimitri joined her by the windows. "What do you think?" He slid his arms around her and pulled her back against his chest. With anyone else, she would have felt uncomfortable and pulled away, but with Dimitri she was far from feeling scared.

"Feels wonderful. It's so peaceful here."

"*I went to the woods because I wished to live deliberately, to front only the essential facts of life, and see if I could not learn what it had to teach, and not, when I came to die, discover that I had not lived.*" Dimitri spoke the words into her ear.

"Henry David Thoreau?"

"My *kiska* is well read."

She turned in his arms and pressed a kiss to his perfectly chiseled jaw. "And my Russian badass is as well."

"Russian badass?" He chuckled, hands gently pressed on her lower back to urge her closer to him.

"It's what I call you in my head." She ducked her chin until she was looking down. He rested his head on top of hers, holding her for a long moment. Was it possible to be in this perfect bubble of his embrace forever?

"Would you like to talk to your parents?" he asked.

His words broke through her hazy, sunny daydreams. "My parents?"

"Royce has them at his home. They have phones that can't be traced. It's safe to talk to them. You can use my tablet to video chat if you prefer."

"Do they know?"

"About your ancestry? Yes. Royce told them."

Nerves prickled beneath her skin, making her shudder. Ever since she had learned the truth, she had felt disconnected from the life she knew, and that included her parents. She was a stranger in her own skin.

"I don't even know what to say. They're probably freaked out."

"They are worried about you. You will always be their daughter, and their love for you will never change." Dimitri's rumbling voice always soothed her. He patted her back. "Come, let's go talk to them." He urged her to follow him to the master bedroom as he grabbed his briefcase.

The master bedroom was only a few rooms away from the main living room. An elegant four-poster bed made the room somehow romantic. The view outside their balcony was one of rolling hills and distant mountains. The cabin's exterior was woodsy, but the rooms inside were luxurious, with plastered walls that softened the cabin's interior. Hand-hewn logs accented the muted color palette of the bedroom. Black Forest trophy mounts and European antiques paired well with rustic design pieces. The doorway of the bedroom and the master bath had fanciful twig work decorating the corners of the beams of the frame, as though the bathroom existed in the forest.

Dimitri set his briefcase on the bed and pulled out his tablet. He placed it on the comforter and called Royce on his cell.

"Elena is ready to talk. I'll call you from my tablet."

Elena climbed on the bed and pulled his tablet onto her lap. Dimitri dialed Royce's number for a video call.

"Come back to the living room when you are finished." Dimitri pulled the door closed behind him as he left.

A moment later, the tablet screen lit up with an incoming call. She accepted and, a moment later, her parents' faces appeared.

"Oh my God, honey," her mother gasped. Tears were already coming down her face.

Elena tried to smile. "Hey, Mom."

Her father's face had new lines on it, making him look years older. "Are you okay?" he asked. "Dr. Devereaux picked us up this morning and drove us to his home. He said you were in danger and we were too."

"Yes." Elena tried to find the right words. "He told you about . . . well, who I am?"

Her mother nodded. "He said that the man you are with, Dimitri Razin, tested your blood against samples from the Romanov family and that you had a . . ." She looked to her husband. "What was it, honey?"

"A twelve point five percent match to Anastasia. So you're her great-granddaughter. Is that right?" Her father checked with her, and Elena nodded.

"So it would seem." Elena still wasn't sure if she believed it, but at some point she would have to. The Russian government believed it enough to try to assassinate her.

"Are you safe?" Her father's eyes were wary. "When Dr.

Devereaux mentioned you are with a Russian man, we didn't know what to think."

He didn't have to explain. It must seem insane for her to be with a man who would remind her of everything she'd been through.

"Dimitri is keeping me safe, Dad. He's amazing. He is like some kind of spy, even though he says he isn't. But he totally is. His friends met up with us, and we are all safe. These guys are badasses, Dad. Seriously. Don't worry. They can take care of me."

"But are you okay being around them?" her father asked more quietly, as though he feared being overheard.

"Yes. I am. And I'm getting better. He's helping." She wanted them to know that Dimitri was helping her feel normal, but she didn't dare elaborate how.

"Where are you?" her mother asked.

"I don't think I can tell you. You can ask Royce. If he tells you, then it's safe, but I don't want to put either of you in any danger."

"We'll be fine. Your father and I are taking a brief sabbatical from our jobs. Everything is fine. Don't worry about us." Her mother's eyes were still bright with tears. "I wish we were with you, honey."

"Me too, Mom. But it's all going to be all right. I promise."

"Call us again soon so we don't worry, okay?" her father said.

"I will if I can, Dad." She imprinted a memory of their

faces in her mind. Her mother's cheery smile, her father's kind, soulful eyes, and most importantly, the look of love they gave her.

"I love you both," she said.

Her mother kissed the tips of her fingers and pressed them toward the screen. "We love you too, honey."

"We'll talk again soon," Elena promised, then ended the call before she lost her resolve. The instinct to run home to them was overpowering. But she couldn't. This was her fight, not theirs. And it was time for her to stop running.

15

Dimitri stood by the fireplace, admiring the flames after he and Maxim had gotten the fire going. But his thoughts soon turned to concern about how best to protect Elena.

"I'm ready to fight."

Dimitri turned abruptly at the sound of Elena's voice. She stood in the doorway that led from the great room to the hallway. She wore a pair of gray yoga pants and a loose T-shirt that hung slightly off one shoulder, revealing an exercise bra beneath.

"You want to train? Already?" Dimitri clarified. He and Maxim exchanged a look.

"Yes. But let's skip the hiding part. I have that covered. I want to learn . . . what did you call it, Maxim? The fighting back during an attack sort of moves."

Dimitri shot his friend another glance.

"She asked," Maxim said with a shrug.

"Please, Dimitri. I need this. I know that learning to hide is important, but I need to have some control in my life. If hiding fails, I need to have some idea of how to fight back." The look of steely determination on her face stunned him. Whatever had happened between her and her parents during their call had set something in motion within her.

"Very well. Let's go." He nodded at Maxim and led Elena to the exercise room at the back of the house. There was a large floormat with two bikes and a treadmill in one corner. They moved the bikes farther to one side of the room, leaving a clear space to practice.

Elena stepped into the center of the mat and held her hands up like she was going to box a cartoon kangaroo. She looked adorable, and it was hard for him to focus on what he was supposed to teach her.

"The first lesson involves being attacked from behind." Dimitri slowly came toward her. When he reached her, he grasped her shoulders and turned her to face away from him. "There is no such thing as a fair fight. You must assume you will be taken at a disadvantage."

Their bodies pressed together. He tried to tamp down the desire that rippled beneath his skin as he breathed in her scent. He refocused his attention on her, on how important this training was. She wouldn't only be learning to fight, but she'd be learning to let people touch her again without panicking.

"The first thing you must learn is the energy of the situation you're in. Self-defense techniques fail when you fight against the energy of the person attacking you. Don't try to fight against the direction your assailant moves you. For example, if you have someone put a hand over your mouth, determine which arm will be free or even both arms." Dimitri placed his palm over her mouth and curled his fingers around her left arm. "Now, you see your right arm is free. If I move my hand to your waist, you have both arms free. You want to keep your response to his action quick and simple. You have two weapons at your disposal: pain and throwing him off balance."

Dimitri grabbed her left arm again, jerking her back against him less gently. She tensed.

"Now, follow my backward energy. Lean back against my body. Let my body stabilize yours. If you are stable, you can use your energy to fight. Now, move with me." He dragged her a step back. After a second's hesitation, Elena relaxed against him, continuing to move back with him step for step and bending her knees.

"Good. Now grab my arm beside your face. You can hold on to me there and be even more stable."

Elena's hand wrapped around his wrist in a viselike grip.

"Here's your first point of attack. Raise your other hand, make a fist, but aim your thumb—like you want to hitchhike—and launch it into my face. Aim for my eyes if you can, but hit any part of my face and it will still startle me. If you hit him in the eyes, your assailant will step back and most likely loosen his grip on you. You want the assailant to lose his focus."

She practiced jabbing at his face in slow motion. Dimitri dropped his hands from her mouth and stepped back, gripping her right arm.

"Now, take your left arm and send it back against my thigh in a hard slap."

She placed her palm on his thigh, and for a second he had to remind himself they were practicing. "Grip my jeans in your fist. Now you will roll your wrist up as you pull down and forward."

"What does this do?" she asked as she followed his instructions.

"It pulls me off balance and will send me stumbling down if you're lucky. Make sure you turn into him if he still has a hand on your mouth. It forces his pressure and energy in a direction he won't expect."

Maxim stepped onto the mat, entering their line of sight. "You cannot stop the force of energy coming at you, but you can control its direction. See how much easier it is to pull Dimitri down? He stumbles forward, his knees jerk as you pull his leg."

"Wow . . ." Elena murmured. "I can't believe that works."

"Maxim is right. Always try to move *with* the energy coming at you. It will make you less tired, and you will be able to fight better," Dimitri explained. He released Elena, and she turned to face him.

"That doesn't seem too hard—"

Maxim grabbed her from behind, latching one hand around her mouth. Dimitri saw the flare of panic in her eyes, but it had to be done. She trusted him to touch her, but Maxim would be recognized as a threat. She thrashed, panicking.

"Use his energy, Elena," Dimitri urged.

She spun into Maxim and launched her hand at his face. He dodged the blow, but it forced him to step back, and she latched onto his leg and pulled down and away from him, forcing him to stumble. She twisted free enough that he had only a grip on her wrist, and without any prompting, she spun back in his direction and kicked. Maxim barely avoided a foot to his groin. He immediately released her, and she stumbled back, her chest rising and falling with shallow breaths. She kept her distance, panting as she eyed them like a frightened animal.

Dimitri held up a hand before Maxim could advance on her again. Neither of them moved now as they waited for her to calm down.

"Deep breaths, *kiska*. You are safe. It's me and Maxim," Dimitri said. Her green eyes were still wild with terror. "Elena." Her eyes flashed away from the threat, Maxim, to Dimitri.

"Breathe with me." He reached out to take one of her hands and placed it on his chest. Then he drew in several slow, deep breaths. Her breath hitched a few times before she settled into a slower rhythm.

"There," he said gently. "You're fine. You did well."

After a moment, she turned back toward Maxim, that determined expression back on her face. "I need to do that again."

"Maxim," Dimitri said, but when Elena seemed to prepare herself for Maxim, expecting him to attack her, Dimitri grabbed her from behind.

She reacted with fear as expected, but she forced it away quicker this time. This time when she got free, her eyes were full of jade fire.

"What's next? What if he has a hold around my neck or something?"

Dimitri and Maxim shared a glance.

"May I?" Maxim asked Dimitri.

Dimitri waved for him to step forward to instruct Elena on the next move.

Over the next half hour, the intense look of dread on Elena's face began to relax, and she occasionally grinned as she successfully countered their moves.

Nicholas entered the room behind Elena without her seeing him. Dimitri knew this would be a good test. She was tired, confident, and relaxed.

Dimitri gave Nick the barest hint of a nod, and the man launched himself at Elena from behind. Nicholas was a charmer, but he fought dirty. He grabbed her by the throat in a choke hold. His other hand strayed up her waist to rest just below her breasts, and Dimitri's heart sank as he saw the old terror fill Elena's eyes.

Then, just like that, her panic cleared and a stone-cold resolve replaced it. She curled into Nicholas, and within half a second, she had used Nicholas's own energy against him, sending him flying onto his back. A groan escaped Nicholas's lips, and he didn't bother getting up from the mat. He muttered a few choice words in Russian.

"Well done, *kiska*," Dimitri said.

The stoniness within her eyes slowly faded.

"Sorry, Nicholas." She reached down and held out a hand to him. Was she even aware that she'd offered her hand so freely? For the last few days, she had been careful to keep her physical distance from his friends. Now she was acting more normal than ever and not shying away from them. He couldn't help but wonder if the training had done more than teach her self-defense. Maybe the repeated exposure of close contact in this particular setting had helped her feel more like her old self again. Whatever it was, he was damned glad about it.

"What's next?" Elena asked.

"Next you shower, and then we eat dinner. You will be exhausted tonight, and you will need proper rest to resume training tomorrow." Dimitri didn't miss the mix of disappointment and relief in her eyes.

He followed her to the master bedroom and watched her collect her things for the shower. She was abnormally quiet, seemingly lost in her thoughts. He placed a hand on her shoulder. She went still an instant before she relaxed, and he started to pull away.

"No, wait, don't—" She reached for his hand, surrounding it with her own. "I'm sorry. I'm still wired from all the training, but I think . . . I think I need to be touched."

Without a word, Dimitri pulled her into his arms. He let her feel the security and warmth of his body around hers.

"Better?" he asked. She nodded against his chest. "Then come find me when you are done, *kiska*." He tilted her chin up and kissed her. He let her feel his hunger, and she moaned softly in response and pressed tighter to him. He wasn't sure how long the kiss actually lasted, but the light was beginning to fade outside when their mouths broke apart. He took far too much satisfaction at the dazed and happy expression on her face as he let her go.

He left her alone to shower and rejoined the others in the great room. Maxim and Nicholas had found a chessboard and were playing. Leo was on the couch nearby, his laptop resting on his thighs as he drank a glass of scotch and studied the major news headlines.

"You cheat," Maxim accused Nicholas with a scowl.

"I do not," Nicholas retorted. When Dimitri joined them, Nicholas shot him a conspiratorial wink that Maxim couldn't see.

"Your bishop was not there. You moved it," Maxim argued.

"I moved it there on my last turn. You weren't paying attention." Nicholas leaned back in his leather armchair, far too smug.

Dimitri chuckled. Some things never changed. Nicholas disregarded the rules and boundaries as much as he could, while Maxim clung to them until they crumbled around him. Dimitri collapsed onto the couch beside Leo and let his head fall back to rest on the sofa.

"Elena did well today. Max couldn't stop praising her when he came in," Leo said.

"Oh?" Dimitri felt a flare of pride. Earning Maxim's respect was hard to do. Not that he was surprised. She was a true fighter, and Maxim would respect that.

"It's good she did so well," Leo added, his tone now serious. "Because I believe we're out of time."

They all turned to Leo. "What? What did you see?" Dimitri asked. His stomach knotted as he wondered what level of threat they now faced.

"Vladimir Andropov is bound for the United States. He lands in Los Angeles in a few hours."

"Shit," Nicholas muttered. "I am not a fan of his."

"Is anyone?" Maxim growled. Viktor had been bad enough, but he was a solo assassin. Vladimir was more dangerous because he wouldn't come alone. He would bring an army.

Dimitri leaned forward, resting his elbows on his knees. "How many came with him?"

"He's alone . . . he didn't bring anyone else with him."

Maxim cursed. That meant he was going to activate sleeper agents already present in the United States, people that Leo would have no alerts set for. They were flying blind now.

"You know what we have to do," Maxim replied. His solemn tone made goosebumps break out on Dimitri's arms.

"No," Dimitri said. "No. I won't even consider it."

"We made a vow," Maxim reminded him.

Dimitri jerked to his feet and stalked toward the tall windows that faced the mountains. The sun had set beyond the peaks, and a purple glow had settled over the mountains sloping toward the cabin.

"This is the best place for it. Draw the men here and end it," Maxim said, his thoughts miles ahead, already planning the battle.

"And Elena?" Dimitri asked.

"We will take the little czarina far away," Nicholas said. "Or, I should say, you will. And we'll find a Jane Doe at the morgue to put in her place. When the reports come in, the Kremlin will assume she was caught in the crossfire and killed. She can live the rest of her life quietly out of sight, under a different name—"

"And what? Live some quiet little life in some town, wearing different contacts, always dying her hair? That's not living. And I won't leave you to fight on your own. We agreed we would take her public, give her a chance to have a life and never fear anyone coming after her."

"That was before we knew Vladimir would come after her, he's too high up in the ranks to make the mistake of leaving her alive. He'll do anything he can to kill her. This is the only way. If we survive the fight, then she'll be safe enough for long enough to get her to New York before the United Nations."

Dimitri had the urge to break everything in sight. How could his friends just agree to put themselves in mortal danger and force him to flee with Elena?

"Then you find another man willing to die for her, and he can take her and you can make a noble last stand with us if it comes to it," Nicholas said. He had risen from his chair and paced halfway toward Dimitri.

This time it was Leo who spoke. "We can't outrun them forever. Vladimir won't be as easy to kill as Viktor. You caught Viktor off guard. He didn't know what he was dealing with. But Vladimir will have put the pieces together by now and he'll bring an army with him."

The men he'd considered his brothers had turned against him. They wanted to throw their lives away so he could flee like a coward.

"My father would never have turned his back on his men," Dimitri shot back.

"Didn't he?" Maxim and Leo got to their feet as well. "Your father abandoned his men to avenge your mother. Don't preach to us about his duty to the cause."

That cut too deep. His father had focused on revenge, and never once did he think about his men or his son. But because it was the truth did not make it easy to accept. Far from it. He grabbed the car keys on the counter and headed for the front door. He had to think, had to do something. He had to . . . he honestly didn't know what.

ELENA WAS ALMOST READY TO STEP INTO THE SHOWER when she heard the slam of a distant door. She slipped on a bathrobe and tiptoed into the hallway, pausing in the doorway that led to the great room. Dimitri's friends were speaking softly and urgently in Russian, and she picked out only a few fragments she recognized.

"Must be done . . . plan for it . . . he will come around," Leo said.

"The little czarina . . . she will be fine. A quiet life . . . settle him down," Nicholas said.

"It's up to us," Maxim said. "We make the plans tonight without him. Once he gets back, we'll tell him what he has to do and he'll fall in line."

A chill snaked up her spine. Dimitri was the one who had left? Why? Was he coming back? Panic overwhelmed her, and she sank back against the wall, clutching her chest.

He was coming back. He wouldn't leave her. But even if he did, she had to go on alone. She was strong enough. She had to be. Too many people depended on her now for fear to rule her life another second.

She pushed away from the wall, got control of her breathing, and stepped into the great room, trying not to think about the fact that she had only a bathrobe on.

"Where is Dimitri?"

Guilt showed on all their faces before they masked it with polite innocence.

"He needed some air," Leo hedged.

"A lot of air," Nicholas added.

"What must be done? What are you planning?" Elena kept her tone calm but commanding. "And if you say *nothing*, I will no longer trust any of you, and I'll second-guess every single thing you ask of me from now on." She was bluffing—she had no real power over these men, and they had to know it—but it was worth trying.

Maxim gave Leo the barest hint of a nod.

"Men are coming for you," Leo said.

She clutched the bathrobe tighter around her neck. "How many?"

"We don't know," Leo admitted. "Likely too many."

"When will they be here?"

"It depends on when they find you. I don't believe they know where you went after leaving Malibu. But they won't stop looking until we give them a reason to stop," Leo explained. He dragged a hand through his dark-blond hair and frowned.

"You want to use me as bait?" she guessed.

"Yes. But when they come, we would be sure you would be long gone with Dimitri," Maxim said.

In a burst of sudden clarity, she understood why Dimitri had been angry enough to leave the house. They wanted him to turn tail and run.

"Dimitri doesn't want to do this, does he?"

"No," Maxim said. "He won't put you in danger, nor will he abandon us to fight where we will be heavily outmanned. But we all agreed long ago to give our lives to this fight."

Elena was silent a long moment. "Dimitri said you were all raised in this life together as children. You couldn't possibly agree to something like that so young."

"When we first saw you at the lodge in Utah, we renewed those vows. We will die for you." Maxim spoke with such fierce pride that it made her chest tight.

"And what if I want you to *live* for me instead?"

It was clear none of them had expected that.

"What if we called in some help and set the bait, like you planned?" She was no master tactician, but she had a few ideas.

Nicholas sent her a sympathetic look. "Elena, we can't risk anyone else. You're too important."

"If I'm so important, then listen to me. I have people I can trust who can help. Let me call them. The more people you have helping you, then the less likely it is we'll die right?"

"You won't be here long enough for that, no matter what Dimitri is getting you out of here after we draw them in." Nicholas tried to cut in gently but his words didn't reassure her at all.

"You want me to hide?"

"Until it's safe to go public, yes," Maxim said.

"Your genes are an academic matter," Leo added. "They are nothing without the story. It is the *story* the government fears and a story must go public. But you can't go out there in front of a hundred cameras until we know we've gotten rid of the main threat and sent a message back to the Kremlin. Then it will be your turn."

"My turn?"

Nicholas nodded. "You must *become* the true descendent of Anastasia—not just as a quirk of your DNA, but to see it as your blood right. The entire world must know you for who you are and accept it as fact." The thought made her dizzy, and she clutched the robe between her fingers, wishing it were a suit of armor.

"The whole world," she said, half to herself.

"It's the only way we can make you untouchable." Leo lifted his computer screen and showed it to her. There was a website that listed a United Nations event.

"We would start here. Announce your heritage to the world at this event. You would step in front of the cameras and become the most protected person on the planet."

She couldn't stop the shiver that came with that knowledge. It created an image in her mind of being everywhere, of being a true force in the world. The right person, with the world's spotlight on them, could sometimes accomplish more than even politicians. She thought of the causes she could champion, the lives she could change . . . if she was brave enough to take that step.

"We just have to keep you alive long enough to get you to that dinner." Maxim's dry tone echoed with grim humor. "Should be easy."

"So, tell me your plan," Elena said.

They only had a brief amount of time to discuss things before Dimitri returned, and there was a lot to do if they were to pull this off and avoid as many casualties as possible. She didn't want to think about losing even one of her new friends.

ROYCE STARED AT HIS PHONE; THE SCREEN FADED TO black after the call ended. He sat at the antique desk in one corner of his bedroom, feeling the weight of recent events in a way he'd never expected.

Kenzie watched him with open concern. "What is it?" She lounged on his bed, hair pulled up in a messy bun. She was tapping on her keyboard as she worked on a presentation for one of their classes. She was so damned adorable. But at that moment, his mind was on other things. *Life-and-death things.*

"That was Elena," he said, still processing her words.

Kenzie abandoned her laptop and sat up, swinging her legs off the side of the bed to look at him. "My Elena?"

He got up from the desk and began to pace. "Yes . . ."

"Okay, you're freaking me out. What's with the pacing?"

"Elena said a bunch of Russian agents are in the US looking for her. They don't know her location yet. We need to help draw them in, take them out if we have to, so that Elena has time to get to the United Nations."

"The UN? Why?"

"She's going to announce to the world who she truly is. They think she'll be safe then with the media spotlight on her."

Kenzie's eyes widened. "That's what the dress is for, isn't it?"

Royce nodded. He hadn't wanted to tell Kenzie the full plan. The less she knew the better, at least to keep her safe. But now they were all in this mess knee-deep.

"How bad is this, Royce?"

He let out a sigh and rubbed his temples. "Think every James Bond villain, but on steroids. What we faced with Vadym's men is child's play compared to what's coming after Elena."

Kenzie swallowed hard. He came over to her, cupping her face in his hands. She reached up and curled her fingers around his wrists, clinging to him.

"What do we need to do?" she asked.

"*Me*, not we. You aren't getting anywhere near this."

A protest formed on her lips, but he leaned down and silenced it with a kiss. He would never let her get near danger like that again. When he finally broke the kiss, she was hazy-eyed with desire. She blinked and her eyes narrowed.

"I hate it when you do that."

He grinned. "Do what?"

"Make me forget about whatever you just said. I'm serious, Royce. I want to help."

"I know, babe. But if you really want to help, then I need you to fly to New York. Get the dress finished and accept an important package mailed to Emery's offices in Manhattan. Then contact every major news outlet and tease them with the story of the century that will be happening at the UN gala. The eyes of the world have to be on her or it won't work."

Kenzie was silent for a brief moment. "Fine. But if you get hurt, I will kill you."

He held up his phone. "I'll be all right. I'm calling in reinforcements."

"Call them, then come to bed. I need one more night with you before all this happens . . ."

He stepped into the hall and called Emery, Wes, Fenn, Hans, and Cody. His friends had all been through hell in the last year, but they would come whenever he needed them. That's what friends were for. They would help you bury a body—or in this case, take on a small Russian army to save the descendent of Anastasia Romanov.

❦ 16 ❧

Dimitri parked his car outside of a bar in town. He didn't get out—he simply stared at the merrily lit windows—yet his thoughts were miles away. He didn't want to admit his friends might be right, that they had to set a trap, and then he would get Elena away to safety. It was the only real option they had.

He couldn't let her go to New York alone, nor could he let her stay and fight. It was too dangerous, and too much depended on her. He rested his forehead on the steering wheel for a long moment before he cursed and turned the engine back on.

He drove back up to the cabin. As he entered the front door, he heard his friends still talking. They quieted as he stepped inside. He fumbled nervously with the keys, not quite ready to meet their eyes. He had never really fought like that before with them.

He cleared his throat. "I . . ."

Nicholas smiled. "Go find your little czarina. She is worried about you."

Leo and Maxim nodded, giving silent signals of forgiveness for his outburst. But he still owed them the words.

"You were right . . . about the plan, and about my father. I didn't want to betray you. I didn't want to leave you." What he couldn't say was that he didn't want to leave them to die. He didn't want to be forced to choose between them and Elena.

"We know," Maxim replied with a rare smile. "Now go reassure your *kiska* that you are well."

Dimitri tossed the car keys at Leo, who set them on the counter before Dimitri walked to the master bedroom. He knocked lightly on the closed door, and it was flung open. Elena leapt into his arms. He chuckled as he caught her. She wrapped her arms so tightly around his back he almost felt his ribs crack.

"Where the hell did you go?" she demanded. Her tone was hot with anger, but she didn't release him.

"Just to town and back."

She lifted her head, glowering at him. "You can't just disappear like that. People worry."

"Did you worry?" His tone was gentle as he brushed the backs of his knuckles over her cheek.

Her lashes fluttered down. "What do *you* think?" Then she looked back up and pinned him with a glare. "Don't you dare do that to me ever again."

"I won't," he promised. He moved them both into the bedroom and closed the door behind them, locking it.

"You should shower." She took his hand and pulled him toward the bathroom.

He couldn't disagree. He had sparred with her that afternoon and needed to wash off his sweat, but he sensed that she was after something more now than simply getting him clean. He allowed her to lead him into the expansive master bathroom, aware of the fact that she wore only a bathrobe. He played with the terrycloth sash that was wound around her waist.

"You haven't showered yet either?"

She shook her head. "I wanted to wait *for you*."

There was such power and emotion behind those last two words, *for you*. Now he understood. She had made her decision, and he would give her what she needed and wanted.

Dimitri held his breath as she moved closer to him, pulling at his sweater. He removed it and let it fall to the ground at his feet. Her hands touched his chest, gently exploring him as she raised her head.

"Please be with me tonight, sir."

That single word turned something on inside him, something he had done his best to bury since Utah.

"This is what you truly want, *kiska?*"

She nodded. "I have been thinking a lot about who I am, who I want to be." She kept her hands on him as she spoke. "I was so broken after . . ."

He caught her chin. "You were never broken, *kiska*."

"You keep saying that, but you're wrong."

"*Kiska*..."

"No, listen, you're missing the point. To keep insisting that I was never broken, it's like . . . well, it's like being broken is a mark of shame. But it's not." She smiled, a soft smile that contained a deeper understanding. "Have you ever heard of *kintsukuroi*?"

Dimitri shook his head. He was a little distracted by the feel of her touching him. No woman had ever affected him like this. He belonged to Elena, now and always. She continued to speak as her hands coasted up his shoulders to touch the sides of his neck.

"*Kintsukuroi* is a Japanese art where you take something broken and repair it with gold—like a shattered piece of pottery. You collect the pieces and fuse them together with gold or silver lacquer. Part of the art of it is the acknowledgment that something can become more beautiful for having been broken. Now that simple pot or base is infused with the might and the glitter of gold."

He gazed at her, spellbound by her words.

"I am done pretending that I wasn't broken. Vadym broke me. But I put myself back together, better, stronger, more beautiful. You helped me achieve that." She caressed his neck with light fingertips. "And now I want you, sir. I want you desperately." She met his eyes. "Be the last piece of gold that puts me back together."

She stepped away from him, but he caught her, holding

her close when she would've moved toward the shower. He nuzzled her neck, feeling the thrum of her pulse against his lips.

"You are my endless wonder," he murmured in her ear before he claimed her lips.

It was a kiss that infused his heart with gold. This kiss burned through him brighter than any star, deeper than anything he'd ever imagined. It was a kiss to build a world upon. His body shook as he parted her lips and delved deeper, wanting to burn her taste into his memory so that it would be carved into the marrow of his bones. Her lips curved into a smile, playful and sweet, as she tugged on the strands of his hair. They moved back toward the shower and separated only long enough for her to turn on the water before he dragged her, giggling, back into his arms.

ELENA FELT LIGHT, AS THOUGH A GENTLE MOUNTAIN breeze could lift her up and carry her to faraway places. She was ready. She wanted this, and she wanted Dimitri. The danger that loomed on the horizon had cast a brilliant clarity on her life as to what truly mattered. She thought back to what her father had once said when she'd fallen off a horse during a jump.

"A person who never falls never gains the strength to get up and try again."

Admitting the fact that she had been knocked down by Vadym had been the first step in finding the strength to get back up. She was raising her fists, ready for the next fight, and she was stronger this time. Knowing that made her more hungry to live her life than to be afraid of it.

She escaped Dimitri's arms long enough to peel the bathrobe off her body before she moved back into the steamy shower stall. Her beautiful Russian badass was speechless as he gazed at her. She didn't think about the scars on her back, didn't worry about any of it. It didn't matter anymore. Dimitri stepped toward her, and she held up a finger.

"I think you're forgetting something, *sir*." She emphasized his title with a grin as she pointed at his pants and boots.

The wolfish gleam in his eyes deepened as he kicked off his boots and socks and then reached for his jeans. He unfastened his belt, slipping it free of his jeans and letting it drop before he unzipped the dark denim and tugged the jeans down. Elena's throat caught at the sight of the corded muscles that led down to a set of muscles that formed a *V* shape, which directed her gaze even lower. He slid his briefs off and then stepped toward her.

All power, all strength, all perfect masculinity. And he was hers.

Elena trembled with excitement as she moved deeper into the shower, hot water cascading down her body. He pursued, a slow dance of predator and prey that excited her beyond imagining. This ritual was as old as time, the mating of bodies and souls.

Dimitri caught her waist and gently pressed her against the cool granite wall of the shower, his flesh against hers, sending waves of heat rolling through her. It was as though the fire inside her moved her into him, fusing them together until his blue eyes glowed with a mix of lust and something softer and deeper.

She basked in the magnificence of his naked form—the raw, sinewy, powerful build of him. He was solid as a wall, massive and unyielding, and it made her feel small and feminine, but not weak. She felt in control, knowing her body caused the same reaction in him. His face hid nothing from her. That was the beauty of domination and submission. She gave up herself to him, yet she had the real power. She could see his desire in his eyes. He found joy in her surrender and their mutual pleasure.

Dimitri's hands slid up her sides, his large, calloused palms gentle, but possessive, as he memorized her every curve with his touch. He branded her in a way no scar left by Vadym ever could.

He captured her mouth, kissing her, leaving no room for her to kiss him back. She could only submit as he took what was his. With a soft growl, he turned her around to face the wall.

"Hands," he commanded, and she placed her palms on the wall.

Then he kissed her neck, the shell of her ear, nibbling

on places that made her legs tremble and threaten to give out. His hands slid up her body to her breasts, which were full and heavy. She arched, pressing them against his waiting palms. Her nipples pebbled into hard points and rasped against his skin. He pinched each peak, the hint of pain heightening her building pleasure.

"Are you mine?" His warm breath tickled her ear. The words felt forbidden, that she could belong to no man, but she did. She was *his*, heart, body, and soul. She nodded, and he punished her with a gentle slap on one ass cheek.

"Use your words, *kiska*."

Every nerve in her body came alive at the command.

"Yes, I am yours, sir." The words were her vow to him. No matter what happened, no matter what her bloodline would bring down on them, she was his.

"Tell me you are priceless, *kiska*. That you are beautiful inside and out." He fisted a hand in her hair, his fingers firm but gentle. *Always* gentle, this beautiful, sexy Russian Dom.

"I'm priceless . . . I'm beautiful inside and out." She spoke the words, her heart swelling. She choked down a sob at the sudden joy that filled her. She *believed* the words.

"Now, tell me what you want, *kiska*." He nipped her ear again, and she whimpered as a flash of arousal weakened her knees.

"I need you, sir. I need you to make love to me. I need you to remind me what it feels like."

He rewarded her by turning her in his arms again and kissing her. It was a slow kiss, one that reminded her of summer days, endless sunlight, and the joy of being alive and having the entire world ahead of her.

"I will *always* give you what you need," Dimitri promised. His eyes held hers, his body cradled hers, and she knew then that she loved this man more than her own life.

He lifted her up in his arms, and she parted her legs, wrapping them around his waist. He braced her against the wall of the shower and guided his shaft into her. She tensed for only a heartbeat as he pressed into her. Even in this, he was a gentle giant. She relaxed against him and he sank in, filling her. She had forgotten how it felt to have a man inside her when she was willing. And with him, she was more than willing. She was desperate with longing.

"My beautiful *kiska*," he whispered in Russian as he began to move inside her.

She wrapped her arms around his neck, their bodies moving together in perfect harmony. She covered his face with delicate kisses as they fused together into something greater than either of them alone could ever be. The weariness of past days and months bled away, and she unfurled in his arms, a flower soaking up his sunlight.

Hypnotized by his touch, his kiss, his body, she was swept to a height of pleasure that was so powerful, she could only desperately gasp as she feared she might die. Her mind blanked as she crested, and every dark corner of her memories were bathed in white light. She was undone, unmade, and reforged by sheer pleasure and love for this man.

He held her, his forehead pressed to hers as he gasped for breath. His body trembled as he slowly set her down on her feet. The hot shower rushed over them as he withdrew from her body but kept her tight in his arms.

She raised her gaze to his, droplets coating her lashes. She wiped a hand across her eyes and stared at him in awe, and he at her.

"I love you," she said. She waited for him to say it back, a brief flicker of fear trespassing through her that he might not feel the depth of what she felt for him. He cupped her face, his thumbs smoothing over her cheeks as he smiled. The tiny lines at the corners of his eyes crinkled.

"I have never not loved you, my little *kiska*. From the moment I first saw you. You were mine, and I was yours." This was his way of saying he loved her, and it was everything she had ever dreamed of.

Elena laid her head against his chest. For the first time, she knew she was whole. Not because she loved someone or was loved back, but because she had embraced herself, broken pieces and all, and put herself back together into something more beautiful. Now she had a life again and someone to share it with.

She wasn't going to let anyone take that away from her.

❄

ROYCE MET HANS BRUMMER AT THE PRIVATE AIRFIELD just as the sun was beginning to set. The middle-aged bodyguard was like an older brother to him, and he smiled as Royce got out of his car. Behind Hans, the private jet was fueled and ready to go.

"Everyone here?" Royce asked as he shook his friend's hand. Hans may have had gray streaking his temples, but he was the best man Royce knew on this side of the ocean who could be trusted with the mission ahead.

"Everyone except Fenn, who's already en route. He was in Denver. Cody's packed up everything we need. We pulled out all the stops and brought the fun guns." Hans's tone was light, but Royce knew the man was taking the situation seriously. He knew better than anyone what kind of men they would be facing. They weren't the spoiled minions of Russian mobsters like Vadym's men. They would be dealing with the most dangerous men Russia had to offer.

"Thank you, Hans," Royce said. "You should be enjoying retirement, not gearing up for another fight."

He knew Hans was ready to retire. The man had become a private bodyguard for Royce's childhood best friend, Emery Lockwood, when Emery and his twin brother, Fenn, had been kidnapped. For twenty-five years Fenn's disappearance had never been solved, and Emery had Hans as his faithful shadow to protect him in case danger struck again. But the Lockwood twins had been reunited, and the danger to Emery was over. The bodyguard had every right to ride off into the sunset in pursuit of the life he had sacrificed to protect Emery.

Hans shrugged. "Elena Allen deserves her life back. She's a good kid. No one should take anything else away from her, especially because of her ancestry."

"I agree." Royce followed him up the steps into the plane. The cabin had a limited number of seats compared to a commercial jet, designed for comfort and pleasure. Two men were already seated at a table. The dark-blond man was Emery Lockwood, and the one who sat across from him was Wes Thorne. Both were Royce's age, in their early thirties.

"Royce," Emery called out as he spotted him.

Hans nodded at the men before sitting in another part of the plane, across from a man in his midtwenties with shaggy blond hair. That was Cody Larson. The man who had saved their lives that day in Ulaanbaatar. Cody looked more like a surfer ready to hit the beach than a man raised on the inner-city streets of Chicago. He knew more about tech than anyone Royce had ever met.

The flight attendants closed the door and started securing the cabin for takeoff. Royce grabbed an empty seat beside Wes and across from Emery.

"Kenzie all settled in Manhattan?" Emery asked.

"Yes, thank you for that. I feel better knowing she's at your penthouse with Sophie."

Emery nodded. "Of course. Sophie's glad to help. With all her media contacts, they'll be ready to launch Elena's story the moment you give the word."

"Speaking of," Wes cut in. "How is Miss Allen? Emery told me that she . . ." Wes cleared his throat. "He told me what happened."

Royce curled his hands into fists. Thinking of what Elena had endured at Vadym's hands still haunted him. Emery and Wes were like him, Doms who shared a natural protectiveness for women, and didn't tolerate abuse of women.

"Dimitri says she's doing much better. But now that she's facing all this"—he waved his hand in the air—"assassination bullshit, I don't know. Hell, news like that would've rattled me. I can't imagine what it's done to her."

"Well, she won't be alone," Emery promised.

"No, she won't," Royce agreed. They were bringing their own army. Although it was small, sure, but it was dangerous as hell.

17

Elena sighed as she stretched in bed. She felt good. No, she felt *wonderful*.

For the first time, Dimitri hadn't slipped out of bed before she woke. That too was wonderful, to feel his large, protective presence in bed with her. She rolled on her side to stare at him, her love for him making her chest ache. She reached out and traced her fingertips along his jaw, then down his throat to his chest. He was exquisite, from his dark hair to his full lips. She traced one of his flat nipples and giggled as he slowly opened one eye to peer at her.

His voice rumbled softly, full of amusement. "You are in a good mood, *kiska*."

"I am." After the previous night, she felt like anything was possible.

"Did you enjoy last night?" He reached over to push a stubborn lock of hair from her face.

"I did. I feel amazing." She was completely naked beneath the covers and so was he. She found his thigh under the sheets and slid her hand up it until she grasped his shaft. He was hard, yet he wasn't pushing for her to do anything about it. He simply watched her with a gentle intensity, as though he could keep it up all day.

"Pin me down," she said. She wanted him to trap her beneath his exquisite body.

He cupped her chin. "Forgetting something?" he asked.

A blush crept across her skin.

"Please, sir, pin me down and take me." She was getting bolder at voicing her desires, and it helped that he only ever responded positively to what she asked.

He rolled her onto her back as he came down on top of her. He captured her wrists in one of his hands and pinned them to the mattress above her head. She parted her thighs, letting him settle into the cradle of her body. He kissed her slowly, softly at first, his tongue teasing her until she was wriggling beneath him, desperate to be filled.

There was something wonderful about being at the mercy of a man she trusted, a man she loved, a man who only wanted to give her pleasure. This was how it was supposed to be.

Dimitri slid a hand between their bodies and guided himself into her. She was still a little sore from the previous night, but it was worth it to feel him enter her, connect himself to her in the most primal way. She'd never understood the idea of *casual* sex. This, the joining of two bodies, was the most intimate thing someone could ever do with another person.

When he was all the way in, he stayed still. She tried to lift her hips, urging him to move. He chuckled and nibbled and kissed her throat.

"So impatient, *kiska*." His warm breath against her ear sent waves of sharp arousal down her body and made her clit throb.

"Dimitri!" she yelped as he nipped her a little harder. "Sir," she corrected on a gasp.

"Yes?" He continued to press his lips in sensitive places on her neck.

God, she wanted him so much it hurt. "Please . . ."

"How do you want it?" he asked.

Elena loved that he asked her, but right now she wanted him to take her as *he* wished. She needed him to be the Dom she'd always wanted.

"I am yours . . . use me." She hoped he would understand. She wasn't ready yet to speak freely of her submissive desires.

He lifted his head, his blue eyes sharp on her face as he studied her.

"*Kiska* . . ." He spoke the word with such gentleness she almost cried.

"Please, sir, you know what I need."

Take me, erase the darkness. Fill it with pleasure.

He adjusted his grip on her wrists, keeping them above her head as he braced his other arm beside her. They locked eyes, his gaze silently questioning whether his pinning her down was too much. Her body blushed at the thought of all the things he could do, things she would trust him alone to do if she were truly bound to the bed. She raised her chin and smiled at him, inviting him to keep going. His lips slid into a wolfish grin. She parted her thighs, and he shifted a little.

He thrust deep and hard inside her, taking his pleasure, and within seconds, she was shooting toward that blinding peak, exploding into glittering pieces of ecstasy. She was a creature of pleasure, not pain. She was satisfaction itself as she came apart. But the moment didn't end. He continued to make love to her, delaying his own satisfaction over and over until she was limp and so happy she was nearly delirious with it. She had just enough strength to roll her hips, inviting him to take his pleasure.

He came after her with a shout that shook the bed frame. Dimitri buried his face in her neck, and she lay limp, boneless, too sated to do anything but smile.

"You will kill me, woman." His muffled grumble made her giggle.

She'd finally found it, the relationship she'd always wanted. A Dom who understood her. Dimitri rolled onto his back, bringing her with him, letting her drape over him like a blanket. She pressed her cheek to his chest, counting his heartbeats with exhausted delight.

Someone pounded a fist on the bedroom door.

"Dimitri. Get dressed. We have company," Maxim said through the closed door.

Elena stifled a shriek of surprise as Dimitri flung the covers off their bodies and got up.

"Who is it?" Dimitri called out to Maxim. There had been nothing urgent in his friend's tone, and so he did not appear to be worried.

"Friendlies. Just wanted you to know," Maxim replied.

Dimitri jerked his clothes on. "Friendlies?"

Elena dropped onto her back on the bed. "That's probably Royce. I called him last night."

"You did what?" Dimitri spun to face her, wearing only his hip-hugging blue jeans. She didn't want him to be upset—she wanted him to come back to bed, even though it wasn't possible now.

"When you left last night, we called him. We need backup if we're going to get out of this. I'm not going to let us fight Vladimir alone." She didn't want anyone to die needlessly, and they needed backup. She'd planned on telling Dimitri today, but she didn't know Royce would drop everything and fly here overnight.

"There is no *us*, Elena. You and I will wait for them to know where you are, and then we'll leave—that's it." Dimitri's eyes were stormy, and Elena knew they were headed for a fight, but she wasn't about to back down.

"Yes, there *is* an us. Your friends will be outnumbered. I wasn't going to run and leave them to die, and you don't want to either. I'm not letting you make me the reason they die."

"So you will risk others who have no reason to fight for this?"

She glared at him, stark naked. "No reason? They have every reason. I'm tired of bullies running the world, and so are they. You want me to be a symbol that people can rally around? Being a symbol is more than just showing up and looking pretty for the press. If I am a Romanov, that has to mean something, or else it means nothing. It stops now. It stops with me. Royce and his friends agree with me. This is something they want to do. The Kremlin doesn't have the right to erase any history, especially mine. If they want to kill me, I will make it hard as hell for them."

Dimitri stared at her for a long moment. "Get dressed. We will continue this discussion later." He grabbed his boots and shirt and stalked out of the room.

"No, we won't," Elena muttered to herself.

She took a hasty shower and dried her hair before heading to the great room. The front door was open, and a group of men now lingered at the entrance. Cold winter air blew in with swirls of snow behind them as they all crowded close together, talking as they carried bags inside.

Elena spotted Royce among them. He and Dimitri were speaking, and the look on Royce's usually charming face was hard as stone. A man with dark-red hair was speaking with Leo, who nodded at whatever he was saying. Another man, this one in his late forties with gray hair streaking his temples, was shaking Maxim's hand while he spoke. She recognized him as one of Royce's men from Mongolia. Hans Brummer, Royce's friend and occasional bodyguard.

Another pair of men who were nearly identical in features were lugging massive black cases inside the house. The only difference she could see between the two was that one had slightly longer blond hair and wore cowboy boots. Elena assumed the cases were filled with weapons.

She'd told Royce to come prepared, and he'd assured her he would bring an arsenal.

"It's like a convention of badasses, isn't it?" someone said from behind her. She jumped and turned to see a man close to her age watching the scene unfold. He grinned, hazel eyes glinting with mischief. His shaggy sandy-colored hair made her think of the young men she'd glimpsed in the distance in LA as they carried surfboards toward the beach.

"Yeah, it's kind of scary," she agreed.

"I'm Cody Larson." He held out a hand. "You must be Elena."

She shook it, noting the jagged white scars on the back of his hand.

"Sorry." He pulled his hand away and tugged the sleeve of his sweater down over the scars. "Some asshole with a metal mallet decided to play whack-a-mole with my hand."

Elena's stomach clenched with sympathetic pain. "What happened?"

"Long story. I'd need half a bottle of tequila before I tell that one." Despite his playful smile, his eyes were filled with pain. "I hear you've had shit of your own to deal with."

Elena nodded, feeling insanely self-conscious. It was one thing for Dimitri and Royce to know the details, but these new men were strangers.

"Who . . . who is everyone else?" she asked Cody in a whisper. "I only know Royce and Hans." Even though he was just as devastatingly handsome as these other men, he was far less intimidating.

"The blond guy in the black boots, that's the boss man, Emery Lockwood. He runs Lockwood Industries in New York. The man next to him in the cowboy boots is his twin brother, Fenn. He runs a ranch here in Colorado. They've been through some serious shit too."

"Wait . . . you mean *those* are the Lockwood twins?" She'd grown up hearing about the infamous kidnapping that had happened twenty-five years ago, before she was born.

"That's them." Cody's face was grim. "And the older man, you know him, Hans Brummer."

"Yes, I met him in Mongolia."

Cody suddenly grinned. "That's right. I was the one who messed with the digital billboards and had them flash in Morse code while you guys escaped."

A memory of that day, of being trapped in the car, of it crashing and her escaping from Vadym and his men, flashed across her mind. Cody's message had helped warn Royce that the traffic lights were being tampered with, giving them the chance they needed to reach the embassy. She threw her arms around him, squeezing him tight, her eyes closed as she fought off sudden tears.

"Wow . . . Yeah . . . Hey." Cody patted her back awkwardly until she released him.

"I'm sorry." She wiped at her eyes. "I didn't know you were the one who did that. You saved us all. Thank you."

Red stained Cody's cheeks, and he rubbed the back of his neck. He tried to play it off. "It's cool. Just all part of the job. So . . . right . . . the guy with the red hair, that's Wes Thorne. He's a sort of an art collector."

Cody chuckled. "I know they look like rich playboys, but trust me, they know their shit. Hans has trained all of us, even me."

That helped her relax a little.

Cody then called out to Emery, "Boss man, where should I set up?"

Emery looked to Dimitri, who nodded at Leo. "Cody, you can work with Leo," Emery said.

Cody smiled at Elena again as he slipped past her and followed Leo into a room down the hall.

Having finished talking to the others, Royce came over and hugged her.

"Thank you for coming," she whispered. "Dimitri is upset I called you for help," she warned him.

Royce gave her a wink. "He's fine with it now, I promise. How are you holding up? Kenzie was so worried when you called."

"I'm okay—getting better. Thank you for sending Dimitri to look after me."

He chuckled. "That was all his idea. He might have been a *tiny* bit obsessed with you. I would never have let him follow you to California if I thought it was a bad idea."

"He's been wonderful," she admitted. *The best thing in my life.*

"Be sure to text Kenzie and let her know you're all right," Royce said to her before he called his friends over to start introductions.

Elena stepped back against the wall as the men paraded past her, each one stopping to shake her hand and introduce himself before Nicholas showed them to their rooms.

When at last only she and Dimitri were left in the hallway, he locked the front door. There was a strange finality to the moment, and it made something flutter in her stomach. Was Royce right? Was Dimitri fine with the others showing up now? Royce turned to face her.

"Are you still mad at me for calling in the cavalry?" she asked him.

He stalked toward her, backing her against the wall, an unreadable expression in his eyes as he placed his hands on either side of her head and leaned in.

"I was never mad, *kiska*, only worried. These men are

my friends as well. They are more than capable of helping us, but I fear for every life under this roof, especially yours." He closed the last few inches between them and kissed her. His seduction was so thorough that when he finally pulled away, she'd completely forgotten where she was. Her beautiful Russian badass smiled down at her, far too satisfied with his effect on her.

"One of these days I'll figure out how to do that to you," she warned.

Dimitri stroked a finger down her lips. "I will enjoy every attempt you make." Then he took her hand in his and led her into the great room, where Maxim was waiting for them.

"We have everyone settled in. I've spoken to Hans, and we think we have a plan, if you want to hear it."

"We're listening." Dimitri gave Elena's hand a squeeze. She squeezed his hand back in silent appreciation. They were in this together.

VLADIMIR STOOD OUTSIDE THE BELLAGIO HOTEL IN LAS Vegas, scowling. He was so close, he could feel it. He had tracked Viktor's movements to Malibu, but he hadn't left the city by any traffic or CCTV cameras. There was only one explanation—Viktor was dead, and Vladimir was convinced that the man in the photographs Viktor had sent to his handler was responsible.

Dimitri Razin, the Russian billionaire Elena had been seen kissing, was more than he appeared to be. There had been a photo of Razin, blurry at best, taken in the lobby of the Bellagio the day after Viktor had taken the photos of Elena and Razin together. Razin was now on Vladimir's radar. Whoever he really was, he had smuggled Elena out of California and had hidden her somewhere. Vladimir had run into a dozen dead ends already. It was nearly evening, and he'd had no luck whatsoever tracking down further leads.

His phone vibrated, and he removed it from his pocket. The number showed his office in Moscow.

"Yes?" he answered with a growl.

"Sir?" It was Viktor's handler. "I think we might have something."

Vladimir waited for the nervous man to continue. "Well?" he snapped when the man didn't speak.

"It's a photograph we picked up on social media. We believe it's the girl."

"How certain are you?" Vladimir's eyes scanned the crowds of tourists funneling into the hotel, just in case.

"It's a seventy-eight percent match."

"Where is she?"

"Colorado, the resort town of Steamboat Springs. She was outside a restaurant."

"Book me a flight there now. I'm headed to the airport. Activate the nearest agents in Colorado. I want at least thirty men to meet me there."

"Yes, sir." The handler hung up.

Vladimir's hands twitched. Soon he would kill the girl and rid himself of the liability her existence posed. It might even result in a promotion if he played his cards right.

18

Elena fell into a rhythm over the next few days. Each day she trained for two hours with Dimitri and Maxim in the exercise room. Then Hans took her out into the woods behind the cabin to practice shooting a gun. Guns made her nervous, but the bodyguard had an easy way about him that put her at ease. He showed her the different kinds of handguns she might encounter, but when it came to firing, she used one with a silencer so the cabins a mile away on either side wouldn't hear the steady stream of gunfire. They didn't want to draw attention to their activities from the local authorities.

"Feel the weight, and prepare for the kick. Remember, squeeze, don't yank." Hans adjusted her stance, and she pulled the trigger. The tin can sitting on a stump didn't move, but she could tell she'd hit the stump below it, so her aim wasn't that far off. She frowned and bit her lip, wishing her aim had been better.

"It's easier to hit a body than a can," Hans said. "The target is much bigger."

"It's even harder to think about hitting a body." She shivered at the thought of taking a life. She wasn't a killer.

Hans took the gun from her hand and flipped the safety on.

"Sometimes you have to let your lizard brain take over."

"My lizard brain?"

He tapped her temple. "Yes, the part of you that developed survival instincts millions of years ago. There's a fancy term that scientists named your lizard brain, but what it boils down to is your gut, your instincts. These men coming after you have one goal: to kill you. There will be no mercy, no chance to reason with them. They will just act. So you must as well."

He was right, but Elena didn't like to admit it. If it came down to it, she might have to kill someone to live.

"The men they send here won't be innocent or novices —they will be hardened killers with blood on their hands. They will murder whoever they are told to without question. That's who you are fighting. Some might argue they are fighting for their country or some other bullshit, but if their government is afraid of a twenty-year-old girl for no reason other than her ancestry . . . well, that government has bigger problems and shouldn't be in charge. Point is, you don't owe these men any mercy."

Elena swallowed hard and stared at the snowy woods. The sunlight had emerged from the cloud bank and lit up the dusting of snow that had fallen the night before like diamonds. Soon these quiet woods would be full of violence.

She pulled her coat tight around her. "Let's go back inside." Hans put a hand on her back, indicating for her to go ahead of him.

Inside, the house had changed. Furniture had been moved around to provide clear pathways, windows had been boarded up on the ground floor, and strange reflective panels had been installed along many of the thinner walls. Cody had explained that they were meant to reflect any heat detection systems from the outside. So if anyone was attempting to get an accurate reading of how many people were in the house, they wouldn't be able to.

Hans set the gun on the kitchen counter, and Elena dropped into a chair next to Leo, who was working furiously on his keyboard. Cody sat next to him, his own laptop open. The two of them spoke occasionally, checking each other's screens and speaking in a tech language that left Elena completely baffled. The two men hooted in triumph, and Cody held up his hand for a high five, which Leo gave with a boyish grin.

"What are you guys doing?" she asked.

Leo turned his smile on her. "Well, we just found a back door in the Department of Homeland Security."

"And I've gotten permission from the boss man to use my new drone." Cody cracked his knuckles and leaned back in his chair with a cocky grin.

"A drone?"

"Yep, the boss man has military contracts. We've been working on a prototype that flies low enough to go unnoticed by most government systems. If we fly that over the woods, I'll be able to see their heat signatures coming up on us. We'll know how many there are and where they are."

"That's incredible," Elena said. It boggled her mind that they actually had access to that level of technology.

"Dimitri asked for you to come find him when you're done," Leo said before he and Cody resumed their discussion.

Elena, not for the first time, was aware that she was the only woman in a house full of dangerous men. It unnerved her a little, even though none of them were a threat to her. She left the kitchen and began searching the house until she found Dimitri in the loft, which had a relaxing den with a sectional and a big-screen TV.

Maxim sat beside him on the couch, and they were speaking together softly in Russian. They stopped when they spotted her coming up the stairs. Maxim got up and nodded at Elena before excusing himself.

Dimitri patted the seat next to him. She came over, glad for a chance to cuddle up. He curled an arm around her shoulders and, not saying a word, she closed her eyes. Just being with him always brought on a wave of peace. She drifted off for a moment, only feeling a little guilty that he probably had better things to do than be her personal pillow.

Sometime later, she was shaken awake by a gentle hand on her shoulder.

"*Kiska*, it's time. You need to eat and drink some water." Dimitri stood over her. Darkness had fallen outside.

"It's time?"

"Yes." Dimitri stroked her hair back from her face. "Leo spotted Vladimir in town a few hours ago. Fenn and Maxim were able to put a tracker on his car and have been keeping tabs on him, waiting to see what he'd do. He's now headed up the mountain."

Elena sat up, rubbing at her face as she tried to shrug off her weariness. Panic was starting to take over.

"How are you so calm?" she asked him.

He gave a wry smile as he stroked her cheek. "Because I've trained for this my whole life. Now come and eat. Then we'll get you ready."

She followed Dimitri into the kitchen, where everyone was eating protein bars and drinking bottles of water. They were all quiet except for Cody, who was calling out updates on where Vladimir's car was.

"He's one mile out, but he stopped alongside the road," Cody said.

Leo frowned and bent over his laptop. Maxim was pulling a Kevlar vest out of a black duffel bag.

"Eat quickly," Dimitri urged. Elena hastily chewed on a protein bar and drank a bottle of water, but her stomach churned. She had to concentrate on something else or risk throwing up. Dimitri took the vest from Maxim.

"Come here." Dimitri led her into the bedroom and helped her remove her sweater, then put the Kevlar vest over her white tank top and covered it with the sweater.

"You will have a backpack with food, water, a space blanket, and a satellite phone. If we get separated, you will have what you need to survive for a few days. There is a list of numbers to call if something happens to me or any of us and you're left alone."

She gripped his sweater, halting him when he tried to turn away. "Nothing is going to happen to you, right?"

He caught her hand in his, kissing her fingers. "We will be all right," he promised, but for the first time, she feared Dimitri was lying.

Emery appeared in the doorway of the master bedroom. "Leo said he picked up on thirty heat signatures moving up the mountain toward us."

"Thirty? On foot?" Dimitri asked.

"Yes. Cody thinks Vladimir met his agents in the woods."

Dimitri urged Elena toward the door. "We must go."

As he turned her toward the garage and away from the other men, she heard Maxim address them in the great room.

"Leave no one alive. If any of them report back, Elena will continue to be in danger. If you have a problem with that, speak up now."

No one said a word.

This last image of the small army defending her was burned into her brain. If she lost even one of them, she would never be able to live with herself.

Dimitri pulled her through the garage door. The cold wind from the winter snow made her nose tingle. It was dark and quiet in the garage, but she saw distant moonlight ahead. The large garage door was open. She knew the plan. They would leave on foot to reach a car they had hidden farther away. The others were to stay behind. This was the only way, get her out before the house was surrounded so their plan to draw in Vladimir and his men could work. Then they had to wait . . . wait to see who survived. It was a plan she hated because if felt like she was just running away, but she knew that if she stayed behind she would be a liability. She had to be at a safe distance so they could focus on removing the threat.

Elena held Dimitri's hand as they hurried through the snowy woods. She turned back at one point, saw the stoic Emery Lockwood standing at the edge of the driveway still watching them. He held up a solemn hand in farewell. A chill of dread raked its way along her skin.

Be safe . . . She sent the silent prayer as she turned to face the woods again. She and Dimitri ran in silence. The only sounds were of their breathing and the crunch of powdery snow beneath their boots. The backpack slung over her shoulders was thankfully lightweight, but she knew if she had to keep going for hours it would begin to feel heavy.

"How far are we going?" she whispered.

"Another half mile," Dimitri murmured back.

The white birch trees that filled the woods seemed to watch them with a thousand dark eyes. She tried not to picture Russian agents crawling through the woods toward her friends. She didn't want anyone dying for her, but there was no real choice. They'd started this fight, and she and her friends had to finish it.

CODY STARED AT THE FIGURES ON HIS MONITOR AS THEY advanced toward the cabin. The trip wires they'd set sent flares into the sky as they were triggered by the enemy. Every major entry point was covered by someone inside the house. The fingers of his scarred hand twitched as memories of old pain came back. He closed his eyes, drew in a deep breath, and pictured himself deep beneath the ocean, the water above him rippling with sunlight.

Hans put a hand on his shoulder. "You okay, kid?"

Cody opened his eyes. "Yeah." He reached for the handgun next to his laptop. "Give everyone the signal."

Hans tapped on the small communication device nestled in his ear. The tap reverberated in Cody's ears as it came through the comm. They weren't to speak using the comms unless necessary since it would be easy for the Russians to pick up any chatter as they got closer.

Cody closed his laptop, slipped it under the table, and put on his thermal goggles, raised up until needed. Then he and Hans took up their positions by a window near the kitchen. A moment later, the window exploded. Cody and Hans dove to the floor as glass rained down around them. Hans shielded Cody's head before he scrambled up and opened fire through the gaping hole where the window had been. Cody crawled across the floor to the other side of the window and peeked up over the sill, sweeping the woods for heat signatures. Two figures were partially visible behind trees. He remembered what Hans had told him.

"If you are to my right, shoot the targets on your right." Cody unloaded several rounds at the figure on his right before he had to duck back down. The explosion of return gunfire was deafening. Someone in the woods shot a flare gun straight at them, blinding him through the thermal goggles.

"Fuck!" He ducked down again as his eyes burned in his skull from the bright flare, and he flipped them up. In a vengeful haze, he reached for a flash-bang strapped to his Kevlar vest and hurled it into the woods.

"Going bright!" he called through the comms a second before the flash-bang went off. More shots came through the windows, shattering wood cabinets and dishware.

Pain tore through Cody's shoulder, and he fell back below the sill, clutching his shoulder and cursing a blue streak. Hans was there, holding a hand to the wound as he tried to see it in the dark.

"You hit?"

"Just a graze," Cody panted through the pain. "I think."

Hans pulled him up to a sitting position and dragged him away from the windows.

The gunfire continued. It sounded like the shots from the woods were getting closer.

"Dammit," Cody gasped. He couldn't finish because Hans was binding his wound with a strip of duct tape.

"Duct tape? Are you kidding me?"

"Handyman's secret weapon," Hans said.

Cody clutched his gun against his chest as he met his friend's gaze. "I knew the odds were bad . . . But . . ."

"What is it you always say from that movie, kid? Never tell me the odds?" Then Hans rushed back into the fray just as the Russians breached the cabin.

ELENA STUMBLED THE SECOND THE FLARES BEGAN arcing in the sky and the shooting echoed in the distance. Dimitri caught her, holding her close. In his other arm, he held a firm grip on a sniper rifle with a flash suppressor. They both stood silent for a moment, listening. Dimitri adjusted his grip on the rifle, his gaze locked on the woods leading back to the cabin. She knew what he was thinking, and she felt it too. Another flare lit the sky as more men set off the snares they'd set up around the cabin.

"Oh God, Dimitri, we have to go back." She turned toward the sound of danger, needing to be there, to stand alongside the men who were risking their lives for her.

"No, we have to keep moving."

Dimitri spun her to face away from the cabin. Her eyes blurred with tears as she tried to follow him.

A few moments later, a deafening explosion behind them sent them both tumbling to the ground. Dimitri covered her body with his. When they got their bearings back, she looked over her shoulder. Part of the cabin was on fire. She saw the agony carved into his features. The urge for them both to go back deepened.

He surged to his feet, lifting her up with him. They started to run even faster toward the escape route they'd planned. In the distance, she saw the SUV ahead of them. Dimitri pulled his gun out and froze, halting her beside him, and then he moved them both behind a tree. He lifted his rifle up, sweeping it across the woods, searching. If he fired, the flash suppressor would keep their location concealed more easily, but any shot fired would still give away their general location.

"Dimi—"

"Shh . . ." He continued to scan the woods.

Elena pressed close to him, blood roaring in her ears. Her eyes scanned the darkness. Between shafts of moonlight, she saw several figures sweeping in on them. They were surrounded. He picked off three men with his rifle before they both faced the awful truth—they were heavily outnumbered.

"Dimitri," she gasped, terror squeezing her chest of all breath.

He held her tight, his lips touching her ear. "Whatever happens, know that I love you, *kiska*." Then he shoved her down into the snow and rushed into the open, drawing the fire of the men advancing on them. Time slowed down, like a nightmare where her legs wouldn't move. Dimitri was hit—once, twice, three times—and fell in a hail of gunfire and lay still twenty yards away.

She was frozen in place, unable to tear her gaze away from Dimitri's body. *No, no, no* . . . She took a step, but bullets fired, digging into the trees around her, and that more than anything forced her back into motion. She had to draw the men and their fire away from Dimitri. If she ran, these men would follow . . . and maybe Royce and the others could find Dimitri. It was the only way she had to save him, even if it was but a sliver of fast-fading hope.

Elena had a mere second to react. She sprinted

toward the SUV, but something arced in the air over her head, and in the next second, the SUV exploded in a fireball.

Elena was blown back, landing in the snow, ears ringing and vision blurred. As she regained her breath, three men dressed in black advanced, guns pointed at her. The man in front pulled off a black ski mask and goggles and tossed them to the ground. He looked older in person than she had expected, but she recognized him from the surveillance pictures Leo had shown her.

"Vladimir," she whispered.

"Ms. Allen." Vladimir nodded at the men on either side of him. They bent and grabbed her arms, hauling her up onto her feet. Somewhere along the way she'd lost her backpack, but that didn't matter now. Nothing did. She wasn't getting away from this.

They dragged her deeper into the woods, and with each step Elena's body grew heavier as the shock of what had just happened wore off. Dimitri was dead. Odds were, most of the other men were too. She didn't want to go one step farther, not now, not ever. Dimitri had become her world, and now she was alone. She didn't think that she would ever love anyone but him. It was strange, but she knew it was the truth. Deep in her heart, there was no other but him.

She jerked free of the men who held her. Vladimir held up a hand when one of the men raised his hand, ready to strike her. The man lowered his arm.

Vladimir scrutinized her. "You look so like your mother."

Her heart began to skitter wildly. "My mother?" She hadn't expected him to speak. She'd been told they'd just kill her without hesitation.

"Your birth mother, of course. I was sent to kill her twenty years ago. She got away. She was pregnant with you, and I assumed she would die in the snowstorm. I never imagined she would survive long enough to get to a hospital. To find you alive after all these years . . ." He frowned. "And to learn what you really are . . ." Vladimir slowly reached out and gripped her hair in his hand as though fascinated.

"A Romanov. Anastasia's blood runs through your veins." He smiled wryly. "So little, too, only twelve point five percent, but it is enough to warrant your death."

Elena was numb as she stared back at him. "I was no one, just a woman living a quiet life. You could have left me alone to live my life."

"Perhaps. But so long as you lived, there was always the risk of someone finding you and using you as a symbol. There have been pretenders before, but even if any of them had been heirs, it was impossible to prove. You, however . . . the proof lies within your very blood for all to see. And that proof gives others hope." He looked at the other two men. "Leave us. I will kill her myself."

The two men walked away into the now silent woods. The fight—her fight—was over. Vladimir raised his gun, aiming at her chest, then changed his mind and began to raise his gun to her head.

Elena's life flickered before her eyes, moments of bliss and pain in equal measure, moments that had changed her forever. Her mother holding her when she'd skinned her knee riding her bike. Her father hugging her the day she'd graduated high school and shown him her college acceptance letter. Dimitri holding her in the waves. Maxim, Leo, and Nicholas kneeling before her, tying their fate to hers. The faces of the men in the cabin as she glimpsed them one last time . . .

A million different memories blended and merged into one single final image, an image that changed everything. It wasn't even her memory, but that of a young woman from more than a century ago. Staring down a firing squad of soldiers in a dark basement, men who believed violence was the only way to change the world.

That girl had survived against all odds, and Elena as her descendant owed it to her to never give up. If Elena died now, everything that girl and all who came after her had gone through would be for nothing.

Elena bowed her head as Vladimir's gun moved toward her head. Then she struck out, knocking his arm up and away, sending the gun deep into a snowbank.

Vladimir recovered fast and lunged for her as she turned to run. He gripped her arm from behind, the other arm going around her throat. Adrenaline spiked through her, but instead of struggling, she turned right into him while jabbing her free hand, thumb out, straight at his face.

He hadn't expected that. With a grunt, he jerked back, and she twisted farther in his direction, giving him a swift knee to the groin. The second her knee connected, he landed a blow to her temple. Elena staggered back, but now that she was free, she bolted.

"Stop her!" Vladimir cried.

Elena heard the other men charge after her. She had abandoned the shelter of the deep woods when the two men circled her from the front, guns raised. She skidded to a stop, hoping to duck behind a tree, but there were none to be found.

Then one of the men who had his gun trained on her turned and shot the man next to him. Elena stared at the fallen man, not quite sure she understood what had happened. The man left standing removed his mask and thermal goggles.

Cody grinned at her. "I always wanted to do that. Pretend to be one of the bad guys, I mean, not shoot some random asshole."

"Cody?" Elena stared at him.

She had a mere second to process what had happened before Cody yelled and tackled her to the ground. Bullets peppered the snow all around them as Vladimir opened fire. Then everything went deathly still. Elena and Cody cautiously raised their heads to look. Vladimir was lying on his side, blood pooling from a hole between his eyes. A dozen feet behind him, Dimitri stood, one hand gripping his side and his other holding a gun.

Elena blinked, trying to clear her vision.

"I've been wondering where the hell you were." Cody got up and helped Elena stand. Her legs shook as she ran to Dimitri and fell against him.

"How many are left?" Dimitri asked.

Cody nodded at Vladimir's body. "He was the last one."

"You're sure?"

"Whole reason I'm out here and not back there."

Elena was barely listening. She was focused on searching him for wounds. She pushed aside his coat, and her fingers came into contact with the Kevlar vest beneath his sweater, which was riddled with bullet holes.

Dimitri hissed as she came across a place where a bullet had grazed him beneath the edge of the vest.

"Sorry . . ." She pulled her hands away.

Dimitri pulled her toward him. "I'm all right, *kiska*."

She closed her eyes, her breath coming shorter and shorter as she started to cry. Dimitri hushed her, making soothing sounds that eventually reached her through the haze of her adrenaline crash. She hated that she couldn't stop shaking now that it was all over.

"Cody . . . how many did we . . . ?" Dimitri couldn't finish.

"No one when I left. Hans got out after the majority of the fight. He told me to find you guys. When I left, everyone was holding their own against the last two they had pinned down, but the fire in the cabin was getting bad. If anyone got trapped inside . . ."

They turned to face the distant cabin, which blazed like a black skeleton against the orange flames.

DIMITRI IGNORED THE PAIN OF HIS BROKEN RIBS AND the slow burn of the two places where he had been grazed by bullets. Adrenaline kept him going as he, Elena, and Cody hurried back to the cabin. Cody touched base with Hans, who gave them the all-clear via the comms to return.

Dimitri spotted Fenn Lockwood as they reached the open garage. Fenn was moving the SUVs into the driveway with Leo and Emery, to keep them away from the flames.

"Maxim! They're here!" Leo roared over the sound of the fire.

From the darkness of the garage, Maxim emerged. He visibly relaxed at seeing them all alive.

"Did we lose anyone?" Dimitri asked.

Maxim shook his head and touched Dimitri's shoulder in concern. "Nicholas and Hans have shoulder wounds, and Emery has a through-and-through on his right arm, but the rest made it out okay other than just minor scrapes. You?"

Dimitri slumped a little. "I've been better." He was exhausted, but he couldn't stop now. Any moment the local authorities would be here. They would have to explain everything, and they didn't have time for that. Elena needed to get out of here fast. The others could handle the locals.

"Dimitri, go. Devereaux's plane is waiting at the airport," Maxim said, as if reading Dimitri's mind.

"We can't leave you."

"The danger for us is over now, but if you don't get her to New York, she will never be safe. Staying to deal with the authorities will only give the Russians another chance at her."

Royce came over and hugged Elena. "Come on, kid, let's get you on that plane." He pointed at one of the SUVs. "Dimitri, move it."

"Keep me informed," Dimitri ordered Maxim. The other man nodded.

His friends were right, Dimitri thought. Elena had to get to New York. The gala was in a few days, and they had to be ready.

Dimitri put an arm around Elena's waist as they got into the back of the SUV. Royce was in the driver's seat and Cody in the passenger seat. Dimitri pulled Elena to his side, ignoring the stabbing pain in his ribs. She was almost deathly still against him, and more than once, he pressed his lips to her forehead, just to feel her shift at his touch. It reassured him she was all right.

By the time they got into Royce's private jet, they both collapsed into a pair of chairs.

"Relax. I'll take it from here," Royce assured him as he and Cody spoke with the flight crew.

Dimitri wasn't used to letting someone else handle things, but he had to acknowledge that he couldn't stay awake. The stress and fear of the last few hours had taken a toll on him.

The flight took a little over three and a half hours, and Dimitri slept through all of it, Elena burrowed against his side. He woke when the plane landed. Elena was still dead to the world, and he hated to wake her. Part of him just wanted to stay right here and hold her forever. But they had to move.

"I have a car waiting for us," Royce whispered as the flight attendant opened the door and secured the stairs of the plane for them to leave. Dimitri tried to lift Elena up, wincing as his ribs protested. He set her back down in the seat, and she stirred and yawned.

He tried not to think about those moments after he had fallen, when the bullets hitting his vest had knocked him unconscious and they'd left him for dead. He had woken to find her gone and had feared the worst. That panicked flight through the woods, until he'd found Vladimir, had been one of the most terrifying experiences of his life.

"Where are we?"

"New York. Can you walk to the car?" Dimitri would

have carried her, but in his condition, he didn't think he would make it very far.

"I can." She descended the steps and walked ahead of him.

Dimitri paused to speak to Royce as they both watched her. "Part of me thinks this is a dream, that we haven't even fought yet." Dimitri rubbed his eyes.

"I know. It's hard to believe the nightmare will soon be over."

Dimitri chuckled. "Don't jinx it," he said in his American tourist accent.

The SUV door opened, and Kenzie emerged. She ran to Elena, hugging her, and then spotted Royce and rushed toward him. Dimitri got down the steps just in time to let Kenzie speed past him and throw herself at Royce.

"You're okay!" Kenzie gasped. "You're all okay."

Royce kissed Kenzie hard and held her tight, his eyes closed as he simply sighed. "We are, sweetheart. We're all okay."

Dimitri swallowed hard and turned to see Elena standing by the SUV. Dawn was breaking over the horizon as he joined her.

She asked as he cupped her face in his hands, "It's really over?" Her green eyes were dark and luminous, reminding him of the soft glow of fireflies.

"Almost. There is still the UN dinner. That will decide everything."

"I can face anything as long as you're with me." She

stood on her tiptoes as he leaned down and captured her mouth with his, love exploding through every cell in his body.

He drew Elena closer to him, and she pressed another kiss to his lips, easing his battered soul. One last battle remained. Now they had to show Elena to the world and hope it would be enough to protect her.

❧ 19 ❧

Three days later
Elena opened the large white dress box that Kenzie had carried into the hotel room. White tissue paper bound by gold ribbons shielded the gown from view.

"Go on," Kenzie urged. "We don't have much time. The gala will be starting soon."

Elena removed the ribbon and tissue paper to reveal a cream silk and blue velvet gown. Gold embroidered the bodice and cream silk underskirt. The blue velvet sleeves were cut open and draped loosely, and the blue overskirt fell in the back in a long, lazy train, embroidered in bright gold thread. She turned to Kenzie in awe.

"This is modeled after the Romanov gowns, the ones the family wore right before . . ."Elena breathed in shock.

"Yes." Kenzie cleared her throat. "You are a Romanov,

and it is time we show the world." Kenzie helped her dress, which she hadn't expected, but the old-world design definitely required a second person behind to fasten up the back. Then Kenzie retrieved one more box.

"There's just one more thing you need."

Elena lifted the lid off the dark-blue box, revealing a diamond-studded tiara nestled in velvet.

"Oh my God . . ."

"It came with a note." Kenzie pulled out a small white envelope from her pocket and handed it to Elena. With trembling hands, Elena pulled out a small note card embossed with the logo of Buckingham Palace at the top.

MISS ALLEN,

This was in my safekeeping. Now it must be returned to the family it rightfully belongs to.

Elizabeth R.

GOOSEBUMPS BROKE OUT OVER ELENA'S SKIN AS SHE looked from the note to Kenzie's face.

"*The* Elizabeth?"

Kenzie nodded. "You are technically related, albeit distantly, to the British royal family. Now let's put it on and get you downstairs."

Kenzie set the box on a nearby table and removed the tiara that had belonged to Alexandra, Anastasia's mother, the last empress of Russia. The tiara was heavy as it settled upon Elena's brow, but she welcomed the weight. If she could have the world accept her for who she was, then perhaps they would listen to what she had to say and help her make the world a better place. It could be the start of something amazing.

She'd come so far in the last three days. Men like Dimitri and his friends had been willing to die for her, because they believed she could make the world a better place. Could she? It was a sobering thought, one that had resonated deep within her. She owed those men and so many others, but she didn't want to help the world out of guilt. She wanted to change the world because she wanted to help.

Kenzie covered her mouth with one hand, tears glimmering in her eyes. "I think you're ready."

"I am," Elena said softly, but it meant much more than Kenzie could ever know. Elena drew in a deep breath and stepped into the hall to meet her destiny.

DIMITRI PACED THE HALL ANXIOUSLY. BELOW HIM, A SET of grand stairs led to a large ballroom where the ambassadors of a hundred nations mingled and sipped wine. Light music played from a small orchestra, and Dimitri felt every note move through him as he waited for Elena to leave her suite of rooms.

"Dimitri, you must be calm." Maxim caught his arm and halted him. "Remember, this appearance is a statement. A statement of fact. It will not do for the press to see you so uncomfortable."

Dimitri nodded, regaining his composure.

A door down the hall opened. Elena emerged, the diamond tiara of her great-great-grandmother resting upon her brow as she walked toward them.

In a blinding flash, he remembered the portrait that hung in the palace that had been his childhood home. The portrait of the young grand duchess, Anastasia. He saw the duchess so clearly in Elena's features now, and he wondered how he had ever missed it. His breath halted in his lungs. Kenzie had outdone herself with the historical re-creation. It was as though Anastasia herself was walking toward him.

As Elena reached him, he and Maxim bowed formally to her. They wore tuxedos so that he and Maxim could blend in a bit easier with the guests attending the dinner. Until Elena had a chance to speak before the members of the UN, there was still the potential of danger.

"How do I look?" Elena's tone was as tense as he felt.

"You look radiant, *kiska*," Dimitri assured her. "Are you ready to change history?"

He offered her his arm. Elena straightened a little, tranquility smoothing over her face. She nodded.

They descended the stairs, and thanks to a perfectly timed press release a few hours ago by Sophie Lockwood's news connections, the last descendent of Anastasia Romanov entered the crowd at the United Nations humanitarian awards gala and had every eye in the room fall upon her with excitement. Dimitri held Elena's slightly trembling arm as face after face turned her way.

The reaction of only one person truly mattered tonight. The Russian ambassador, Fyodor Turgenev. His junior advisor leaned in to show him something on his phone and to frantically whisper in his ear. The ambassador's eyes moved from the phone's screen to Elena as she proceeded through the room. Within seconds, men and women crowded Elena, desperate to speak with her. The secretary-general of the United Nations, Mr. António Guterres of Portugal, reached Elena first and bowed.

"Miss Allen. I was just informed by my staff that you are scheduled to address the guests before we present the awards. If you would follow me." He waved for her to follow him, and Dimitri let go of her arm. She proceeded alone with the secretary-general toward the main dais.

The Russian ambassador sidled up beside Dimitri.

"Very clever of you, Mr. Razin," the man said softly, just loud enough for Dimitri to hear. Dimitri smirked. There was nothing the man could do to him here.

"I'm sure you're aware of what happened in Colorado. Not one of your agents survived."

"I have no idea what you're talking about."

"Of course not. Nevertheless, I think you will find it will not be so easy to get to Elena again after this."

"She is certainly about to catch the world spotlight," Turgenev conceded. "For a time."

Dimitri played with the golden phoenix ring around his pinky finger, drawing the ambassador's attention to it. "Look around this room, Ambassador. Every man and woman bearing one of these rings here tonight stands between you and Miss Allen. The White Army is back, and our numbers are greater than you realize." It had been a true miracle earlier that day when Leo had told Dimitri that he'd managed to contact more than three hundred members in the last week, and they'd all promised to come for the event. Dimitri had never seen so many men and women from the White Army in one place before. According to Leo, there were nearly ten thousand members spread out across the globe, and all knew of Elena and had sworn to aid her in whatever cause she chose to fight for.

The ambassador cast a glance around. Nearly a hundred men and women in the ballroom had their eyes trained on him rather than Elena. Each wore the same signet ring.

"What is it you want, Razin? She will never rule Russia. The age of monarchs is over. Even in countries that cling to the traditions, they are merely powerless figureheads. The house of Romanov can never be restored."

Dimitri flashed him a dangerous smile. "She doesn't want or need a throne. But she will claim the hearts of every man and woman out there who believes in a better future. The strongest rebellions burn with the fire of hope."

The ambassador scowled. "You may be protected here, but you won't have this protection on Russian soil." Then the ambassador spun on his heel and stalked away, shoving several delegates out of his path. Dimitri smiled and turned his attention to the dais as Elena began to speak to the crowd.

"Tonight, we celebrate the humanitarian awards. People who promote the welfare of all mankind and prevent suffering are honored tonight. But we face a grave crisis in this modern age. I was held captive for two months in Moscow, a victim of sex trafficking. A problem that we have become comfortable lying to ourselves about, pretending it rarely, if ever, happens. I have come to tell you the truth.

"This is a worldwide problem, one that grows with each passing day. Women are targeted in every country at almost every age. And while it seems unfathomable to those present here, it is not a problem that is going to go away.

"However, the people in this room have the power to change that. I am here today to ask you what you can do, what your nation can do, to make the world a better place. To respect and enforce the human rights these United Nations are supposed to stand for."

She didn't mention her ancestry. That was never the plan. The media had been told enough and would uncover the rest on their own. But this wasn't about grandstanding. The message tonight couldn't be seen as being about her. It was about all those who couldn't be there to speak. This was her true calling, to speak for those without voices.

As Elena continued to speak, Dimitri was spellbound by the changes she had undergone. Gone was the frightened college girl who jumped at every shadow. The woman before him rivaled even the empress she was descended from. She was grace, dignity, and courage. A beacon of hope.

Leo, Maxim, and Nicholas stood next to Dimitri, and the tight knot of concern he'd had began to ease.

"I wish my father and mother could have seen this," he murmured to his friends. "He would say we're witnessing the birth of something wondrous."

Leo placed a hand on his shoulder. "She is magnificent."

Dimitri's throat tightened with emotion. She *was* magnificent, and he would spend the rest of his life devoted to loving her.

EPILOGUE

Four *months later*

Elena reclined on the deck of the sailboat, watching Dimitri work the ropes that moved the sails. He was shirtless and barefoot, wearing only a pair of navy-blue-and-white swim trunks. The setting sun made the light sheen of sweat glisten on his muscled physique, reminding her of the pleasant—more than pleasant—day they had spent in bed at a small bed-and-breakfast in the town of Camden off the coast of Maine.

Dimitri had spent hours worshiping her body, and she was delightfully exhausted . . . if a little sore from it. Not that she minded. He knew what she needed and never hesitated to give it to her.

"What are you thinking about?" he asked as he secured the sails and came to sit beside her on the deck. She lay back, gazing at the gold sky that was surrendering to evening purples.

"I was thinking about you," she answered honestly.

"Ah. And what do you think of me?"

He leaned over to kiss the tip of her nose, and her heart melted at the playful smile on his lips. He had relaxed so much in the last few months, becoming the person he was meant to be. A man who smiled more, laughed often, and did not stare at the shadows with worry in his eyes.

"That day in Colorado, when I saw you get shot . . . I never even had the chance to say again that I loved you. That was all I could think . . . that I wished we had had more time." Her words suddenly choked her a little.

"We have time now, *kiska*," he promised her. "Time enough to say *I love you* and perhaps a bit more." He trailed his fingertips along her collarbone above her sensible one-piece bathing suit.

"I love you," she said again, needing him to hear the words.

He leaned in to kiss her and nuzzled her cheek. Nothing else could be so perfect in the world as lying in the sun beside him and feeling him kiss her like this.

After her speech in front of the United Nations, she'd been swamped by the press. Naturally, the question of her ancestry was grabbing the spotlight, but Dimitri's friends had already arranged for all the proof they could ask for to be made available.

With that settled, the hot topic became her experience as a captive, something she did not want to relive so publicly, but she knew it was a necessary step to get the narrative pointed in the direction she wanted. It didn't take long to turn her personal tragedy into the story of countless others. People were starting to listen, not because of who she was, but what she had to say.

She'd spent months working with several countries on strategies to stop human trafficking, including increased communication between police agencies and refugee arrangements for those rescued far from home. Far from just being the public face of this crusade, she'd poured herself into study, understanding the difficulties involved in tackling this problem and proposing solutions.

Then, at Dimitri's insistence, they'd taken a much-needed vacation to see her parents in Maine. She'd had to hide her laughter the first time her parents had met Dimitri. Her mother's eyes had nearly popped out of her head, and her father had just gaped at Dimitri as they'd shaken hands. It was easy to forget how tall and intimidating Dimitri was to everyone but her.

She closed her eyes again, wanting to tell him all that lay in her heart. "I was thinking . . ."

"Yes?"

"Well, Royce said he'd help me transfer my college credits to his university, and I could finish my degree on Long Island. It's a lot closer to my parents and our friends." She wanted to ask him what his plans were. He'd vowed to be with her always, but did that mean playing house while she went to college and juggled her new life?

Dimitri didn't say anything; he simply pulled back to watch her. So she continued.

"The United Nations votes soon on the new human trafficking proposal, and they have asked me to come back to advocate for it, but I feel it's not enough. There's so much more to be done, isn't there?" She felt that she had been given a new lease on life, a new chance to begin again where so many others could not, and she believed that came with the responsibility to help others.

"Only if you wish to, Elena. No one demands it of you. You began the change, and if you want, that is enough." He continued to stroke her skin in soothing patterns that always seemed to draw the tension out of her body.

"I wish to keep going, to keep fighting." She gazed up at him. "But only if you are by my side. Do you want to stay with me? I mean, Nicholas, Maxim, and Leo are going back to Russia for a while, and I didn't know if you'd want to go with them . . ." The last thing she wanted to sound was desperate for him to stay.

"They won't stay long. Leo is going to see to the sale of my properties there and ship my possessions here. I spoke to Royce about houses on the Gold Coast on Long Island, and I believe there are several places worth looking at. I thought that after we're bored of making love in every little inn along the coast, we could go and tour a few of these American *palaces*."

His smile deepened, and a hint of a dimple peeped out of one cheek.

"Really?" Her heart gave a wild flutter. "You want to move to Long Island?"

He rolled his eyes. "Of course. I want to move wherever you are, and for the moment, that would be Long Island."

She curled her arms around his neck, pulling him down into a slow kiss as she thanked him without words. Then he moved back a little and sat up.

"Stay there," he said before he disappeared belowdecks. When he came back up, he held out one hand, a small black box in the center of his palm.

"What's this?" She took the box warily, but he was still beaming at her.

"Last week, I spoke with your father. Even though he agreed I didn't need his permission, I still wished for his blessing." He chuckled. "I'm far too bound by tradition not to ask."

With trembling fingers, she opened the box. A simple engagement ring with a marquise-cut pale-blue gem stared back at her.

"It's alexandrite. The official gemstone of Imperial Russia. The stone changes color depending on how the light hits it."

Even now, the gemstone changed color as she removed it from the box. Dimitri took the ring and grasped the fingers of her left hand with great tenderness.

"Tell me that you will marry me."

It sounded more like an order than a request, and she couldn't help but giggle.

"You're always telling me what to do." She kissed the corner of his mouth, and he let out a sigh as he cupped the back of her head and claimed her mouth, leaving her momentarily forgetting what they'd been talking about.

"Will you?" he asked this time.

"I will," she said with a smile and watched him slip the ring over her finger. "But I believe you had better kiss me again, just in case I need further convincing."

"That is one order I will let you give me for the rest of our lives, *kiska*."

She curled her arms around his neck as he pulled her onto his lap. Their mouths met in a kiss that she would tell her daughters and granddaughters about someday. It lasted longer and burned hotter than any star in the sky. It was a thing of fairy tales made real. If loving Dimitri had taught her anything, it was that love, real love, was a permanence of mind, heart, and soul.

Love was hope. Love was a rebellion. Love left no room for hate or fear.

Love was unstoppable.

THANK YOU SO MUCH FOR READING DARK DESIRE. IF this story touched you, please consider leaving a review on the store where you purchased it. Want to know more about what happens to Hans and Cody? Be sure to stay tuned for their stories as the Surrender series continues! And if you were intrigued by the trio of Russian hotties, Maxim, Leo and Nicholas, then I'm excited to say they will also have stories in their own series!

To keep up with their release news, follow me here:

BOOKBUB

MY NEWSLETTER

PRIVATE FACEBOOK GROUP

If you haven't read the first three books in the Surrender Series, turn the page to read the first 3 chapters of The Gilded Cuff, the story of Emery Lockwood, the reclusive billionaire who falls for a journalist with a tragic past to match his own.

THE GILDED CUFF
CHAPTER 1

EMERY LOCKWOOD AND FENN LOCKWOOD, EIGHT-YEAR-OLD TWIN SONS OF ELLIOT AND MIRANDA LOCKWOOD, WERE ABDUCTED FROM THEIR FAMILY RESIDENCE ON LONG ISLAND BETWEEN SEVEN AND EIGHT P.M. THE KIDNAPPING OCCURRED DURING A SUMMER PARTY HOSTED BY THE LOCKWOODS.

—*New York Times,* June 10, 1990

Long Island, New York
This is absolutely the stupidest thing I've ever done.

Sophie Ryder tugged the hem of her short skirt down over her legs a few more inches. It was still way too high. But she couldn't have worn something modest, per her usual style. Not at an elite underground BDSM club on

Long Island's Gold Coast. Sophie had never been to any club before, let alone one like this. She'd had to borrow the black mini-skirt and the red lace-up corset from her friend Hayden Thorne, who was a member of the club and knew what she should wear.

The Gilded Cuff. It was *the* place for those who enjoyed their kink and could afford to pay.

Sophie sighed. A journalist's salary wasn't enough to afford anything like what the people around her wore, and she was definitely feeling less sexy in her practical black flats with a bit of sparkle on the tips. Sensuality rippled off every person in the room as they brushed against her in their Armani suits and Dior gowns, and she was wary of getting too close. Their cultured voices echoed off the craggy gray stone walls as they chatted and gossiped. Although she was uneasy with the frank way the people around her touched and teased each other with looks and light caresses, even while patiently waiting in line, a stirring of nervousness skittered through her chest and her abdomen. Half of it had to do with the sexual chemistry of her surroundings, and the rest of it had to do with the story that would make her career, if she could only find who she was looking for and save his life in time. Her editor at the Kansas newspaper she wrote for had given her one week to break the story. What she didn't know was how long she had to save the life of a man who at this very moment was in the club somewhere. She swallowed hard and tried to focus her thoughts.

Following the crowd, she joined the line leading up to a single walnut wood desk with gilt edges. A woman in a tailored gray suit over a red silk blouse stood there checking names off a list with a feather pen. Sophie fought to restrain her frantic pulse and the flutter of rebellious butterflies in her stomach as she finally reached the desk.

"Name, please?" The woman peered over wide, black-rimmed glasses. She looked a cross between a sexy librarian and a no-nonsense lawyer.

A flicker of panic darted through Sophie. She hoped her inside source would come through. Not just anyone could get into the club. You had to be referred by an existing member as a guest.

"My name's Sophie Ryder. I'm Hayden Thorne's guest." At the mention of her new friend's name the other woman instantly smiled, warmth filling her gaze.

"Yes, of course. She called and mentioned you'd be coming. Welcome to the Gilded Cuff, Sophie." She reached for a small glossy pamphlet and handed it over. "These are the club rules. Read over them carefully before you go inside. Come to me if you have any questions. You can also go to anyone wearing a red armband. They are our club monitors. If you get in too deep and you get panicked, say the word "red" and that will make the game or the scene stop. It's the common safe word. Any Doms inside should respect that. If they don't, they face our monitors."

"Okay," Sophie sucked in a breath, trying not to think

about what sort of scene would make her use a safe word. This really was the most stupid thing she'd ever done. Her heart drummed a staccato beat as a wave of dread swept through her. She should leave... No. She had to stay at least a few more minutes. A life could hang in the balance, a life she could save.

"There's just one more thing. I need to know if you are a domme or a sub." The woman trailed the feather tip end of her pen under the tip of her chin, considering Sophie, measuring her.

"A domme or sub?" Sophie knew the words. Dominant and submissive. Just another part of the BDSM world, a lifestyle she knew so little about. Sophie definitely wasn't a domme. Dommes were the feminine Dominants in a D/s relationship. She certainly had no urge to whip her bed partner.

She liked control, yes, but only when it came to her life and doing what she needed to do. In bed? Well...she'd always liked to think of an aggressive man as one who took what he wanted, gave her what she needed. Not that she'd ever had a man like that before. Until now, every bedroom encounter had been a stunning lesson in disappointment.

The woman suddenly smiled again, as though she'd been privy to Sophie's inner thoughts. "You're definitely not a domme." Amusement twitched the corners of her mouth. "I sense you would enjoy an *aggressive* partner."

How in the hell? Sophie quivered. The flash of a teasing image, a man pinning her to the mattress, ruthlessly pumping into her until she exploded with pleasure. Heat flooded her face.

"Ahh, there's the sub. Here, take these." The woman captured Sophie's wrists and clamped a pair of supple leather cuffs around each wrist. Sewn into the leather, a red satin ribbon ran the length of each cuff. The woman at the desk didn't secure Sophie's wrists together, but merely ensured she had cuffs ready to be cinched together should she find a partner inside. The feel of the cuffs around her wrists sent a ripple of excitement through her. How was it possible to feel already bound and trapped? They constrained her, but didn't cut off her circulation, like wearing a choker necklace. She wanted to tug at the cuffs the way she would a tight necklace, because she was unused to the restriction.

"These tell the doms inside that you're a sub, but you're unclaimed and new to the lifestyle. Other subs will be wearing cuffs; some won't. It depends on if they are currently connected with a particular Dom and whether that Dom wishes to show an ownership. Since you're not with anyone, the red ribbons tell everyone you're new and learning the lifestyle. They'll know to go easy on you and to ask permission before doing or trying anything with you. The monitors will keep a close eye on you."

Relief coursed through Sophie. Thank heavens. She

was only here to pursue a story. Part of the job was to get information however she could, do whatever it took. But she wasn't sure she would be ready to do the things she guessed went on behind the heavy oak doors. Still, for the story, she would probably have to do something out of her comfort zone. It was the nature of writing about criminal stories. Of course, tonight wasn't about a crime, but rather a victim—and this victim was the answer to everything she'd spent years hoping to learn. And she was positive he was in danger.

When she'd gone to the local police with her suspicions, they'd turned a blind eye and run her off with the usual assurances that they kept a close eye on their community. But they didn't see patterns like she did. They hadn't read thousands of articles about crimes and noticed what she did. Somewhere inside this club, a man's life was hanging by a thread and she would save him and get the story of the century.

"Cuffs please." A heavily muscled man reached for her wrists as she approached the door that led deeper into the club. He wore an expensive suit with a red armband on his bicep, but his sheer brawny power was actually accented, rather than hidden, by his attire. It surprised her. She'd expected men to be running around in black leather and women fully naked, surrounded by chains, whips, and the whole shebang.

The man looked at her wrists, then up at her face. "You know the safe word, little sub?"

"Red."

"Good girl. Go on in and have a good time." The man's mouth broke into a wide smile, but it vanished just as quickly. She smiled back, and bowed her head slightly in a nod as she passed by him.

She moved through the open door into another world. Instead of a dungeon with walls fitted with iron chains, Sophie found the Gilded Cuff was the opposite of what she'd anticipated.

Music and darkness ruled the landscape of the club, engulfing her senses. She halted abruptly, her heart skittering in a brief flare of panic at not being able to see anything around her.

The dungeons and screams she'd expected weren't there. Was this typical for a BDSM atmosphere? Her initial research had clearly led her astray. It wasn't like her to be unprepared and The Gilded Cuff certainly surprised her. Every scenario she'd planned for in her head now seemed silly and ineffective. This place and these people weren't anything like what'd she'd imagined they would be and that frightened her more than the cuffs did. Being unprepared could get you killed. It was a lesson she'd learned the hard way and she had the scars to prove it. The club's rule pamphlet the woman at the desk had given her was still in her hands and a slight layer of sweat marked the glossy paper's surface.

I probably should have glanced at it. What if I break a rule by accident?

The last thing she needed to do was end up in trouble or worse, get kicked out and not have a chance to do what she'd come to do. It might be her *only* chance to save the man who'd become her obsession.

Sophie made her way through an expansive room bordered with roped-tied crimson velvet drapes that kept prying eyes away from the large beds beyond them when the curtains were untied. Only the sounds coming from behind the draperies hinted at what was happening there. Her body reacted to the sounds, and she became aroused despite her intention to remain aloof. Around here, people lounged on gothic-style, brocade-upholstered couches. Old portraits hung along the walls, imperious images of beautiful men and women from ages past watching coldly from their frames. Sophie had the feeling that she'd stepped into another time and place entirely removed from the cozy streets of the small town of Weston, on the north shore of Long Island.

The slow pulse of a bass beat and a singer's husky crooning wrapped around Sophie like an erotic blanket. As if she were in a dark dream, moving shadows and music filled her, and she breathed deeply, teased by hints of sex and expensive perfume. Awareness of the world outside wavered, rippling in her mind like a mirage. Someone bumped into her from behind, trying to pass by her to go deeper into the club. The sudden movement jerked her back to herself and out of the club's dark spell.

"Sorry!" she gasped and stepped out of the way.

As her eyes adjusted to the dim light, bodies manifested in twisting shapes. The sounds of sexual exploration were an odd compliment to the song being played. A heavy blush flooded Sophie's cheeks, heating her entire face. Her own sexual experiences had been awkward and brief. The memories of those nights were unwanted, uncomfortable, and passionless. Merely reliving them in her mind made her feel like a stranger in her own skin. She raised her chin and focused on her goal again.

The cuffs on her wrists made her feel vulnerable. At any moment a dom could come and clip her wrists together and haul her into a dark corner to show her true passion at his hands. The idea made her body hum to life in a way she hadn't thought possible. Every cell in her seemed to yearn now toward an encounter with a stranger in this place of sins and secrets. She trailed her fingertips over the backs of velveteen couches and the slightly rough texture of the fabric made her wonder how it would feel against her bare skin as she was stretched out beneath a hard masculine body.

The oppressive sensual darkness that slithered around the edges of her own control was too much. There was a low-lit lamp not too far away, and Sophie headed for it, drawn by the promise of its comfort. Light was safe; you could see what was happening. It was the dark that set her on edge. If she couldn't see what was going on around her, she was vulnerable. There was barely enough light for her to see where she was headed. She needed to calm down, regain her composure and remind herself why she was here.

Her heart trampled a wild beat against her ribs as she realized it would be so easy for any one of the strong, muscular doms in the club to slide a hand inside her bodice and discover the thing she'd hidden there, an object that had become precious to her over the last few years.

Her hand came to rest on the copy of an old photograph. She knew taking it out would be a risk, but she couldn't fight the need to steal the quick glance the dim light would allow her.

Unfolding the picture gently, her lips pursed as she studied the face of the eight-year-old boy in the picture. This was the childhood photo of the man she'd come to meet tonight.

The black and white photo had been on the front page of the *New York Times* twenty-five years ago. The boy was dressed in rags, and bruises marred his angelic face; his haunted eyes gazed at the camera. A bloody cut traced the line of his jaw from chin to neck. Eyes wide, he clasped a thick woolen blanket to his body as a policeman held out a hand to him.

Emery Lockwood. The sole survivor of the most notorious child abduction in American history since that of the Lindbergh baby. And he was somewhere in the Gilded Cuff tonight.

Over the last year she'd become obsessed with the photo and had taken to looking at it when she needed reassurance. Its subject had been kidnapped but survived and escaped, when so many children like him over the years had not been so lucky. Sophie's throat constricted, and shards of invisible glass dug into her throat as she tried to shrug off her own awful memories. Her best friend Rachel, the playground, that man with the gray van...

The photo was creased in places and its edges were worn. The defiance in Emery's face compelled her in a way nothing else in her life had. Compelled with an intensity that scared her. She had to see him, had to talk to him and understand him and the tragedy he'd survived. She was afraid he might be the target of another attempt on his life and she had to warn him. It wouldn't be fair for him to die, not after everything he'd survived. She had to help him. But it wasn't just that. It was the only way she could ease the guilt she'd felt at not being able to help catch the man who'd taken her friend. She had to talk to Emery. Even though she knew it wouldn't bring Rachel back, something inside her felt like meeting him would bring closure.

With a forced shrug of her shoulders, she relaxed and focused on Emery's face. After years of studying kidnapping cases she'd noticed something crucial in a certain style of kidnappings, a tendency by the predators to repeat patterns of behavior. When she'd started digging through Emery's case and read the hundreds of articles and police reports, she'd sensed it. That prickling sensation at the back of her mind that warned her that what had been started twenty-five years ago wasn't over yet. She hadn't been able to save Rachel, but she would save Emery.

I have to. She owed it to Rachel, owed it to herself and to everyone who'd lost someone to the darkness, to evil. Guilt stained her deep inside but when she saw Emery's face in that photograph, it reminded her that not every stolen child died. A part of her, one she knowingly buried in her heart, was convinced that talking to him, hearing his story, would ease the old wounds from her own past that never seemed to heal. And in return, she might be the one to solve his kidnapping and rescue him from a threat she was convinced still existed.

She wasn't the boldest woman—at least not naturally —but the quest for truth always gave her that added level of bravery. Sometimes she felt, when in the grips of pursuing a story, that she became the person she ought to be, someone brave enough to fight the evil in the world. Not the tortured girl from Kansas who'd lost her best friend to a pedophile when she was seven years old.

Sophie would have preferred to conduct an interview somewhere less intimate, preferably wearing more clothing. But Emery was nearly impossible to reach—he avoided the press, apparently despising their efforts to get him to tell his story. She didn't blame him. Retelling his story could be traumatic for him, but she didn't have a choice. If what she suspected was true, she needed the details she was sure he'd kept from the police because they might be the keys to figuring out who'd kidnapped him and why.

She'd made calls to his company, but the front desk there had refused to transfer her to his line, probably because of his "no press" rule. Thanks to Hayden she knew Emery rarely left the Lockwood estate but he came to the Gilded Cuff a few times a month. This was the only opportunity she might have to reach him.

Emery ran his father's company from a vast mansion on the Lockwood estate, nestled in the thick woods of Long Island's Gold Coast. No visitors were permitted and he left the house only when in the company of private guards.

Sophie tucked the photo back into her corset and looked around, peering at the faces of the doms walking past her. More than once their gazes dropped to the cuffs on her wrists, possessively assessing her body. Her face scorched with an irremovable blush at their perusal. Whenever she made eye contact with a dom, he would frown and she'd instantly drop her gaze.

Respect; must remember to respect the doms and not make eye contact unless they command it. Otherwise she might end up bent over a spanking bench. Her corset seemed to shrink, making it hard to breathe, and heat flashed from her head to her toes.

Men and women—submissives judging by the cuffs they bore on their wrists—were wearing even less than she was as they walked around with drink trays, carrying glasses to doms on couches. Several doms had subs kneeling at their feet, heads bowed. A man sitting on a nearby love seat was watching her with hooded eyes. He had a sub at his feet, his hand stroking her long blond hair. The woman's eyes were half closed, cheeks flushed with pleasure. The dom's cobalt blue eyes measured her—not with sexual interest, but seemingly with mere curiosity— the way a sated mountain lion might watch a plump rabbit crossing its path.

Sophie pulled her eyes away from the red-headed dom and his ensnaring gaze. The club was almost too much to take in. Collars, leashes, the occasional pole with chains hanging from it, and a giant cross were all there, part of the fantasy world created amid the glitz and old world décor.

Sliding past entwined bodies and expensive furniture, she saw more that intrigued her. The club itself was this one large room with several halls splitting off the main room. Hayden had explained earlier that morning the layout of the club. She had pointed out that no matter which hall you went down you had to come back to the main room to exit the club. A handy safety feature. A little exhalation of relief escaped her lips. How deep did a man like Emery Lockwood live this lifestyle? Would she find him in one of the private rooms or would he be part of a public scene like the ones she was witnessing now?

She was nearly halfway across the room when a man caught her by her arm and spun her to face him. Her lips parted, ready to scream the word "red", but when she met his gaze she froze, the shout dying at the back of her throat. He raised her wrists, fingering the red ribbon around her leather cuffs. His gray eyes were as silver as moonlight, and openly interested. Sophie tried to jerk free of his hold. He held tight. The arousal that had been slowly building in her body flashed cold and sharp. She could use the safe word. She knew that. But after one deep breath, she forced herself to relax. Part of the job tonight was to blend in, to find Emery. She couldn't do that if she ran off and cried for help at the first contact. It would be smarter to let this play out a bit; maybe she could squeeze the dom for information about Emery later if she didn't find him soon. For Sophie, not being able to get to Emery was more frightening than anything this man might try to do to her.

"I see your cuffs, little sub. I'm not going to hurt you."

His russet hair fell across his eyes and he flicked his head: power, possession, dominance. He was raw masculinity. A natural dom. He was the sort of good-looking man that she would have mooned over when she was a teenager. Hell, even now at twenty-four she should have been melting into a puddle at this man's feet. His gaze bit into her. A stab of sudden apprehension made her stomach pitch, but she needed to find Emery and going along with this guy might be the best way to get information. He tugged her wrists, jerking her body against his as he regarded her hungrily. "I need an unclaimed sub for a contest. Tonight is your lucky night, sweetheart."

CHAPTER 2

ELLIOT AND MIRANDA LOCKWOOD WERE
VISIBLE DURING THE TIME THE KIDNAPPING IS
SPECULATED TO HAVE OCCURRED. THE TWINS
WERE LAST SEEN IN THE KITCHEN BY THEIR HIRED
NANNY FRANCESCA ESPINA, AGE FIFTY-FOUR YEARS, WHO
HAD SUMMONED THE BOYS TO THE KITCHEN FOR DINNER.

—*New York Times*, June 10, 1990

Sophie barely had time to protest at the dom's tight
hold on her wrist before he dragged her across the room
to where a group of people circled a couch against the
wall. She could have said "red" and stopped whatever game
he'd intended to play so she could keep searching for
Emery, but the word died on her lips. A large crowd of
people all turned to face her, amusement flashing in their

eyes. The crowd's focus on her was not comforting in the slightest. She was prey, for a so-called contest, in a BDSM club. Searching the faces for Emery's, she prayed she'd be lucky enough to find him. If not, she'd use her safe word and get free of the man and his "contest."

Holding her, he grinned darkly at the onlookers. "Found a newbie. She'll be perfect."

Sophie again jerked to get her wrist back and failed. She stifled a gasp as he promptly smacked her bottom with an open hand. Her gaze darted across the crowd, trying to seek out Emery's familiar face. He had to be here somewhere. Most of the club members had moved in to watch her and this dom.

"Stand still, bow your head," he commanded.

To her shock she obeyed instantly—not because she naturally bowed to anyone who shoved her around, but because something inside her responded to the commanding tone he'd just used on her. He seemed like a man who would enjoy punishing her, and she knew enough about this lifestyle to know she never wanted to end up over a spanking bench, even if the idea did make her insides flare to life.

"Bring her here, Royce." A cool, rich voice spoke, pouring over her skin like whisky—slightly rough, with an intoxicating bite to it. When this man spoke, the voices murmuring around her stopped and a hush fell over the area.

The crowd around her and the man, Royce, parted.

Another man, sitting on the blue brocaded couch, watched them. His large hands rested on his thighs, fingers impatiently drumming a clipped beat. Royce shoved Sophie none too gently, sending her to her knees right at the man's feet. She reacted instinctively, throwing her hands out to balance herself, and her palms fell on his thighs and her chest collided with his knees.

Air rushed out of her lungs in a soft *whoosh*. For a few seconds she fought to regain her breath as she leaned against the stranger for support. The large muscles beneath his charcoal pants jumped and tensed beneath her hands, and she whipped her palms off him as though burned. She'd practically been in the man's lap, the heat of his body warming her, tempting her with his close proximity. Hastily she dropped her head and rested her hands on her own thighs, waiting. It took every ounce of her willpower to concentrate on breathing.

She still didn't look at his face, focusing instead on his expensive black shoes, the precision cuffs of his dark charcoal pants. Her eyes then tracked up his body, noting the crisp white shirt and thin, blood red tie he wore. It was loosened beneath the undone top button of his dress shirt. She had the sudden urge to crawl into his lap and trail kisses down his neck and taste him.

"Raise your eyes," the voice demanded.

Sophie drew a deep breath, letting air fill her, making her almost light-headed. And then she looked up.

Her heart leapt into her throat and her brain short-circuited.

Emery Lockwood, the object of her darkest fantasies, the ones she'd buried deep in her heart in the hours just before dawn, was looking down at her, predatory curiosity gleaming in his gaze. He trapped her with a magnetic pull, an air of mystery. She was caught in invisible strands of a spell woven around her body and soul.

The boy's soft angelic features were there, hidden beneath the surface of the man before her. He was the most devastatingly, sensual man she'd ever seen. His high cheekbones, full lips, and aquiline nose were all parts of the face of a man in his early thirties. But his eyes—the color of nutmeg and framed with long dark lashes any woman would kill to have—were the same as those of the wounded eight-year-old boy in her photo. Although she could see that they'd hardened with two decades of grief.

He was masculine perfection, except for the thin, almost invisible scar that ran the length of his sharp jaw line. Even after twenty-five years, he still bore the marks of his suffering. She ached with every cell in her body to press her mouth to his, to steal fevered kisses from his lips. Her fingertips tingled with the need to stroke over the scar on his face, to smooth away the hurt he must have endured.

"Do you know the rules of our game?" Emery asked. As he spoke, his gaze still held her in place, like a butterfly caught beneath a pin and encased in glass. Hands trembling, she pursed her lips and tried to remain calm and collected. It was nearly impossible. The heat of his intense regard only increased as the corners of his mouth curved in a slow, wicked smile. Oh, the man knew just how he affected her!

Emery leaned forward, caught her chin in his palm, and tilted her face up to look at him. Her skin burned deliciously where his palm touched her. He pulled her, like the moon calling to the tides, demanding devotion and obedience with the promise of something great, something she couldn't understand. Her senses hummed with eagerness, ready to explore his touch, his taste. Like a minnow caught in a vast current, she was pulled out to deeper waters, helpless to resist. In any other situation, she wouldn't have been so off balance, and wouldn't be letting herself get sucked into this strange game she sensed she was about to play. But here in this dark fantasy of the Gilded Cuff, she didn't want to look away from him.

"The rules are as follows: I give you a command, you obey. I have to make you come in less than two minutes. I cannot do more than stroke any part of your body covered by cloth—no touching between your legs and no touching of your bare breasts. You are to look into my eyes and do whatever I say so long as my commands are within the rules. If you come, I win; if you don't, Royce wins."

Sophie struggled to think clearly. There no way she would have agreed to this anywhere else, but in the club, this was the sort of game the doms played... the sort of game Emery played, and he wanted to play with her. A shiver of desire shot through her, making her clit pulse. How could she refuse?

"Uh... permission to speak?"

"You will call me Sir, or Master Emery."

"Sir," Sophie corrected. She wanted to kick herself. She had read enough about this lifestyle that she should have remembered to address him formally, but in all honesty the way he was looking at her—like something he wanted to eat—she couldn't remain entirely rational.

"Permission to speak granted." Emery's voice dropped into a softer tone, approval warming his hazel eyes.

"What happens to me, Sir? Only one of you can win."

Royce shared a glance with Emery.

"She's a smart one, this little sub. Well, Emery? What do you think?"

Both men focused their intense gazes on her. It took everything in her not to look away.

"Punishment by the one who loses. But what form? Flogging?" Royce suggested.

Sophie flinched.

"No whips," Emery seemed to conclude, his eyes reading her tiniest reaction.

Emery ran a palm over his jaw, which was shadowed with night stubble. The look gave him a rugged edge, reminding her of the men back home in Kansas.

The tension in the crowd seemed to heighten as the subject of punishment continued. Emery continued to stare at her, his eyes seemingly unlocking the puzzle she presented. "She's new. Why not a spanking?" he murmured softly.

That caught her attention. Her clit thrummed to life, pulsing in a faint beat along with her heart. The twinge of uncomfortable pain in her knees was temporarily abated by this new distraction. Her eyes immediately settled on Emery's large, capable hands. She could practically feel the width of his palm striking her bottom.... Trouble. She was in so much trouble.

"Definitely spanking." Emery smiled. "My favorite form of punishment. It will be a disappointment when you come in my arms, and I shall have to allow Royce the plea-sure of laying his palm to your flesh."

"Cocky bastard," Royce retorted. "She might resist you. I bet she's far less submissive than she looks, and given her clothes, far too self-conscious to come in front of people. When I win, you'll owe me your best case of bourbon."

Her knees were aching, pain flaring like sharp little needles through her skin and deep into her bones. She shifted on them, trying to favor one over the other, and then hastily switched, but it didn't help. There was no way she was going to make it much longer on her knees.

Emery's hazel eyes lit up with the challenge. "Like hell! When she comes, and she will, you'll owe me your best case of scotch."

As the men continued to posture and argue, Sophie sat

back on her heels, her knees aching something fierce. Like metal rods were jabbing up between her knees into her nerves.

Screw this. I'm getting up. Surging to her feet, she breathed a sigh of relief as blood flow pumped through her legs.

The people gathered around her gasped. Both men stopped arguing and turned to face her, gazes dark with anger. It wasn't the lethal sort of anger she'd come across before, not like the murderers she'd interviewed for her crime stories. That anger was a terrifying anger, pure hatred. It rolled off those criminals in waves. The kind of anger that truly good people never felt, it was the sort of rage that consumed the soul and blackened the heart until only a killing machine was left its place.

With Royce and Emery, however, it was merely the anger of a parent or a mentor at a charge who'd clearly disobeyed a direct order. She knew the outcome. Punishment. She could read it on their faces, and it aroused them both. Hell, it aroused her.

"You weren't given permission to rise." Emery spoke slowly, as though trying to decide whether he would give her a chance to apologize or to just skip straight to the punishment.

Even as she opened her mouth she knew it was a bad idea.

"My knees hurt. This isn't carpet; it's rock. *Hard* rock."

Emery's jaw dropped. The people around them stepped back.

Royce was silent for a long moment, and then burst into long, hooting laughter. He doubled over, palms on his thighs, as he struggled to catch his breath. "Damn, this is going to be fun."

"Fun," Emery muttered and shook his head. "Back on your knees, until we decide what to do with you."

"Yeah...no thank you, Sir." Sophie challenged. "I'll stay on my feet until you're done."

He was up and on his feet and before she could react he had turned her to face the crowd and bent her over.

Whack! His palm landed on her butt. The impact stung, but it faded almost instantly to a warm, achy feeling. Her legs turned to jelly and she trembled helplessly against a shocking wave of pleasure that began to build inside her abdomen.

The glare she launched in Emery's direction had no effect. When he released her and took his seat again, she spun to face him. His narrowed eyes shot her pulse into overdrive.

"You have a safe word, little sub?" Royce asked.

She wracked her brain for one, knowing it had to be something she could remember when she was panicking because it was the word that would get the doms to stop whatever they were doing if the interaction became too unbearable.

"Apricot," she decided. Being highly allergic to the fruit made it a word she wouldn't forget easily.

Her unusual choice of safe word had both men raising their brows. In that instant they could have been brothers. They mirrored each other the way only true friends could. A pang of envious longing cut through Sophie's heart and she sucked in a breath as she thought of Rachel.

"What's your name, little sub?"

"Sophie Ryder." When his brows lowered she hastily added, "Sir."

Emery patted his thigh with one palm. "Let us begin the contest. You will come and sit on my lap and I will command you."

Sophie's stomach pitched so deep it felt like it hit her toes. Emery leaned back, his arms rested on the back of the couch. He looked every bit a prince, a leader of a pride of lions, merely waiting for his conquest, his prey. His relaxed position only made her feel more helpless. She knew he could move fast, catch her in his arms and have her bent for punishment again in seconds if she dared to resist him. Her nipples pearled beneath the unforgiving leather of the corset, rubbing until they ached. She clenched her hands to stop them from shaking.

Here we go, you can do this. Sophie approached him and sat across his lap. She wriggled, trying to find a comfortable position, unable to ignore the feel of his muscular thighs beneath her.

He cocked one eyebrow imperiously, as though her restlessness had somehow offended him.

"Do not *squirm.*" He issued his first command.

She stilled instantly. Her only movement was her breasts rising and falling with her breaths.

"Look at my eyes, *only* my eyes." His tone softened, but the rough edge still scraped over her, making her hungry for the promise she found in his gaze. The voices around them faded and she slipped deeper and deeper into his dark spell.

He would be a rough lover; carnal, quiet. He wouldn't whisper sweet words, wouldn't utter harsh arousing statements. He'd simply take her, take her again and again, the grinding, the pounding. The soft silence punctuated by uneven breaths, the stroke of rough hands over her sensitive skin. Everything a sensible, modern woman shouldn't want from a man in bed. He'd be all animal in all the right ways.

She'd never been with someone like him before, might never be again, and the thought was an intoxicating one. To be at the mercy of such power, such electrifying sexual control and surrender it all to him... Her mouth was suddenly dry, her pulse tapping Morse code for help as she tried to maintain a semblance of calm. Would she be able to give in to him? To let him guide her through the dark lust that so often took hold of her when she had no way of releasing it? Yes... She could let go with him, and the uncertainty of what would happen when she did was half of the excitement that lit a fire in her veins.

His hands settled on her hips, fingers slowly stroking back and forth, teasing her skin beneath the leather miniskirt. What would it be like to have his hands on her bare flesh? Fingers exploring between her legs.

"Tell me what you'd like, Sophie." Emery leaned his head down, his brow touching hers, eyes still locked on her face.

She gulped, her mouth dryer than the Gobi Desert.

"What would it take to make you lose control? Do you want a hard fuck? A desperate pounding? Or would you like to have your hands bound, lying face down on a large bed, softness against your belly and my hardness above you, in you?" His erotic whispers were so soft, so low that no one nearby could hear what he was saying to her. The images he painted were wild, vivid, yet blurry—like a strange combination between Van Gogh and Monet. Sweet and sensual, then dark, exotic and barely comprehendible. Emery was an artist in his own way, an erotic painter of words and pictures.

"I'd take you slow, so slow you'd lose all sense of time. You'd focus only on me, on my cock gliding between your thighs, possessing you." His words were slow and deliberate, as though he'd given them years of thought, but the slight breathless quality to the whisper made her realize she was not the only one affected.

The first quiver between her thighs was inevitable. She

shifted, restless on his legs, despite his command not to move.

His breath fanned her lips. "Oh, god," she murmured.

He smiled, unblinking, and licked his lips. She wanted that tongue in her mouth, tangling with her own. She craved his hands on her bare flesh.

"Please..." she moaned. He moved his hands down from her hips, to her outer thighs, barely exerting any real pressure. That made it worse. The hint of his touch, the promise of the pressure she craved. Sophie wanted him digging his fingers into her skin, holding her legs apart as he slammed deep into her.

"Take a deep breath," he issued another command.

She obeyed. Her heartbeat seemed to expand outward from her chest until the pulse pounded through her entire body so hard she swore he could feel it beat through her skin wherever he touched her. The throb between her thighs nearly stung now—her need so great, his effect so potent.

"When I take you, no matter the position, you will like it. I'll bend you over a couch." He stroked one finger on her outer thigh, made circular patterns. "I'll push you up against a wall."

With little panting breaths she wriggled, trying to rock her hips against his lap, but he held her still. She nearly screamed in frustration at being denied what her body frantically needed.

The finger moved higher, past her hip, up to her

ribcage. "Spread and bound open on my bed." His fingertip quested up past the laces of her corset. "You'll twist and writhe, unable to get free. At my mercy, Sophie, my mercy. You will beg and when I'm ready, I will grant your every desire, just as I take mine."

She couldn't breathe. The orgasm was so close. She could feel it, like a shadow inside her body, breathing, panting, waiting to be set free. She was ready; she wanted to climax in his arms, wanted to forge that connection which would tie her to him. Terrifying, shocking, intimate, but damn if she didn't want it more than anything in the world at that moment. Wanted it more than her story, more than the interview, more than easing her pain from the past. She needed pleasure. His pleasure.

The feathering touch of his fingers, Emery's erotic murmurs now incoherent with breathless anticipation against her neck as they both strained toward the great cliff, eagerly craving the fall back to earth. Why wouldn't he touch her where she needed it? The slightest pressure on her inner thighs, the rhythmic stroke of his hand against her clit, anything would do it if he could only...

"Time!" Royce's triumphant call shattered the glass bubble that had cocooned them for the last two minutes. Murmurs of shock from the surrounding crowd broke through.

"Damn." Emery's eyes darkened. Anger, but not at her, flared at the lines of his mouth. He bent to press his lips against her ear. "You were close, weren't you, darling? So close I almost had you." His body was trembling beneath hers, the little movements wracking his arms and chest. The press of his arousal beneath her bottom far too evident. He'd been there, right alongside her, dying to come. Together. And it hadn't happened for either of them; two minutes hadn't been enough time.

Sophie's legs shook as cold reality slashed through her. The climax her body had been prepared to give Emery faded away. In its wake little tremors reverberated along her limbs, made worse by the tension in her entire body that hadn't found release. She tried to breathe, to let her shoulders drop and her muscles relax. It was going to take a while to come down from this.

Almost had her? No. He definitely had her, practically wrapped up with a bow on top, totally and completely his. No question.

CHAPTER 3

THE KITCHEN IS NOW THE OFFICIAL CRIME SCENE WHERE THE ABDUCTION IS BELIEVED TO HAVE OCCURRED. THE CRIME SCENE WAS LITTERED WITH BROKEN COKE BOTTLES, BLOOD, AND HALF-EATEN SANDWICHES ON THE BOYS' PLATES.

—*New York Times*, June 10, 1990

"So, my best case of bourbon?" Emery raised his face to look at Royce, who stood in front of the couch.

"If you don't mind." Royce's eyes twinkled with devilish merriment, but he clapped a palm on Emery's shoulder with gentle camaraderie. "I'll be by the house later to pick it up."

"I'll have it ready for you," Emery assured him, and

then turned his attention back to Sophie. "Now, little sub, let's see about that punishment."

A sensuous light flickered at the back of his eyes, like a lighthouse's beacon fighting to shine through the depths of a storm. Every emotion—a thousand of them—shuttered and then exploded behind his gaze. To Sophie it felt as if she was seeing the entire world captured in one rapid blink...and then it was gone. His eyes were heavy with desire and nothing else.

Oh dear. "I...uh..." How inadequate words were! What could she say to persuade him against punishing her?

Emery rose from the couch in a fluid movement with Sophie still clasped in his arms. She had only a moment to marvel that her weight didn't seem to bother him at all before he was carrying her through the group of people. There was a door ajar halfway down one of the halls that branched off the center room. He nudged it open with his foot. It was completely empty save for a thick rug spanning the entire room and a wooden piece of furniture that she knew from her research was a spanking bench.

At the sight of the bench Sophie went rigid; her limbs locked up, her hands balled into fists. Only a sliver of her panic came from fear. The rest of her wanted to know too badly how it felt to be bent over that, with his hand smacking her ass until she cried out. *That* scared her: how much she wanted to experience something so dark and sinful. Emery set her down and started to close the door. He left it open about an inch or two. Someone could come in, could get to her if she needed help. Still...Sophie shot a glance at the bench. There was no way in hell she was going to bend over that and...and...let herself go with him. She'd never been able to do that with anyone and she couldn't start with someone like him. He was tall, blond, and brooding. She'd make a fool of herself if she gave in to him. What would he think of her if she got aroused by a punishment? That she was just like any other woman in the club? The thought stopped her cold.

She didn't want to be just another woman to him. She wanted to be something more; she wanted him to trust her, to open up to her. Letting him spank the hell out of her might not be the best way to earn his trust....

Then again, maybe it would.

I wish I knew what I was doing. She cursed inwardly. With men, she was always awkward and unsure of herself, and now her typical failings seemed magnified because he affected her too strongly.

"Look, I'm sorry, but this whole scene just isn't for me. I shouldn't have come here." She edged toward the door. Maybe if she got far enough from the bench, he'd forget about punishing her and she could talk to him about the abduction. If he thought she was scared enough to leave, he might back off in his determination to spank her and she'd have her chance to speak.

Emery sidestepped, blocking her access to the exit. She saw the outline of well-defined muscles; he was much bigger and stronger than she was. To her sheer humiliation, something inside her started to purr with delight at the thought of that strength and size directed at her, for her protection and more importantly, her pleasure.

He placed a hand on the side of her neck where it connected to her shoulder. His thumb moved slowly back and forth against the base of her throat, as though questing for the frantic drum of her pulse. His lips moved, flirting at the tips with a smile.

She couldn't take much more of this. If she didn't get away, she'd let him take her over to that bench and she'd surrender to him. That couldn't happen.

"Please, let me leave." Her tone, thankfully, sounded stronger than the whimpering inside her which begged to stay, to let him bend her over the bench and do wicked things to her.

"If you want out, say your safe word." His sharp tone was edged with a challenge. Something deep inside her responded.

She knew enough of D/s relationships to know that subs weren't powerless; surrendering to a dom was their choice, one that had to be based on trust. Emery's challenge for her to surrender was tempting, too tempting if she was honest with herself. She'd never wanted to surrender to a man, but the idea of willingly letting one overpower her? Her thighs clenched together, her sensitive nerves inside jumping to life. Could she give in? Gain power by giving him power?

"I'm waiting for your answer."

When Sophie hesitated, Emery threaded his fingers through the black satin ribbons that laced the front of her corset. He tugged one bow's string with careless ease, so at odds with the cool, dispassionate expression on his face as he began to loosen the laces and peel her corset apart. A haze of heat settled over her skin and fogged her mind. Sophie prayed he'd keep going, would pull her corset open like they were in some torrid romance novel, and bend his head to her breasts to...

His fingers caressed the tip of the folded up photo. She jolted back, the memory of where she'd tucked his photo slamming into her. He couldn't see it; he'd never understand. Emery's hand shot out, caught her wrists, and lifted them above her head. In a move as smooth as the steps of a slow dance, he maneuvered her back against the wall by the door. One thick, muscled thigh pressed between hers, and he kept her wrists trapped above her. His other hand moved back to her corset, dipped between her breasts and retrieved the photo. His thumb and index finger deftly unfolded it and the wide-eyed interest of natural curiosity on his face morphed to an expression of narrowed suspicion.

He released her wrists, stepped back several feet and stared at the image in his hand. He was so still he could have been carved from marble — his eyes dark with horror, his tanned skin now alabaster white.

A long moment later he drew a deep measured breath and raised his eyes to hers.

"Where did you get this picture?" Each word seemed dragged out between his clenched teeth. He changed before her eyes, the prince transforming into a beast. Wounded rage filled his eyes, morphing with the promise of vengeance.

The pit of her stomach seemed to have dropped out. She felt as if she was falling, that awful sensation of losing control, of being seconds away from a sickening crash. This was what she'd come to talk about, come to warn him about, and she wasn't ready. It would hurt him to drag this out in the open again and she wasn't prepared, not after the way they'd been so close just seconds before. The truth was, she didn't want to lose him, not this sexy, addictive man. And she would lose him if she brought up the past. Like all victims he'd retreat into himself and pull away from her even as she tried to help him.

"The newspaper," Sophie replied breathlessly.

Emery continued to stare at her, his long elegant fingers curling around the photo, crumpling it. "Why do you have a picture of me from twenty-five years ago?" When Sophie opened her mouth he waved a hand at her. "Think carefully how you answer, Ms. Ryder. I'm not above lawsuits, and I have a very, very good lawyer."

Sophie bit her lip, tasted a drop of blood and licked at the sore spot before she replied. She'd only rehearsed this a thousand times yet now she didn't know where to begin.

"I wanted to be able to recognize you, because I wanted to interview you. I'm a freelance investigative journalist. I specialize in crime stories, primarily those about kidnappings." She knew she'd made a mistake the moment the words left her mouth. She felt incredibly small in that moment, like a mouse cornered in a lion's cage. Should she have started with the part where she thought his life was in danger? That would've made her sound crazy, and she needed his trust more than anything.

Emery's eyes turned dark as wood that had been consumed by flames and burnt to ash.

"You people are all the same." His tone was deadly calm. Quiet. The hand holding the photo started to shake. His fingers clenched so tightly that his knuckles whitened. The shaking spread outward; his shoulders visibly vibrated with his rage.

Sophie sucked in a breath. He wasn't withdrawing... He was going to lash out. The oppressive wave of guilt that cut off her air warred with a new, unexpected apprehension. This looked bad, she knew it. The sneaky reporter trying to get the scoop on a story that defined this man's worst moment in his life. God, she'd been an idiot to think she could waltz in here and start chatting about his kidnapping.

Goosebumps rippled along her bare arms and her muscles tensed. Despite the anger she could feel rolling off him in waves, he seemed to rein in that silken thread of self-control and loosened his fingers. The photo stayed crinkled in a tight ball, completely destroyed. When she swallowed, it felt like knives sliced her throat.

Emery spoke again, much to Sophie's dread. "Invade my life, my privacy. You know nothing of what I've endured or what happened to me and my..." the words faded but Sophie sensed he nearly said "brother."

Her eyes burned with a sudden rush of tears. His pain was so clear on his face, and it made her think of herself, of the way she felt when she thought of Rachel.

"Mr. Lockwood—" She had to explain, to show him she only wanted to help.

He threw the crumpled photo at her feet. He might as well have slapped her. Would he be more willing to listen if he knew she was here to save him? But how could she get him to listen long enough to explain everything?

Summoning her strength, she stepped toward him. "But you survived. I think people want to know the truth, know how strong you are." Why couldn't he see what a miracle his escape was? He'd survived a horrific experience and was stronger, stronger than she was. Losing Rachel had destroyed her innocence and shattered her world.

A ruthless laugh broke from his lips. "Strong? Strong?" He shook his head from side to side, a wild smile splitting his face suddenly. "I'm strong now. I *wasn't* strong then. If I had been strong, Fenn would be here." When his eyes grew hollow Sophie realized how much that admission must have cost him. He blamed himself for whatever had happened to his brother, thought Fenn Lockwood's death was his fault. And she'd played right into reinforcing his delusion that an eight-year-old boy should have been able to stop kidnappers. That was ludicrous.

"At least you're here. You're alive and you have a good life." The words were hollow; Sophie didn't know what else to say so she repeated what her therapist had told her years ago, after Rachel was taken.

"It's a half-life, nothing more." Emery's soft utterance cut open her soul. He understood, felt the same way she did, if not more.

She'd poured her heart into what little life she felt she had left, but it wasn't enough to fill the empty space where Rachel should have been. She couldn't imagine what it must be like for Emery to have lost his twin. A sibling, a person he'd shared a womb with, had been raised alongside for eight years. Whatever had been between them had been destroyed, one life ended, the other haunted.

"I'm not going to agree to an interview. Your homework should've told you that. Now if you'll excuse me, I've had enough of the club tonight."

Sophie's heart cracked down the middle. She'd failed. But there was more to it—the loss of something else, something deeper and infinitely more important: his trust. She'd never met this man before today, didn't fully trust her, yet she hated that she'd let him down, abused what little trust he'd started to give her. It was like losing him, even though she sensed he'd never belong to anyone. He seemed so distant, buried beneath the past and that made him danger- ous. A wildness emanated from him that made him seem like the sort of a man a woman couldn't own, couldn't claim, not matter how hard she wanted to or tried to. Her grandmother used to say you could never harness the wind.

Foolish woman that she was, Sophie just had to try. She waited a breathless moment that seemed to hang on the edge of forever. He needed her to submit to him; he needed the control between them. She could give it to him, right now, even if it was only temporary.

"Mr. Lockwood, please." Guided by some instinct, she grabbed his hand and fell to her knees at his feet, head bowed. "Please..." She knew the second his gaze shifted to her. The hairs on the back of her neck rose, her skin prickled, and arousal flooded through her, making her damp, and her breathing shallow. Even though he was upset with her, his focus heated her blood.

There was a long pause before he spoke. "Please, what?" Emery's voice was dom-like—cool, calm, commanding, not hard or biting like moments before. He shifted his feet, angling his body toward her—a few inches only, but it was enough to show she was getting through to him again. There might still be a chance.

She swallowed thickly. "Please, Sir."

"And what do you request of me?" He pulled the hand that she clutched free of her grasp, but moved it to the crown of her hair, stroking. His palm moved down to her neck, fingers threading and pulling tightly enough to make her arch her back to ease the pressure. It forced her face upward, and she had to look into his eyes. He stood over her now, his towering posture not threatening but completely dominating. She didn't cower but kept herself submissive, giving him what he needed.

No one understood. No one knew the agonizing grip of pain at losing someone you loved. But Emery did. And she wanted him to talk to her, to tell her how he'd survived with a broken heart. But when he turned to look at her, eyes so full of echoing pain, she came to a realization. He wasn't stronger, at least not in this. He was just as wounded as she. They were both lost. He without his brother, she without Rachel. Lives taken from them that could never come back. Memories tarnished by other men's evil, leaving them with nothing more than a child's fear of loss and death.

She didn't think he could give her the answers she needed. But he could give her the story, provide the details which might give her enough information to solve who was behind his kidnapping. She was so close to figuring it out. She could catch whoever was responsible and prevent them from harming Emery or anyone else ever again. It would have to be enough.

"I want your help to make the monster who did this to you pay. He's still out there. You know that." She paused, licking her lips. "And he could come after you again. It's why you've kept bodyguards and security high for the last twenty-five years," she guessed. Her reports always showed the same man shadowing Emery the few times he'd been photographed outside his home.

Emery's lips pursed into a thin line and his brows drew down over his eyes, which were more the color of choco-late-kissed honey now.

"You think you can catch a man who's eluded police and the FBI?"

Her heart jolted. He'd just admitted his captor had been a man. The reports said three masked men, but he made it sound like only one man was involved. What had happened to the other two? More puzzle pieces shifted.

"I'm a skilled reporter. I've focused on criminal stories for years, Sir. If you let me, I can use whatever you tell me to solve the case. I *know* I can." She prayed he'd hear the sincerity and resolve in her tone. She meant every word. She'd protect him and catch the bastard who'd hurt him. As penance for Rachel. As penance for every child she couldn't save.

He seemed to consider her request.

"What would you do for me in return?" His eyes promised he meant something sexual. Something that might shatter her lonely world into pieces and leave her craving him for the rest of her life.

"D-do for you?" Sophie stuttered. That was becoming an irritating habit she needed to fix. The man had the ability to tie her in knots when he got her thinking of other things besides her job.

"I'm a dom, darling. Your needs should involve me, and

your thoughts should be about what I need and want. If I am nice and give you what you need, you must give me something in return. And no... I'm not talking about money or anything so trivial as that. My story, as you call it, is worth something beyond money. I will need something just as important from you in return."

She hesitated. What could she give him? She had nothing to offer. Nothing but...herself. She could give herself to him. A scolding voice in her head warned her that it would be a devil's bargain. But she silenced the voice. Damn the consequences; her body wanted him. Never had she crossed a line before, never had she wanted to. She was tired of being the good girl, tired of playing it safe. The hint of danger and the thrill of dark passion in Emery's eyes was an escape, one she needed more than her next breath.

"I'll give you anything. Name it and it's yours. I came here knowing what to expect." She threw a glance around the room, eyes touching briefly on the spanking bench before settling back on him.

He chuckled and brushed the pad of one thumb over her lips. "That's a dangerous offer." His hand dropped to her neck, his fingers curling around her throat, the touch a warning, but he didn't hurt her.

"What if I demand you strip completely and I tie you to a St. Andrews cross and fuck you senseless? Or if I require you to walk through the main room and accept any intimate touch another dom wishes to give you?

Would you agree to that? There are a thousand things I could ask of you that would not just push your limits but break them. You were spooked at the sight of one little bench, and that tells me everything I need to know. You may have studied domination and submission, but you haven't lived it. The importance of this particular lifestyle is that one must always be safe, sane and consensual. Your offer shows no consideration for any of those, and half the doms outside would do things you might not consent to. You have natural submissive tendencies. It's clear from the way you responded to my commands, but we aren't in a vanilla sex world, Sophie. While this life demands trust, it is a dark world, full of fire, passion, loss of control. Are you truly ready for that?" The bite to his tone made her arousal sharp; her womb clenched in eagerness, even as she felt a cold sweat dew on her body as trepidation set in.

Sophie breathed deeply. He'd warned her, hadn't just accepted her blanket offer. *Trust.* Even as scary as what he'd mentioned sounded, she also longed for a taste of that forbidden passion. She was hungry for it. But she needed to trust him in return.

"Would you really do those things?" She glanced away then forced her eyes back. He was watching her, the way a hawk at the tallest branches of a tree might survey a rabbit in the field below. Yet he was close, so incredibly close to her he could have kissed her.

With a sigh, Emery shook his head. "Absolutely, unless of course that fell within your hard limits. I'm not a saint, and I have only the semblance of being a gentleman, but I would respect your safe word. Sharing my bed would push you right to the edge of your limits. Lucky for you, I'm in no mood to bed a woman who inherently denies her submissive nature."

"You think I'm a real submissive?" Sophie could hear the shock in her own voice. Was she truly? More importantly, could she trust him to keep his word and respect her safe word if she needed to use it?

"You are submissive. To the right man, you are. When I held you in my arms and commanded you to focus only on me, you did it without hesitation, without question. You submitted to me and it was a beautiful thing to behold. You're too strong for most, but you still crave submission. Being a sub doesn't mean you're weak. It only means you need to surrender. Many weak people crave power, crave to hurt others, to take control, but they are still inherently weak individuals."

Sophie knew that was the truth. She had met killers and murderers—pathetic examples of humanity. They were too weak to stand up for themselves when it mattered, and the resulting loss of power or control turned them toward paths of violent retribution on innocents. Such behavior was more common than it should be.

A sudden thought struck her. "What if...I let you teach me how to surrender?"

Curiosity flitted shadowlike in his eyes, but his wariness was stronger.

"I'm not sure I come out on top in this bargain. You might prove to be too much trouble." Emery moved over to the spanking bench and sat down on the edge, seemingly unbothered by its real purpose. Sophie's face heated with a treacherous blush.

It should have surprised her how much she did want to please him. He seemed an intricate puzzle and knowing her behavior was a partial key; she couldn't help but wonder what doing his bidding would unlock.

He leaned back, crossing his legs at the ankles, and looked at her. She was still on her knees, hands clenched together, fingers knotted. Sophie studied him, traced the perfectly tailored suit that clung to his body like a second skin. He was every inch the rich recluse she'd heard him to be.

People spoke of him in sad whispers, their eyes full of pity. But when Sophie met Emery's gaze, she couldn't pity him. Sympathize? Yes. Pity? No. His expression of domination demanded obedience, respect, and not one second had passed where he'd let that expression falter, except when he'd stared at the picture from his past. Only then had she seen the other Emery, the one trapped in childhood memories. The one she had to save. For that was clear. Part of this man before her needed to be saved.

"I'm not sure bedding you is worth my tale of woe." His tone sounded almost taunting, rather like he was reciting Shakespeare. He was mocking her!

Embarrassment flooded her face with heat, but her

pride was pricked. Without a second thought she slipped off one shoe and threw it at him.

Thunk! It bounced off the solid wall of his muscular chest and dropped to the floor. He didn't move an inch except to drop his eyes to the shoe, and then raise his gaze again. She could feel it passing over her body as he did so.

"You just threw a shoe at me." His eyes flashed fire, but his lips twitched.

"Yeah? Well, you just implied I'm not good in bed!" Muttering to herself, she bent to remove her second shoe, wanting nothing more than to chuck that one at him too. She was completely unprepared for his reaction.

One second she had her hand on her remaining shoe, the next he'd spun her around to face the wall, his body pressing tight against hers from behind. Both her wrists were caught in one of his hands at her lower back. He rolled his hips, rubbing against her bottom, grinding a very hard erection against her miniskirt. Emery put his free hand on her stomach, his large palm making her feel incredibly small.

"You have an unusual way of expressing your temper." His low growl summoned deep shivers from the base of her spine. "Some doms like to paddle that temper out of their subs, then they pound the sub into delicious submission until the sub is dying of pleasure." He punctuated this with a sharp arch of his hips again. Her clit throbbed and her breath quickened.

Images rose in her mind—him dragging her skirt up to

her waist, tearing away underwear and taking her hard from behind. Sophie jerked when her knees smacked together and she wobbled. Emery held her upright, rubbing her stomach, the pressure arousing rather than soothing.

"Don't tell me I've struck you speechless." His husky laugh was rich as scotch and burned her to the core.

He nuzzled her ear, then nipped at it. An explosion went off somewhere below her waist and Sophie sucked in a breath. Her blood pounded in her ears, and a dark mist seemed to roll across her vision as she sank into him and his teasing kisses and touches.

"I'm having trouble...thinking," she admitted through the fog that seemed to curl around the logical part of her mind. All she could focus on was his breath on her cheek, his tongue flicking inside her ear and the stinging jabs of arousal that spiked though her lower spine and zoomed straight to her clit. She was empty, needed something inside her, needed him. Her body actually hurt with the wild craving to have him. All it would take was his thrusting into her softness and giving it to her hard enough, and she'd die from the pleasure.

"You respond well to me. Perhaps you are worth a few nights." He licked a path up from her shoulder to a spot beneath her ear, and then feathered kisses before blowing softly on the now sensitive shell of her ear. Her hands shook violently in his hold.

Then he was gone. He'd released her and stepped back.

Sophie fell forward a few inches, her body resting against the wall as she fought to regain her composure. The stone against her cheek was cool and slightly rough, like the craggy rocks of a castle's keep. It lent a dungeonlike atmosphere to their sparse surroundings, more than chains and whips and other objects might have. She was at his mercy, his to torture or to pleasure, or perhaps a combination. Her clit pulsed to life at the thought of both.

"Very well. Unlace your corset."

The command was so abrupt that Sophie balked instantly. There was no way she'd do that, and it didn't have anything to do with modesty.

"You can't obey a simple command?" One golden brow arched over his eye.

"It's not that I don't want to obey…"

"Are you plagued by modesty?" His lips tilted down, but a glimmer of amusement danced briefly across his face.

"I'm not plagued, I'm naturally modest. But that's not why I can't unlace the corset."

Emery sighed and crossed his arms. "I suppose I'll give you one easy out today. Tell me why you won't open your corset and I will release you of the command to actually unlace it. Can you do that without issue?"

"Just tell you?" She could do that, couldn't she?

"For now. Someday you will show me." He raised one hand to his hair, raking his fingers through it, mussing the blond waves. It made her ache to do the same. To lie beside him in bed and know that she mussed up his hair, that she had grasped the thick shimmering strands and tugged while in the midst of passion.

"I don't like delays, Sophie," he warned.

Swallowing a shivery breath, she nodded, more for herself than him. "I've got scars." There. It was out. No going back.

"What kind of scars?" Emery's voice was soft, velvety, like he wanted to soothe her.

His question confused her.

"Scars. There isn't any other kind."

Emery's eyes trained on her. "I mean, are they scars from abuse? From an accident?"

"No abuse. Surgery."

"What did you have surgery for?"

"Explaining that isn't part of the bargain," Sophie replied. She'd agreed to submit, not tell him her every secret.

Emery stood up and left the bench to come toward her. He moved so fast she had no time to react. He snatched her wrists and dragged her over to the bench, bending her over it and spreading her knees with one thigh. He pulled her wrists back behind her body and pinned them there with one of his hands. When he pushed his leg up against the apex of her thighs beneath the skirt she whimpered. The soft, expensive fabric of his suit rubbed erotically against the sensitive skin of her thighs.

"Lesson one: never lie to your dom, or any dom. Punishment is always the result, or worse, the dom severs the relationship and releases the sub. Now, let's try this again. What was the surgery for?"

"All right!" Sophie hissed. She was madder than a wet cat, but she knew he had her beat. Still, she jerked and jostled against the bench, testing his hold. Tight. No way to get out of this.

"Stop." His bark made her flinch and go slack. "Tell the truth. I have ways of making you talk if you think to keep quiet."

Did he mean he'd spank it out of her? She wish she knew, then again, maybe she didn't want to know. Her eyelashes fell against her cheeks and darkness captured her vision, thankfully making her feel alone enough to utter the truth. "I had an accident and got cut. The surgery was to sew the cuts back together. Is that a personal enough answer for you?" She flinched, waiting for a blow.

"I didn't want a personal answer, only a truthful one. And I don't *ever* beat answers of anyone, especially a sub who surrenders to my care." Although his words suggested a chastisement, he didn't seem angry, rather puzzled and hurt that she'd assumed he'd beat it out of her.

"How did you know I was afraid you would hit me?" she whispered.

"You flinched after you lashed out verbally. I've seen that before in other submissives. You expected me to spank you, but know this, I don't ever react with violence, only with erotic punishment. There is a difference and I will teach you."

Very slowly, he withdrew his leg from between her thighs and released her wrists. Sophie lay for a moment, unsure of what to do. But rather than standing, Emery sat on the floor and reached for her. He took her in his arms and laid her on the floor beside him. Sophie gasped as he settled over her. If she hadn't been so distracted by his close proximity she might have laughed. Emery Lockwood did not strike her as the type of man to prefer the missionary position.

But Sophie was distracted; he invaded her space, gently took hold of her wrists again and secured them to the floor above her head. He slid one hand down her ribs, over her belly and then between her knees, parting them so his hips could sink into the cradle of her legs. He rocked his pelvis forward, rubbing against her, showing her she couldn't shift, couldn't move unless he wished her to.

It had been ages since she'd been this close to a man, with every inch of their bodies touching except their lips, and his were so temptingly close. The last time hadn't affected her like this. Her universe was shrinking around this one single moment, to just the two of them. Their gazes locked.

"This is personal. My past is personal, Sophie. Everything you want from me and what I want from you is personal." His free hand slid up from her hip to rest on her lower ribcage. He toyed with the loose ribbon of her corset. She could feel him tug, tease, but not undo the laces any further. Still, he could if he wished; he could pry the corset open and see her scars, her ugliness.

Sophie's breath hitched, her breasts rising rapidly as she struggled to breathe.

Concern darkened his eyes. "You're like a frightened little sparrow, your chest heaving as you beat against the cat's paw holding you down. *Relax*, Sophie," he murmured. "Otherwise I might lose my already tenuous control. As a dom, I am aroused by your apprehension. I love bringing a woman to the fine edge between trust and fear. I'd never hurt you, but still I'm determined to push your boundaries, test your limits, and I know that scares you just as much as it arouses you." His once silky tone was now gruff and a little ragged.

The truth of his words was like a whip cracking in her mind, more sharp and agonizing than anything she'd ever felt on her skin.

Sophie bucked her hips, trying to dislodge him. "Damn you!" His large erection dug into her, making her womb throb.

As though he could sense her rising need and frustration, Emery's eyes swirled with lust and hunger.

"So you have scars and they upset you," he observed.

She raised her chin, glowering at him. "Well, it's humiliating. Men don't like my...my..." To her own shame, her voice wavered.

"They don't like your breasts?" The sheer look of incredulity on his face startled her.

"Uh huh." Sophie shut her eyes, shame smashing her insides like a sledgehammer through fine china.

God, let this humiliation be over quickly. Every other man had left her alone after hearing this. Emery wouldn't be any different. He was too sexy, too gorgeous to ever settle for a scarred woman like her, not when he could have his pick.

Emery held still, didn't make a sound or move until she opened her eyes. When she did finally look up at him, he dropped his head a few inches, his nose touching hers, nuzzling her cheek.

"I'm not like other men, Sophie. Scars are a sign of strength, survival. Someday you'll be brave enough to show me, and I'll prove you have nothing to be ashamed of. Now, I am willing to accept the deal you proposed. Are you willing in return?"

She bit her lip. It had been her idea; she had to see it through. She wanted to see it through, even if it scared the living daylights out of her.

"Yes. I'll do it. Your story, my submission."

Want to know what happens next? Grab the book HERE!

OTHER TITLES BY LAUREN SMITH

Historical
The League of Rogues Series
Wicked Designs

His Wicked Seduction

Her Wicked Proposal

Wicked Rivals

Her Wicked Longing

His Wicked Embrace

The Earl of Pembroke

His Wicked Secret

The Last Wicked Rogue

Never Kiss a Scot

The Earl of Kent

Never Tempt a Scot

Boudreaux's Lady

Escaping the Earl

Lost with a Scot

The Seduction Series

The Duelist's Seduction

The Rakehell's Seduction

The Rogue's Seduction

Standalone Stories

Tempted by A Rogue

Devil at the Gates

Seducing an Heiress on a Train

Sins and Scandals

An Earl By Any Other Name

A Gentleman Never Surrenders

A Scottish Lord for Christmas

Contemporary

Ever After Series

Legally Charming

Tempting Prince Charming

The Surrender Series

The Gilded Cuff

The Gilded Cage

The Gilded Chain

The Darkest Hour

Love in London

Forbidden

Seduction

Climax

Forever Be Mine

Standalones
Cocktail

Paranormal
Dark Seductions Series
The Shadows of Stormclyffe Hall
The Love Bites Series
The Bite of Winter
His Little Vixen
Brotherhood of the Blood Moon Series
Blood Moon on the Rise
Brothers of Ash and Fire
Grigori: A Royal Dragon Romance
Mikhail: A Royal Dragon Romance
Rurik: A Royal Dragon Romance
The Lost Barinov Dragon: A Roya Dragon Romance

Sci-Fi Romance
Cyborg Genesis Series
Across the Stars
The Krinar Chronicles
The Krinar Eclipse
The Krinar Code (Written as Emma Castle)

ABOUT THE AUTHOR

Lauren Smith is an Oklahoma attorney by day, author by night who pens adventurous and edgy romance stories by the light of her smart phone flashlight app. She knew she was destined to be a romance writer when she attempted to re-write the entire *Titanic* movie just to save Jack from drowning. Connecting with readers by writing emotionally moving, realistic and sexy romances no matter what time period is her passion. She's won multiple awards in several romance subgenres including: New England Reader's Choice Awards, Greater

Detroit BookSeller's Best Awards, and a Semi-Finalist award for the Mary Wollstonecraft Shelley Award.

To Connect with Lauren, visit her at:
www.laurensmithbooks.com
lauren@laurensmithbooks.com

facebook.com/LaurenDianaSmith
twitter.com/LSmithAuthor
instagram.com/Laurensmithbooks

Made in the USA
Las Vegas, NV
29 December 2021

39771810R00229